PRAISE FOR

WOMAN ON THE EDGE

"One woman's struggles with motherhood and another's desperate desire to be a mother collide in this explosive debut. **A white-knuckle read** that welcomes a bright new talent to the world of psychological suspense."

Mary Kubica, *New York Times* bestselling author of *The Good Girl*

"A shocking premise and two intriguingly damaged characters whose story lines hurtle toward each other, colliding in a powerful, moving climax. **A propulsive read!** Samantha M. Bailey is a writer to watch in the thriller genre."

Robyn Harding, bestselling author of *The Party* and *The Arrangement*

"Begins with a shocking, tragic event and doesn't stop there. **An impressive debut** that will keep you reading until the final twist."

Samantha Downing, *USA Today* bestselling author of *My Lovely Wife*

"**A fast-paced, twisty roller-coaster ride** in which a desperate widow, a guilt-ridden new mother, and the secrets of the past collide—with a baby's life hanging in the balance. . . . I couldn't race to the end quickly enough! An exciting, binge-worthy debut."

Kristin Harmel, bestselling author of *The Winemaker's Wife* and *The Room on Rue Amélie*

"From its first chapter—its first line!—*Woman on the Edge* will grip you like so few novels manage to do. From the moment two women's lives collide on a subway platform to the shocking finale, **you'll be dizzied by the twists and turns the story takes.** Some writers toil their entire career trying to master this kind of adept plotting, but Samantha M. Bailey nails it in her first effort. *Woman on the Edge* stayed with me for days after I turned its final pages. A truly thrilling debut."

Amy Stuart, bestselling author of
Still Mine and *Still Water*

"Begins with a bang and takes the reader on a tense, emotional journey of love, betrayal, and loss, and straight into the heart of a mother willing to do anything to protect her child. Infused with **riveting, hold-your-breath suspense,** this masterful debut needs to be your next binge-read. A knockout page-turner."

Heather Gudenkauf, *New York Times* bestselling
author of *The Weight of Silence* and *Before She Was Found*

"**A captivating thriller** . . . Bailey masterfully spins a chilling tale of deceit and duplicity that will have you guessing until the very end. Filled with unexpected twists, tight prose, and penetrating characters, this novel heralds the arrival of an immensely talented author."

Lori Nelson Spielman, *New York Times*
bestselling author of *The Life List*

"This is the page-turner you've been looking for! Bailey's writing is gripping and emotionally resonant at once, and her debut novel, **perfect for fans of Lisa Jewell and Kimberly Belle,** will keep you on the edge of your seat until the final sentence."

Marissa Stapley, bestselling author of
The Last Resort

"A tale so tightly told that you won't swallow or exhale for the entire duration. **Dark, riveting, utterly gripping!**"

Roz Nay, bestselling author of *Our Little Secret*

"**One word: exhilarating!** *Woman on the Edge* was impossible to put down as the twisty thrills kept on coming—and kept me guessing— leaving me breathless. Fans of Shari Lapena will no doubt gobble this one up in a heartbeat."

Hannah Mary McKinnon, bestselling author
of *Her Secret Son* and *The Neighbors*

"Gripping from the first page to the last, *Woman on the Edge* had me **nail-biting and breathless** all the way through. But even after you've turned the final page, this riveting and deeply felt thriller from debut author Samantha M. Bailey won't relinquish its hold on you."

Laura Sims, author of *Looker*

"With the narrative acceleration of a runaway train, *Woman on the Edge* kept me at the edge of my seat for its entire zigzagging ride; I had to remind myself to breathe. Bailey's confident prose and dark sat- ire enrich the ingenious plot, and her authentic characters—whether damaged, yearning, or downright diabolical—make this compulsory reading for fans of suspense. **An exceptional debut!**"

Sonja Yoerg, *Washington Post* bestselling author of *True Places*

"**Exhilarating and evocative** . . . *Woman on the Edge* had me gripped. This book effortlessly ticks all the boxes: wonderful world build- ing, realistic characters, and a gripping plot that made me keep flipping the pages. It's about obsession and madness, motherhood and trauma. This is a debut you'll want to slip straight to the top of your to-read pile!"

Christina McDonald, author of *The Night Olivia Fell*

"Readers, clear yourself a block of time for this one, because once you pick up *Woman on the Edge*, you won't want to set it down. From its breathless first chapter to its startling conclusion, Bailey is in control, delivering **a gripping plot, palpable tension, and characters pushed ever closer to the brink** in this unmissable debut."

Paula Treick DeBoard, critically acclaimed author
of *Here We Lie* and *The Drowning Girls*

"A glowing debut that starts with a bang and never lets up, *Woman on the Edge* weaves the stories of two women, both on the edge, who find themselves at different times the protector of a baby girl. **Unrelenting suspense** and a taut, propulsive plot add up to a first-rate, **heart-pounding mystery**. I loved this one!"

Emily Carpenter, bestselling author of
Burying the Honeysuckle Girls

"Opens with an ingenious setup: a woman on the subway hands her baby to a total stranger, then jumps in front of an oncoming train. But were they really strangers, and did she really jump? Suspicions swirl in this propulsive debut, and the truth is revealed in twisty, page-turning increments that culminate in a whopper of an ending. **A clever and addictive read** from a bright new talent."

Kimberly Belle, *USA Today* bestselling author of *Dear Wife*

"Every mother's worst nightmare comes to life in this taut, razor-sharp thriller. Bailey's genius is in her story's structure. By alternating the voices of two narrators—a new mother driven to the edge of insanity and a woman crawling out of the emotional abyss of her devastated life—gruesome clues reveal the sinister events that led one to abandon her infant in the arms of the other before ending her life. **Crackling with suspense**, the blistering pace of Bailey's story will keep you turning pages late into the night to find out who—if either—is telling the truth."

Josie Brown, bestselling author of
the Housewife Assassin series

"A knockout premise, breakneck pacing, and a twisty plot with two strong women at its core make *Woman on the Edge* irresistible. I read it in one sitting, absolutely riveted by this propulsive tale of motherhood, loss, and betrayal. **A must-read for thriller lovers.**"

Daniela Petrova, author of
Her Daughter's Mother

"Samantha M. Bailey's highly anticipated debut **grips you from its first line**. Quick-paced with roller coaster-like twists and turns, *Woman on the Edge* is a thrilling story of two women whose lives, in one brief moment, are forever changed. You'll be breathless as you tear through the final pages. Loved it!"

Liz Fenton & Lisa Steinke, bestselling authors of
The Two Lila Bennetts

"**Page-turning, up-all-night, expertly tracked** . . . *Woman on the Edge* is a twisty tale where paranoia, double takes, reversals, and deceit bend to the awe-inspiring power of a mother's love. Not to miss!"

Julie Valerie, author of *Holly Banks Full of Angst*
and the Village of Primm series

WOMAN
ON THE
EDGE

A NOVEL

SAMANTHA M. BAILEY

PUBLISHED BY SIMON & SCHUSTER

New York London Toronto Sydney New Delhi

SIMON &
SCHUSTER
CANADA

Simon & Schuster Canada
A Division of Simon & Schuster, Inc.
166 King Street East, Suite 300
Toronto, Ontario M5A 1J3

This Simon & Schuster Canada edition November 2019

SIMON & SCHUSTER CANADA and colophon are
trademarks of Simon & Schuster, Inc.

For information about special discounts for bulk purchases,
please contact Simon & Schuster Special Sales at 1-800-268-3216
or CustomerService@simonandschuster.ca.

Interior design by Joy O'Meara

Manufactured in the United States of America

1 3 5 7 9 10 8 6 4 2

Library and Archives Canada Cataloging in Publication
Title: Woman on the edge / by Samantha M. Bailey.
Names: Bailey, Samantha M., 1973– author.
Identifiers: Canadiana 20190130032 | ISBN 9781982126742 (softcover)
Classification: LCC PS8603.A44347 W66 2020 | DDC C813/.6—dc23

ISBN 978-1-9821-2674-2
ISBN 978-1-9821-2675-9 (ebook)

To my parents, Celia and Michael,
who filled my childhood with books,
so much love, and the belief I could do
anything if I worked hard enough.

Mom and Dad, this one's for you, because of you.

No language can express the power and beauty,
and heroism and majesty of a mother's love;
it shrinks not where man cowers, and grows stronger where
man faints, and over the wastes of worldly fortune sends the
radiance of its quenchless fidelity like a star in heaven.

—EDWIN HUBBELL CHAPIN

CHAPTER ONE

MORGAN

Monday, August 7

"Take my baby."

I flinch at the brittle, scratchy voice. I'm standing on the subway platform as I do every day after work, waiting for the train to come. I used to try to smile at people, but I'm warier now. Ever since my husband, Ryan, died, no one knows how to act around me, and I don't know how to act around them. I usually keep to myself, head down, which is why the voice surprises me.

I look up. I thought the woman was talking to a friend, but she's not. She's disheveled, wearing faded black yoga pants and a stained white T-shirt. She's alone, and she's talking to me.

She clutches a sleeping baby to her chest with one arm. She knows she has my attention now. She presses up against me, and my purse bangs into my side. Then she digs sharp nails into my bare wrist. "Please, take my baby."

Icy fingers of fear run up my back despite the sweltering heat inside Grand/State station. The woman is on edge, and so am I—literally, at least. I always stand on the edge of the platform so I can be first on the train. One hard push is all it would take for me to fall onto the tracks. As bleak as the last eighteen months have been, no matter how ostracized I've become after Ryan's suicide, I've made a new life for myself. I don't want it to end here.

I gently extract my arm from her tight grip. "Sorry, could you . . ."

She steps even closer to me, so close that I'm on the blue strip. Her eyes are wild, lips so bloody and raw, like she's been chewing on them. She clearly needs help. I pull my long black hair around my face, lower my gaze to the gray speckled tiles, and say, "We should step back a bit. Here." I put a hand out to guide her away from the edge, but she won't move.

She's making me so nervous. As a social worker, I recognize the signs of distress, signs I should have noticed in Ryan. If I hadn't been the loyal, obtuse, willfully blind wife I never thought I'd become, my husband might have turned himself in and gotten help before it was too late. He might have realized that even though he'd be found guilty of embezzlement, there were worse things to lose. Like life itself. If I'd noticed anything ahead of time, I might not be paying for the crimes I didn't even know he'd committed until he was dead.

I might even be a mother myself now, like this woman in front of me.

She looks awful. Clumps of matted dark curls stick out haphazardly from her scalp as though her hair has been hacked with a chain saw. I look away quickly.

"I've been watching you," she says to me in a strangled voice.

She squeezes the sleeping baby so tightly, too tightly, and I fear for the safety of the child. The woman's eyes—ringed with such dark circles it's like she's been punched—flick back and forth.

"Are you looking for someone? Is someone supposed to meet you here?" Then I curse myself for getting involved when I should just give her my boss Kate's number at Haven House, the women's shelter I work for. I'm not the lead counselor and head advocate at the shelter anymore. I've been demoted to office manager. I wish I'd never met Ryan. I wish I'd never fallen for his crooked smile and self-deprecating humor. And I have no recourse. I still have a job. I did nothing wrong, yet I lost so much, including everyone's faith in me. My faith in myself.

She is not my client to counsel. Who am I to counsel anyone?

Her haunted eyes land back on me, and on her gaunt face is a look of pure terror. "Keep her safe."

The baby is fast asleep, her tiny nose and mouth pressed too closely to her mother's chest. She's unaware of her mother's suffering. I feel myself unwittingly absorbing this woman's pain, even though I have enough of my own to contend with. I'm about to give her the shelter phone number when she speaks again.

"I've been watching you for a long time. You seem like a nice woman. Kind. Smart. Please, Morgan."

My head jolts back in shock. Did she just say my *name*? It's impossible. I've never seen her before in my life.

The woman kisses her baby's tufts of hair, then stares at me again with those piercing blue eyes. "I know what you want. Don't let anyone hurt her. Love her for me, Morgan."

I know what you want?

"How can you possibly know anything about me?" I say, but my voice is drowned out by an announcement to stay back from the platform's edge. The woman's cracked lips move again, but I can't hear her over the wind roaring through the tunnel.

I'm truly panicked now. Something about all of this just isn't right. I feel it in my gut. I need to get away from this woman.

People surround us, but they don't seem to notice that something strange is going on here. They are commuters in their own world, as I was just a few minutes ago.

The woman's eyes sweep the platform once again. Then her arms reach out. She launches her baby toward me; my hands catch the infant by instinct. I look down at the child in my arms, and I tear up. The yellow blanket she's wrapped in is so soft against my skin, the baby's face serene and content.

When I look back up at her mother a second later, the train is shrieking into the station.

And that's when she jumps.

CHAPTER TWO

NICOLE

Before

Nicole tapped her gold Montblanc Boheme Papillon pen—a gift from her husband, Greg—on the last page of Breathe's glossy winter catalog. Something was off. The model leaned into warrior pose, showcasing the new line of straight-leg yoga dress pants. Nicole squinted at the picture. Yes, there was a wrinkle on the model's knee. That wouldn't do. This ad campaign was her last major project before she went on maternity leave at the end of the day. As founder and CEO of one of the bestselling athleisure and wellness companies in North America, she had final approval on everything that Breathe produced. She wouldn't walk out of work until this catalog was perfect.

Nicole sighed. How was she going to stay away from the office? She'd never even taken a vacation without her phone and laptop. She hadn't really taken a vacation at all, come to think of it. She'd be away only six weeks, she told herself. A month and a half that she'd negotiated with her nemesis, Lucinda Nestles, executive chairperson of Breathe, and the other board members. She wanted to start her life as a mother off right, but she couldn't imagine not working. In a lot of ways, Breathe was her first baby. Now, she was carrying her second. It would be okay, though. Tessa, her best friend and Breathe's chief product officer, would keep her apprised of all affairs while she was gone.

She pushed the wireless intercom to call her office manager. "Holly, can you ask Tessa to come see me as soon as she gets in?"

"Yes, of course," Holly replied.

Nicole pulled her thick chestnut curls off her face and laid a hand on her swollen belly. She felt a foot or maybe an elbow protruding. The reality of her impending motherhood both excited and terrified her. It wasn't something she'd planned. She'd gone to her doctor to get relief from what she believed was a serious bout of the stomach flu. Instead, she learned she was thirteen weeks pregnant. She was always so busy with work she'd forgotten to track her period, and the stress of her job made it irregular. The shocking news had sent a hot flash of fear through her chest. But the moment the ultrasound technician ran the sensor over her stomach, filling the air with the noise of what sounded to Nicole like a herd of galloping horses, she felt hope and anticipation. A chance at redemption. This was an opportunity, a chance to absolve herself of the past. A chance to bring forth a new life—for her baby and for herself.

She smiled now when she thought of the night she'd shown Greg the sonogram. She had waited until they'd come home from the launch party for Breathe's ten-minute-wellness app. Right after they'd settled on the couch to debrief, as they did after every Breathe event, she slipped the black-and-white photo in his hand.

"What's this?" he'd asked, his brow furrowed.

She wasn't sure how he'd react, exactly, but she knew it would be okay. "Our baby."

"What?" he'd whispered, as though any louder would make the news more real.

His eyes grew huge, and he paled so quickly she thought he might pass out.

"I know we never planned this, but it's happened." She reached for his hand and entwined her fingers with his. Her husband loved when she touched him. He adored her. He put her needs above his.

He still looked stunned, but his eyes softened. "I'm going to ask this only once, and then I'll be right by your side no matter what you answer. You want this baby?"

She looked right into his eyes. "I want this baby. We can give a child everything, Greg. We'll be great parents. We'll figure it out. We always do."

He smiled then and looked again at the paper. "I don't see it."

She'd laughed and pointed out the tiny bean in the picture.

He cocked his head at her. "You always said you never wanted kids."

Greg was right.

"I didn't know how much I wanted it until it happened."

"I assume we'll get a nanny. You're not going to stay at home, obviously."

Nicole flinched. She'd never hire a nanny. And she'd never tell Greg the reason. So all she said was: "I'll see how much time I can take, and Breathe has a day care on-site."

He nodded but still looked floored by the massive life change they'd never planned for.

On their first date—mere hours after she'd slammed into the back of his Audi because she was rushing to a meeting—she'd told him she never wanted children, as a baby at the next table screamed throughout their entire meal. He'd laughed it off and said he would leave the decision in her hands. Empowering her even then. And when he'd winked, it had sent sparks through her. They'd discussed the possibility once more right after they'd gotten married a year later, but Nicole was firm: They were both career-focused, and kids would weigh them down. She never did tell him why she'd been so adamant she'd never be a mother. Greg was her rock. She never wanted to be a failure in his eyes. She loved him deeply, and now she realized that a baby would bring them even closer.

At the seventeen-week sonogram, his sweaty hand gripping her clammy one, the technician had announced, "It's a girl!"

Greg kissed her cheek and whispered, "I'll never let her date, you know."

And Nicole closed her eyes, letting the news wash over her. Her life had come full circle. One girl lost, and one gained.

Now at almost forty weeks, the end of her pregnancy, the bean had grown into a baby whose sharp, little limbs jabbed Nicole daily, letting her mother know she was there. She was alive.

Nicole felt so much gratitude for Greg. For the kind of man and husband he was. For the way he had given her a family once again. She looked at the photo she'd snapped that morning. It was of the gorgeous creamy-white crib she'd dog-eared in the Petit Trésor catalog. Greg had surprised her by setting it up in the nursery the night before while she was sleeping. It must have taken him hours.

This morning, he looked ready to drop when he led her into the room. "Surprise!" he said.

"Oh, Greg, I love it. Thank you!" And she hugged him hard, hoping he'd be able to stay awake for his full workday. Yes, Breathe had made them rich, but Greg was successful in his own right, a stockbroker, not a kept man.

Her reverie was interrupted by Holly, who walked into her office. She placed Nicole's mail in a neat pile next to her purple computer. "Tessa's on her way."

Nicole shook her thoughts from her personal life and all the changes that were about to happen. "Great. I reviewed the updated website, and we'll need to make a few tweaks. The Chaos to Calm program looks too busy." She thought for a second. "Can we get the e-team to streamline it to five yoga poses instead of seven? And check with sales for the latest orders on the fall line of track jackets. If they're where they should be, Tessa can roll out the app with marketing to coincide with the release of the brochure."

Holly nodded and handed her a white envelope. "I opened all your business mail but not this one. It looks personal, and I didn't want to pry. Maybe it's just a fan letter after the feature in the *Tribune*?"

Nicole's pulse instantly sped up. She could hear her heart pounding in her chest. She saw the familiar shaky scrawl across the front of the white envelope that Holly held out to her. It bore her maiden name—Nicole Layton. It was postmarked Kenosha, Wisconsin. The place where her life had fallen apart nineteen years ago. Not a fan letter. Not in the least.

Nicole hadn't wanted her pregnancy mentioned in the *Chicago Tribune* for precisely this reason. She didn't want anyone from her past to know she was having a daughter. Lucinda insisted the article would be great PR: Nicole, a powerful, pregnant CEO who touted balance, would prove women really could have it all. The story was about the company's visionary accomplishments: Breathe's empowering and healing mindfulness workshops, its singular line of body products created "for women by women," and the company ethos about women leading balanced lives. A portion of the proceeds of all Breathe products went to a foundation that provided support and counseling for orphaned teenagers—teens just like Nicole herself. Her parents were killed in a car accident during her senior year of high school, so she knew what it was like to feel alone, to have nothing and no one. What she didn't know was that the newspaper would fail to respect her wishes, that it would mention her pregnancy and that she was expecting a girl.

The story had come out a week ago, and every day since, she wondered if another letter would arrive. And now it had.

She reached for the envelope and clutched it. "Thanks, Holly," she said, managing to keep her voice on an even keel. She hoped the sudden sweat coating her skin wasn't evident. "Can you get me the latest numbers from San Francisco for the Stream collection? The tankinis aren't selling as well as they should. I need the numbers before my board meeting. This is my last one before my leave."

"I can't imagine a board meeting without you. How are we going to do this?"

"You'll be fine. You've got Tessa and Lucinda, and the entire staff here. You won't miss me at all."

"Just promise you won't Skype in wearing a Breathe nursing bra."

Nicole laughed. "Not much chance of that," she replied.

Holly left, closing Nicole's office door behind her.

The false smile on Nicole's face faded instantly. She debated ripping the envelope into little pieces. Not reading the words inside meant not knowing what threats lay ahead for her. But something in her made her want to know. Her throat tightened.

The first such letter she ever received was delivered the fall of her freshman year to her residence at Columbia College. It contained three typed sentences.

I know what you did. You were supposed to keep her safe. One day you will pay.

Razor-sharp fear had sliced at her chest, and her fingers had gone numb. One white envelope arrived every year after that, without fail, until five years ago, the letters suddenly stopped. She'd hoped Donna had finally healed from that horrific summer, like Nicole had tried to, and that she'd really stopped harassing her. But it seemed that wasn't the case. Nicole's hand shook as she held the envelope now. Donna, who'd draped herself over her baby like a protective cloak. Who'd fretted over her child's every sneeze. Who'd repeatedly pop into little Amanda's room as she slept, making sure the remote-control-operated butterfly mobile spinning above the crib still played its lullaby on a continuous loop. Donna was a mother who loved her baby girl as much as Nicole already loved her unborn child. But Donna had lost hers forever. How could any mother ever heal from that?

And now, here was a new envelope. With it still clutched in her hand, Nicole heaved herself out of her desk chair. With a full-grown baby inside her, it had gotten harder to move around. But besides her massive belly, she was still fit and toned thanks to daily yoga, which she did right in her office. She encouraged all her employees to take time in their workdays for themselves.

She laid the envelope beside her and slowly lowered herself onto the yoga mat under the floor-to-ceiling window, easing from a prenatal lotus pose into cat pose. Focusing on her breath, she whispered, "My heart is centered and open. I love myself and allow my heart to connect with the hearts of others. I forgive myself and want to live with gratitude and grace." Her baby stretched in her womb, and she embraced the bond she felt with her unborn daughter.

Nicole was ready. She sat up on her mat, grabbed the envelope, and opened it. Then she slid the white paper out.

You don't deserve a baby girl. You're a murderer. You can't keep her safe.

The typed words smudged with Nicole's tears. So Donna had read the *Tribune* article and knew she was having a girl.

Nicole put the letter back in the envelope, then pulled herself up by gripping the edge of the windowsill. With the envelope in hand, she pressed her hot cheek to the cool glass that overlooked West Armitage Avenue. She watched the women entering and exiting Breathe's first storefront, adjacent to the corporate offices, which took up all four floors in the slate-gray building at North Halsted in Lincoln Park.

Her daughter fluttered inside her.

Now Nicole's chest tightened, and her breath released in shallow gasps. Black dots flitted across her vision. She reached out a palm to steady herself against the window, the traffic below only agitating her vertigo. She couldn't faint at work.

"Nic?"

She quickly crumpled the paper into a ball and looked over her shoulder to see Tessa's tiny frame in her office doorway. In seconds, Tessa was at Nicole's side, a gentle hand on her back.

"You're okay. Deep breath in. Good. Now let it out. Again." Tessa breathed with her. "Once more. Good."

Tessa knew how to calm her. Nicole trusted her with her work, with her secrets, with her health.

"Thank you, Tessa," she said.

"We just have to breathe. It's you who taught me that, Nicole."

She smiled to herself. "I guess that's what friends are for—to keep each other breathing."

"Exactly," Tessa said, her wide, kind smile filling her face. "I can't remember the last time you had a panic attack."

Nicole remembered it vividly. It was four years ago when she and Tessa were reviewing the catalog for Breathe's first baby skin-care line. As Nicole flipped to the shot of the beatific mother sitting in a rocking chair, cradling her swaddled infant, she suddenly gasped for air, clutching at the excruciating pain in her chest. The mother in that photo had reminded her of Donna. The memory of that traumatic summer bubbled to the surface before she could stop it. She'd been so ashamed. Tessa was an employee, a product designer then, and Nicole hadn't wanted to blur the lines.

But Tessa had been so understanding. A yoga teacher and holistic-wellness graduate, she taught Nicole how to manage her panic attacks. Her calm, soothing voice and light touch had worked. Over time, Nicole was able to go off her antianxiety medication. She and Tessa bonded. Tessa had risen in the ranks to chief product officer, and Nicole's right hand. She felt close enough to Tessa to tell her almost everything about that summer nineteen years ago in Kenosha. And telling that secret released such a heavy burden, a burden that was weighing on Nicole in increasingly frightening ways. In a sense, her friend Tessa—because she did become a friend, so much more than just an employee—had saved her life.

Besides Nicole's older brother, Ben, who she rarely saw, Tessa was the only person who knew anything about what had happened all those years ago. She didn't want Greg to know any of it, or about her panic disorder. To him, she was strong, capable, and a leader. That was the woman Greg loved, and Nicole refused to show him anything else.

Nicole's breathing slowed, and the vise grip on her chest loosened.

"Want to tell me what precipitated that?" Tessa asked.

Nicole turned to lean her back against the window and looked at Tessa's young, beautiful face. Her long, white-blond hair in its ubiquitous braid and her petite figure. She was only twenty-nine to Nicole's thirty-six, but at times, she was so much wiser than her years. Type B to Nicole's type A. Tessa had no significant other, no kids. Her life was how she wanted it. Free and unencumbered. Nicole often envied her. She didn't seem to need other people, not the way Nicole did. And she certainly never seemed to feel alone.

Nicole pushed herself away from the window. This was supposed to be the happiest time in her life. Another new beginning. She wasn't going to let Donna ruin everything, again.

So Nicole lied when she answered Tessa's question. "I guess I'm just feeling nervous about the birth. And I think leaving Breathe in Lucinda's hands is making me anxious, too. It's my company, and it's been everything to me. It's hard to imagine that for the next six weeks I won't be here."

"But I will be here. And Lucinda believes in Breathe. She's thrilled to be acting CEO in your absence."

That made Nicole grin. When she'd taken Breathe public, she'd negotiated a permanent placement as CEO, barring any unforeseen circumstances. Lucinda had voted against it, and she'd lost. Now, at least for a few weeks, Lucinda was getting what she wanted. Once

Nicole was back from maternity leave, she would have to reward Tessa for her loyalty, maybe promote her to VP.

"If you could see her in the board meetings . . ." Nicole said to Tessa. "Anyway, you're right. It will all be fine."

Tessa laughed. "You okay to make the meeting?" she asked.

"Of course." Nicole straightened. She was a CEO, for God's sake. She'd taken her company public when she was only twenty-eight. How could she be undone so easily? The past was the past. It was just a letter. Words couldn't hurt her now.

"Tessa, I'm fine. I can totally make the meeting."

"Okay. Swing by my office when you're out, and we can go for dinner to celebrate your last day."

"I'd love to, but Greg and I are having a date night. I could go into labor at any time, so we want to make the most of these last few days together."

Tessa smiled and walked out of her office. Nicole went to her desk and shoved the letter in her drawer. But as she collected herself and prepared to leave for her final board meeting before she became a mother, Donna's message rang ominously through her.

You can't keep her safe.

A horrific thought occurred to Nicole: *What if she's right?*

CHAPTER THREE

MORGAN

The brakes grind with an earsplitting screech against the metal tracks. I scream and scream and scream and when I open my eyes, the train has barreled right into the station. And it's too late.

"Help me! That woman just jumped! Oh my God! I have her baby!" I cry. My arms and legs shake so violently I'm afraid I'll drop the baby. I barely look down onto the tracks, but when I do, I see the woman's limbs splayed at all the wrong angles, and I know she's dead. I look away, afraid to see more. The flashing red lights of the train bouncing off the walls blind me. I hear alarms, and yet all the sound feels far away, as if I'm underwater.

Swarms of people howl, push, and shove. The train's doors open, and commuters spill off until there's no room left to move on the platform. People are panicking, yelling, pointing down at the woman on the tracks. Where are the police? Where are the paramedics? Even though I know there's no hope, they at least have to try.

Fighting not to throw up, I wrap my arms around the baby's back and turn us both so we can't see her mother.

One person after another surround me until I'm so hot I can barely breathe. I see their lips move, but I can't take it all in. It's too fast, too intense.

"Who was she?"

"Why did she jump?"

"Was she a friend of yours?"

"Is the baby okay?"

They're all firing questions I can't answer. Sweat pours down my face, and I need air, but I'm swallowed by the crowd, frantic to move.

I feel a thud against my back, and I stumble. "Call nine-one-one! Help!" I scream again as I fall forward.

A hand grabs my arm and pulls me away from the edge.

"Please, please help me," I cry to the man in a Chicago Transit Authority uniform I find beside me. I'm afraid I'm going to pass out and drop this precious child. He steadies me with one hand on the baby's back and the other around my shoulder.

I can't get enough air into my lungs. I lean into him. "I— She—"

With a sickening wave of panic, I realize that the baby could be injured. I frantically peel away the yellow blanket she's wrapped in. I brace myself, afraid I'll see blood and bruises, but it's all baby-smooth skin of chubby arms and legs. A perfect baby in an ivory onesie who presses her little rosebud mouth to the shoulder of my thin white dress.

My knees buckle. Then the baby is taken from my arms, and a sudden coldness rushes through me.

"This is the woman, Officer!"

"Ma'am, are you okay? Did you witness the incident?" a police officer says as he drapes a blanket over my shoulders.

"She was talking to the lady right before she jumped."

"She took her baby!"

A cacophony of voices thrashes in my ears. I watch as the baby is handed from a male officer to a female one. Then they both disappear in the crowd, and the baby who was a moment ago safe in my arms is gone.

The officer by my side leads me away from the tracks. When we're farther up the platform, he pauses to let me lean against the hard tile of the wall.

My teeth chatter. I don't know what to do. I don't know what just happened. Where are they taking that poor child? Why would her mother do that?

Take my baby.

Morgan.

Had the woman really said my name, or had I imagined it? I clutch my head, soaked with cold sweat, and watch the other witnesses comfort one another and emergency personnel race down to the track level. It's almost as if I'm not really here. I have no clue who that woman was. I can't stop crying.

The officer stands beside me, watching me with interest. "Why don't we go to the station where it's quieter and we can talk?" he asks gently.

The station? No. I never want to go back to that place.

I was taken there after I found Ryan lying on the floor of his home office, a shotgun dangling from his fingertips and a bleeding hole in his stomach. My husband was dead by his own hand. I knew nothing then. I know nothing now.

Why is this happening?

I have no choice but to follow the officer as he marches through the mob. I have no choice but to look down when I pass the dank, dark pit of the tracks, where the mother's mangled body is being lifted onto a stretcher. Her arms are askew, her legs crushed, and her face covered in blood, so much blood her features are no longer visible. Bile rises to my throat and I gag. My legs are so weak, I'm barely able to walk.

Love her for me, Morgan.

"It's impossible," I say out loud.

The officer doesn't hear me over the chaos and yelling and directions being shouted at everyone.

I taste my fear, metallic and cold, swirling in my mouth. My steps are heavy as I trail behind the officer through Grand/State, past the traumatized onlookers, past the tracks, my head bowed because it feels like everyone is watching me. But it's a feeling I've grown used to since Ryan left me the way he did. I'm Ryan Galloway's widow. The wife of a thief and a suicidal coward. Now I'm the last woman another suicide victim spoke to. The person she begged to help her.

I pull my battered black purse closer to my chest. Then I notice something purple stuck to one side.

It's a Post-it note. I didn't put it there. I slip my hand over it and curl it into my palm. The officer leads the way up a flight of stairs. I stop and wait as he clears the mobs of people so I can follow. While he's distracted, I turn the paper over in my hand. On it, in large loopy script I don't recognize, one word is written, a name.

Amanda.

CHAPTER FOUR

NICOLE

Before

A fierce contraction tore through Nicole's lower back. On her hands and knees on the plush, private hospital bed, she again refused the epidural the nurse and Greg kept urging her to have. For four years, she'd gotten through every panic attack, even the most recent ones, with no medication. Because of Tessa. She would deliver her baby into this world drug-free.

"She doesn't want drugs. I promise we can help her through it. Put your hand here on the small of her back." Tessa kneeled beside her on the left side of the bed. Greg stood to her right.

Nicole felt the heel of Greg's large palm dig into the exact spot of her most excruciating cramp. She breathed out on a moan.

"You've got this." Tessa wiped the sweat from Nicole's forehead.

Greg's hand stilled. "You're in so much pain, Nic. Are you sure you want to do this? There's no shame if you change your mind and need meds."

Nicole turned her head to her husband, grimacing. "It's supposed to hurt." She wanted it to hurt. She wanted to feel every moment of her labor.

This was her family. Greg and Tessa were both here with her, supporting her. She could do this.

As another spasm seized her, she breathed in and out five times, like Tessa always told her to, focusing on the agonizing wave of torture until it faded.

"Thank you. I don't know what I'd do without you two," she managed when the pain subsided a little.

Nicole reached for Tessa's hand and squeezed. "I'll hold your hand for as long as you want, but don't break my bones!" Tessa joked.

"Here." Greg slipped his fingers into Nicole's. "Squeeze with all your might."

The moment of calm was interrupted by a loud, frenzied beeping. A team of nurses rushed in, jabbing the fetal monitor above the bed and pushing Greg and Tessa out of the way.

"What's wrong? What's wrong with my baby?" Nicole frantically gulped air. Her lungs compressed.

"Your baby's heart rate is plummeting. Everything is going to be fine, but you need an emergency C-section."

She struggled to understand.

"What's going on? Is my wife going to be okay?" Greg's voice was panicked, not his usual affable tone, which frightened Nicole even more. She was the one who panicked, not him. He was the calm one. He was her rock.

"She'll be fine, but we need to get her to surgery. Please, we need to do this right now."

Tessa marched back to Nicole's side. "She doesn't want a C-section. That's not the plan!"

"Please, Tessa. Listen to them," Greg said. "It's okay."

Nicole caught sight of her husband's face. What she saw sucked any remaining oxygen from her lungs. He looked . . . hopeful. Like perhaps it would be a good thing if he didn't become a father today. Or any day. No, it wasn't possible. It was ridiculous. She was in pain, in agony, and she was seeing things that weren't there. She was sure she imagined it, because just a moment later, he was beside her and sweetly kissed her forehead. "I love you, Nic. It's going to be fine. I'm not leaving your side."

She couldn't do or say anything else because a mask was placed over her face. Nicole was unconscious before she could ask if her daughter was going to survive.

———

The sharp odor of antiseptic filled Nicole's nostrils. She tried to sit up. Numb from the chest down, she couldn't move, so she groped around on the bed for anything that could leverage her. Something hard and cold was placed under her chin and she vomited.

"Nausea from the anesthesia. It will wear off. I'll put an anti-nausea in your drip, so you don't throw up again," a soft voice said.

She moved her head to the side and saw a woman in pink scrubs smiling kindly at her. And that was when it all came back to her, why she was there, what was going on.

"My baby. How's my baby? Is she—"

The nurse grinned. "She's fine. She's just fine." Then she wheeled a clear bassinet close to the bed. A tiny infant with wisps of dark hair lay sleeping on her back. Her paper-thin eyelids fluttered. Nicole couldn't believe this delicate, perfect baby was hers.

"Congratulations, Mommy. Would you like to meet your daughter?" The nurse picked up the baby and laid her on Nicole's chest, holding her there with a small, steady hand.

Without warning, massive sobs erupted from Nicole, startling the nurse.

"It's overwhelming, love, I know. She's perfectly healthy. Six pounds, nine ounces, and twenty-two inches long. And beautiful from head to toe. You'll be numb for a while and a bit groggy. I'll take her now, but I'll bring her to you to breastfeed soon so she gets the colostrum."

The nurse took the baby back before Nicole was ready. She was processing slowly; everything was happening too fast, and it was hard to make it stop.

"Where are my husband and best friend?" She gazed at her daughter in the nurse's arms. Her nose was so tiny, and her perfect mouth was a wonder. Nicole tried to control her tears, but she couldn't. She was a mother. A rush of love, so engulfing, so complete, spread through her entire body until the ferocity of it almost hurt. Then a tide of grief came over her as she remembered holding Amanda with such care so many years ago.

"They're waiting just outside. You need to recover a little bit more before any visitors can come in."

Her daughter was so still in the nurse's arms. Terror climbed up her throat. "She's breathing, right? Is she breathing?"

The nurse gave her a reassuring look. "She's breathing just fine." Nicole felt the tension leave her body. No matter how hard she fought it, she was slipping into sleep. When she next opened her eyes, Greg was sitting on the edge of the bed, with empty arms.

She shot up, her stomach screaming in protest, a burning and pulling. "Where's the baby?" she cried.

"Careful, Nic. You have to take it easy." He pointed at the bassinet under the window. "She's right there, and she's gorgeous."

Seeing the tiny figure swaddled in pink slowed her racing heart. She had given birth to a healthy daughter, and despite the frightening surgery, she was a mother. She reached for her husband's hand. "Do we really have a baby?"

Nicole's heart melted at the sight of Greg's awe-filled eyes. "She looks exactly like you. She's beautiful," he told her.

She knew when he met their daughter, he'd fall in love.

He let go of her hand and went over to the bassinet, then lifted their baby out and brought her to the bedside. She looked so tiny in his large arms. Nicole laughed out loud because Greg held her so delicately, as if worried he might break her.

"I'm not sure when I last held a baby. She's so small."

"Babies are tough," she said, then wished she could take the words back. She knew better than anyone how fragile they really were.

He laid a kiss on their baby's forehead, and she felt another flood of affection for her husband. Then he carefully handed her their daughter.

Nicole cradled her newborn, stroking her soft, round head and funny strands of black hair. "She's ours, Greg." To her daughter, she whispered, "We're going to take such good care of you." Then she looked up. "Where's Tessa?" She couldn't wait for her best friend to meet the baby. Hold her. She'd never seen Tessa with a baby before. Auntie Tessa was going to spoil her rotten.

"She went to get you some food from that vegan place you love. She said there was no way you'd eat hospital food."

Nicole laughed. "She's right. I just can't wait for her to meet our little Quinn."

They'd decided before she was born to name the baby Quinn, Nicole's mother's maiden name. Hearing it said out loud brought both joy and sorrow, and she felt the tears well in her eyes. How she wished her mother were sitting beside her, telling Nicole how proud of her she was.

Greg looked perplexed. "Why does the name card on her bassinet say 'Amanda'?"

Nicole stared at him, sure she'd misheard. "What do you mean?"

"There's a little card on the side of her bassinet. I like the name Amanda, too. Whatever you want to name her is fine by me."

She looked over at the bassinet and saw the name card, squinted to read the small type.

Amanda Markham.

No, no, no. How? That name. Why was that name on her baby's bassinet?

She felt a panic attack coming on. She had to stop it before Greg saw it happen. Now wasn't the time. This was the most beautiful moment of their marriage. *Gratitude, faith, and trust*, she repeated silently, inhaling and exhaling, to clear her crown chakra.

"Honey, are you okay?"

She struggled to stay steady. "Take her, please. I think my blood pressure's a bit low. I feel a little faint."

Greg put their daughter back in the bassinet and rushed to Nicole's side. "Nic? What's going on? Why are you freaking out?"

It had to be a clerical error, just a terrible, cruel, stupid coincidence. After five deep ins and outs, Greg's face came back into focus.

She wanted her baby back. Wanted to touch her. Feel her breathe. Nicole flung the covers off, pain radiating up her sternum, and tried to move out of the bed. Something pulled at her arm. The IV. "The baby. Please. I need my baby!"

"Honey, it's okay. I'll get her. The labor was intense. You're still really . . . emotional." He put their daughter back in her arms, then walked over to the bassinet, where he picked up the name card.

"Has a nice ring to it, don't you think?" Greg said, holding the card for her to see.

Amanda Markham.

Fighting the unbearable heaviness in her chest, Nicole turned away and lay back against the pillows. She put her fingers to the baby's neck. *Thump, thump, thump.* Every beat reassured her that her child was breathing, was alive, was hers. Her own breathing slowed, and she kissed her daughter's velvety cheek. She reveled in the softness and newness of her.

"I'll keep you safe. I'll love you forever. Nothing bad will ever happen to you," she promised her baby. Then she looked at Greg. "Sorry. I'm all out of sorts after the surgery. Quinn is her name. That's my decision. My mom would have been the best grandmother in the world. It means a lot to me that she takes her name."

Greg approached the bed and gently sat beside his wife and daughter. "You deserve whatever name you want. Quinn it is."

Before she could think any more about the name card, she heard the click of heels near her room. Expecting Tessa, she looked to the doorway and saw a woman outside. At first, Nicole couldn't process the flash of flaming-red hair, the exact color of Donna's hair, nearly twenty years ago.

Greg stroked his fingers along Nicole's temple. "What? You look like you just saw a ghost."

"Who was that?" she whispered.

"Who was who?"

"The woman at the door."

He observed her, saw her getting nervous again. "Well, it wasn't Tessa. I don't think she'd be back that fast." He glanced at the door. "There's no one there, babe. You're coming out of surgery, that's all. The meds are playing tricks on you. Can I get you anything?"

"I'm fine." It was a lie. A red-hot lie. "I'm just anxious for Quinn to meet her auntie."

She had so much more to be anxious about.

You don't deserve a baby girl. You're a murderer. You can't keep her safe.

Nicole looked out the door again, but the redhead was long gone.

CHAPTER FIVE

MORGAN

I shove the purple Post-it in my purse before I follow the officer up the concrete steps out of Grand/State, holding carefully onto the sticky black railing. Amanda. Is that the baby's name or the mother's? A cool gust of wind slaps my cheeks when we exit onto West Grand Avenue. Dusk has started to fall, and the sun is an orange ball of fire behind the station. Media vans and police cars by the dozen are parked carelessly in the bike lanes.

The officer stops at a police car, and I finally get a good look at him. He's short and wiry, and I realize we're almost the same height. Still, he's intimidating.

"I'm Officer Campbell. Can you tell me your name, please?"

"Morgan Kincaid." I whisper it because my throat is raw, as if sandpaper is grating against it.

He helps me into the back of the police car, his hand on my head as I slide in. I want to tell him not to touch me, but I don't. I feel like a criminal.

My grief engulfs me during the ride, and I stare out the window. But it quickly evolves into dismay when Officer Campbell turns onto North Larrabee. The trees transform from lush, emerald canopies to sparse and sad-looking branches, hunched over as though they sympathize with me. Brown-brick industrial buildings line both sides of the street, with parking lots and run-down shops leading the way to the dull gray concrete imposition that is the 18th District.

My dress sticks to the cracked black leather seat, and I unpeel myself before pulling my phone out of my purse. I shoot off a quick text to Jessica Clark, my attorney. She's the one who protected me when my entire world caved in, when Ryan was gone, and all my friends and family turned their anger on me. Maybe I don't need her this time. I did nothing wrong. But I don't trust the police.

I text her quickly.

Only a few seconds pass before she texts back: On my way.

I feel faint, and I'm afraid to collapse on the back seat. I should have pushed through that crowd and run away from that woman. But what would have happened to the baby? I wind the ends of my hair around and around my finger, letting the strands cut into my flesh.

Love her for me, Morgan.

I couldn't have gotten away.

Officer Campbell pulls into the police garage, and I unclasp my seat belt and then trudge behind him through the sally port, where he says my name into the speaker on the concrete wall. We ride the elevator to the interview rooms, and I avoid looking at the thick metal bars behind us that block potentially dangerous prisoners from the police. I don't want to be here.

"Ms. Kincaid, will you follow me, please?" Campbell's uniform strains against his biceps as he takes a paper from a sergeant manning the front desk.

I cringe at the thin layer of grime covering my dress and skin, but when I run my hand across my face, I smell the scent of the baby—powdery and fresh—and I hope she's okay.

I follow him through the station, the repetitive drone from the fluorescent lights making my head pound. The last time I was here was eighteen months ago. I was in a stupor of raw grief, my clothes and hands drenched in Ryan's blood.

Don't let anyone hurt her.

I will tell Officer Campbell everything. I'll simply recount every word the mother said. I'll tell him about the note, too, once he takes me wherever we're going now. How I have no idea how she did it, but that the mother stuck it to my purse before jumping.

We pass various offices. In one, I see an officer taking a call. He rushes up to close his door as we pass. Could he be calling the woman's partner or family? I know what it's like to be the person on the other end of the line. I got that same call from the hospital after my father died. I can almost feel the fall to the floor, the hunching over with knees to chest, the shivering, the despair. I know the voracity of blame and guilt, the emptiness of regret. No one forgets the moment when your entire life is ripped apart, crushed by the shocking truth. I feel a rush of empathy for the family the woman has left behind, especially her beautiful little baby girl. Then it occurs to me: If the woman had a family, why did she give her baby to me?

If anything ever happened to me, the police would have no family to call. My mother lives in Florida, and we barely speak. I actually can't remember the last time we talked. We saw each other six months ago, after my father's funeral. We sat awkwardly in the living room of my childhood home, cups of lukewarm tea in our hands.

"I'm moving to Miami to live with Aunt Irene. I have to sell the house, now that your dad is gone."

I understood the unspoken message. She couldn't afford the mortgage because my husband had stolen all their money, investing it in his corrupt hedge fund without their knowledge. My father's massive heart attack was, according to my mother, all my fault.

"I didn't know anything about what he was doing," I told her, hundreds of times. I'd said it to so many people. I repeated it by rote every time suspicion clouded the eyes of my friends, colleagues, and loved ones, all of whom had trusted Ryan with their investments. The only one who ever believed I had nothing to do with it was my father. But he's gone now. Gone forever.

Officer Campbell leads me through the station until we arrive at an unremarkable interview room, thankfully one that's new to me. Before dismissing himself, he says, "A detective will be with you shortly to get your statement. Do you want a coffee? Water?"

I take a seat in a hard swivel chair and shake my head. He leaves, and a few moments later, I hear footsteps and look up. I recognize the woman at the door. And from the look that registers on her face, she recognizes me, too. It's Detective Karina Martinez, the same detective who came to the crime scene in my home as I sat trembling beside Ryan's lifeless body. She was the one who led me away and questioned me about why he'd killed himself and about the millions of dollars he'd stolen.

She puts a *Chicago Tribune* and an open bottle of water next to a Kleenex box on the scratched laminate table. Then she takes the seat across from me and pushes her bangs off her high forehead. Her round face is smooth, not a single wrinkle. I wonder if she's still the youngest detective in this district. I'm aware of the camera blinking red from the corner of the ceiling, recording my every gesture. I cross my legs, then uncross them. I don't know how I'm supposed to behave. I feel guilty, even though I've done nothing wrong.

I clamp my lips shut.

Martinez pushes the bottle of water toward me. Then she leans closer. "So here you are. Again." She locks eyes with me, as though she's exhausted by the very sight of me.

Her demeanor is alarming. My palms start to sweat.

"Morgan, how have you been?"

I don't know what to tell her. Jessica would tell me not to say anything until she arrives, but surely I have to answer her. "I'm okay. Hanging in."

Martinez nods. "Can you state your name and address for the record, please?"

My hands quiver. "I think I should wait for my attorney."

"Your attorney is on her way? Interesting. You realize this is just a witness statement."

That's what I thought, too. So why is she acting like I'm guilty? I relent under the pressure. I give my name and address.

"Can you tell me exactly what happened today on the Grand/State platform?" she continues.

I swallow hard to buy myself some time, hoping Jessica will walk through the door and help me. Martinez trains her brown eyes on me and pulls her ponytail tighter.

I remind myself that the truth is on my side. What do I have to be worried about? Martinez just wants to know what happened. And there were so many witnesses. So many people must have seen that woman give me her baby and then jump.

I take a deep breath, open my mouth, and it all comes pouring out. "I was taking the train home at the same time I always do. I wasn't paying attention to my surroundings, so I was surprised when a woman grabbed my arm and asked me to take her baby."

Martinez arches her perfectly tweezed eyebrows. "Did you know who she was?"

I shake my head. "No. I'd never seen her before in my life. She seemed . . . not okay. I pulled my arm away, because she was scaring me. We were so close to the edge I was afraid for her and for the baby, but I didn't know what to do."

"Did you walk away? Or ask anyone for help?"

I shiver. I wish I had. "It all happened so fast. She was in front of me, and her eyes were darting every which way, like she was looking for someone on the platform. Like she was scared. Then she told me not to let anyone hurt her baby." I pull my purse closer to me. I won't tell her the woman said my name. I won't tell her about the note with the name "Amanda" on it.

"How did the baby end up in your arms before the woman landed on the tracks?"

My heart pounds inside my chest. "She shoved her into my arms. I was shocked and held her. I was actually worried I'd drop her, so I held her tightly. As I was looking down at that beautiful little baby, her mother jumped." My voice hitches, and tears spill down my cheeks. "I . . . I couldn't even stop it. It all happened so fast."

Martinez hands me a Kleenex, but there's nothing gentle about the way she thrusts it at me.

"I don't think you're telling me everything," she says.

I flinch. "Everything I've said is the truth."

"It's not what you've said that's untrue. It's what you're not saying, Morgan. Officers on-site at the platform have taken witness statements. People saw it all happen. And they heard her, the woman who jumped. Morgan, they heard her say your name."

Dread presses on my chest. I scratch my collarbone and wonder to myself why I kept that detail from her. "Yes, but I wasn't even sure I heard right. It was all so scary and sudden. I'm telling you the truth. I'm telling you what I know. I'd never seen her before. I'd never met or spoken to her ever before. I don't know who she was or how she knows me or why she talked to me at all."

There. I've told her everything, everything except the purple note. What if she knows about that, too? Should I wait for Jessica, or should I pull that out of my purse and confess?

Martinez takes a breath, crosses her arms. "Were you wearing a name tag today, maybe for work? Or personalized jewelry? Anything that would tell her your name?"

I think it through. I come up blank. "No."

Martinez stares hard at me, then picks up the *Chicago Tribune* sitting at the edge of the table. She slaps it open. She points at an article. "You know the victim, Morgan. She's Nicole Markham, the CEO of the Breathe clothing line. So what's your relationship with her?"

I can't silence my gasp. In the photo is a beautiful woman with chestnut curls. Her legs are long and lean in silver heels, and she's dressed in a tight, stretchy coral skirt and fitted white V-neck shirt. She looks the very picture of a high-powered, totally together female CEO. Is this really the same panic-stricken, bedraggled woman who pleaded with me to love her baby before jumping to her death? I can see it's her, but the transformation is horrible, a makeover played out in reverse.

And of course I know the company Breathe. Who doesn't? I even own some of their signature yoga leggings. But I'm not familiar with Nicole Markham. It's not like I know her personally. Why would this power maven, a complete stranger, ask *me* to keep her baby safe? How did she know me? And safe from what?

Then an idea hits me. "My name was in the news for a bit after Ryan died. Maybe she knew me from that?"

I don't say, "Now that my name is falsely connected to embezzlement," but I'm sure Martinez gets my point. "Or maybe Breathe has a connection to Haven House, where I work?" Few people even know the shelter exists; its location in a nondescript brown building on West Illinois Street is well hidden to safeguard the women and children who escape there.

Martinez taps the heel of her black pump on the floor. "We'll look into the Haven House files." She tosses me a glance that seems sympathetic, but it doesn't quite reach her eyes. "It must be hard being alone. Now that your husband is gone."

It is. I have no friends or family in Chicago anymore. After Ryan died, I realized my only friends during our marriage were his friends. He'd cheated them all and made me out to look like an accomplice. Even the friends I'd had from college and work winnowed away in the aftermath of his suicide. I was alone, with only my pain and loss for company. But I won't tell Martinez any of that because she's fishing for something. I don't know what.

Martinez's lips curl in distaste when I don't say a word.

"Morgan, it's always been a bit hard for me to believe that you didn't know your husband was stealing from his investors and defrauding the Light-the-Way Fund, a charity *you* founded. You lived with him, day in and out. You seem like a sharp woman. It's true we could never exactly prove that you knew what he was up to, but there's something about you that always seems so . . . unforthcoming. And here it is once more." She leans back, looking again at Nicole Markham's photo. "The CEO of Breathe is dead, and you were holding her baby on the edge of a subway platform. She said your name. Can you see why I think you knew each other?"

For Martinez to use my horrific, traumatic experience to trip me up suddenly infuriates me. I bolt out of my chair, knocking the water bottle over.

I point my finger at her. "Everyone thinks they know everything about me, and you know nothing," I say, my voice choked with more tears I don't want to shed.

Martinez eyes my raised finger. The clack of high heels in the hall diverts my attention. I shakily sit back down, my whole body sagging with relief when Jessica enters the room.

Jessica's so tall that even though I'm more than average height, I always feel short next to her. Her dark skin is smooth and clear, her belted teal dress, like all her clothing, so well suited to her. The first time we met, I asked if she was once a model.

She and Martinez greet each other politely, then Jessica pulls out the chair beside me and sits down, putting her hand on my shoulder.

Martinez fills her in about the woman who jumped and how I'm a "witness of interest." Jessica lightly lays her fingers on my back. "You all right, Morgan?"

Her gentle touch unravels the emotions I've barely kept in check since I got to the station. The woman's shredded lips, wild eyes, and desperation flash like a movie scene in my mind. I sob with grief, for this baby, for her mother I didn't know, and for myself.

Jessica pats my shoulder until my hiccupping stops.

To Martinez, she says, "I need a moment alone with my client." She looks up at the ceiling. "Without the camera on."

"Fine." Martinez stands, leaves, and closes the door behind her.

The room seems smaller now, and I feel so light-headed that I pull back from the table and bend my head to my knees.

Jessica waits until I lift myself to a seated position. "So I'm putting things together here." She looks down at the newspaper on the table. "I heard on the news that the CEO of Breathe committed suicide at Grand/State after giving a stranger her baby. You're the stranger?"

"Yes and no."

Jessica's eyes widen. "Time to tell me everything."

"I was waiting for the train when this woman grabbed my arm, told me to take her baby and love her. She looked so frightened, Jessica, like someone on the platform was after her. Then she said my *name*. She said, 'Love her for me, Morgan.' I told Martinez everything but that part. Then she said she'd heard already from other witnesses. It's like she's out to get me, and I was just standing there, waiting for the train." I drop my head into my hands. "I don't know why I didn't tell her right away." I look up. "I'm sorry."

She groans. "It's okay. You're under stress. I'm sure seeing all that brought up some horrible memories."

Ryan, the wound oozing with blood, the gun in my hand. *No, no, no, it can't be. This can't be happening.*

"Yes, it did," I admit. "And she chose me to protect her baby. And I—"

"Shh. I get it. It's okay. You were in shock. You didn't do anything wrong. And you know that it's my job to defend you. We've been through this before, Morgan. So now, let's just say you've talked enough. You're traumatized. You're not yourself. You can't talk to

Martinez anymore, to the media, to anyone again—not without me present."

She scoots her chair a little closer. "So, we don't have a lot of time here right now. If there are any other details that are important—anything else you've left out—it's time to tell me."

I push my hair back from my face, damp with panicky sweat. Then I rummage inside my purse for the Post-it and give it to Jessica. "I found this stuck to my purse, after. Maybe it's the baby's name?"

Jessica eyes the note curiously, turning it over in her hands. "No. The news said the baby's name is Quinn."

Not Amanda. Quinn. Such a beautiful name for the tiny girl I had held in my arms.

"So who's Amanda?" I ask. "And what if Quinn is in danger? Her mother suggested she was. She begged me not to let anyone hurt her baby. She was so antsy, like she was being followed. I think we should show this to Martinez, no?"

She gives a quick, sharp shake of her head and hands the note back to me. "Absolutely not. You put that note away right now. I'll have my investigator, Barry, do some digging. But until we know why Nicole said your name on the platform, or why she talked to you at all, telling Martinez anything will only make it sound like you had something to do with this. From what you've told me, Nicole Markham did not look or sound well."

Jessica's too close to me. I'm boxed in with nowhere to go.

"Is there a chance Nicole knew Ryan? Could she have been involved in his fraud?"

My stomach churns. Even though I think about Ryan all the time, I hate talking about him. "I still don't know everyone he stole from. He could have defrauded Nicole, or someone she knows. She could have borrowed from the wrong people to make up for the loss. She could have been in on it with him and never gotten caught. I don't know anything." My voice breaks. "He left me nothing but questions and hurt and anger. I never really knew him at all."

Something suddenly dawns on me. "Jessica, what if I'm in danger?"

"Relax. Nothing's pointing to that. Even this note isn't evidence that anyone wants to hurt the baby, you, or Nicole. Maybe her baby wasn't safe with *her*." Jessica stands, paces in the small room. Her face softens. "I know this is hard. But you have to stay calm."

"How can I stay calm when Nicole said my name, asked me to love her baby, then died right in front of me?"

She taps a pink fingernail to her lips. "We'll figure out why she approached you and if you're at any risk, okay? And I'm sure the baby has been taken somewhere safe."

She knows without my saying it that I'm worried about the baby. I feel like Jessica has infiltrated my deepest thoughts. She knows me so well.

Jessica sighs. "I'll do my best to find out more about Quinn. But right now, my goal is to get you out of here as soon as I can. Okay?"

I fall back into my chair.

"Fine. Whatever you say."

Jessica goes to the door, opens it. I see her signal down the hall for Martinez. Martinez glides back into the tiny space. Jessica glances at me, and I put my hand on my knee. I'm trembling from the inside out.

"Can I go home now?" I ask. I just want to be home.

"Not yet. I have some more questions, and you're going to need to answer them before you can go."

A look of trepidation passes over Jessica's face. "Can we please talk outside, you and me?"

Both women leave the room, closing the door behind them. For a moment, I'm left by myself, but before I can get used to it, they're back.

Martinez takes a seat behind the table. Jessica leans against the wall. She gives me a look, which means "say as little as possible."

Martinez is settling in slowly, taking her time.

"Martinez, we don't have all day," Jessica says.

The detective's espresso eyes sear into mine. "The victim landed on her back. Most people don't commit suicide by jumping backward."

I don't understand. I press my lips shut and grab the arms of the chair to stop my hands from shaking. I replay those final seconds in my mind. Did I see her jump or didn't I? My mind draws a blank.

Suddenly, I'm catapulted back to another time, back to the moment when I walked into Ryan's home office and found him on the floor. My heart, my life, shattered into a million pieces. The wet, sticky sensation of Ryan's blood on my wool pants comes rushing back to me, my hands covered in crimson after I pried the gun from his fingers. I was petrified the whole time that it would go off again. I tried to stanch the flow pouring from the gunshot blast in his stomach, willing my husband to take a breath. But it was too late. Sure, my marriage wasn't perfect. Ryan and I had our struggles. I wanted a child; he didn't. There were tensions. But I never wanted him to die.

And now this poor woman is dead, too. How did I not see what unfolded right in front of me? Why is it all so opaque?

"Morgan, did you grab that baby before you pushed her mother off the platform?"

The accusation hits me like a hard slap across the face. I look up at Martinez. My entire body goes cold, and I fight not to throw up all over the floor. She's asking me if I *murdered* Nicole Markham.

"What?" I'm staring at Jessica, wondering how the hell it is that I can be asked such a thing. Jessica intervenes.

"Nicole put her baby in my client's arms; my client did not *take* her from Nicole. And if Morgan hadn't been there to hold that baby, the child would have fallen to the ground or, worse, onto the tracks. She might have been hit by the train, too. So what kind of a question is this exactly? Morgan *saved* a baby. Lots of bystanders saw it happen. She's a hero." Jessica arches an eyebrow at Martinez.

Martinez smiles, a dimple deepening in her left cheek. On anyone else, it would be sweet. On her, it's a threat. "I don't think 'hero' is quite the word for Morgan."

She's right about that. A hero would have recognized the depth of Nicole's pain and would have known what to do right away, would have stopped this desperate mother from ending her life. I stood there, useless, gaping like a fish, as she dropped her baby in my arms. A hero would have figured out her husband was using her and countless others for his financial gain and would have stopped it from happening. It might be the only thing Martinez and I agree on: I'm no hero.

Martinez stands and pushes back her chair. What she says next chills me to the core.

"So you insist you don't know Nicole Markham, yet she called you by name. I have only one more question for you: How badly do you want a baby?"

"Don't answer that, Morgan." Jessica turns to Martinez and barks, "That's enough. Unless you're charging my client, we're leaving."

Martinez gestures to the door. "You're free to go. We'll be chatting again soon, I'm sure. It's amazing what you can get caught doing when you think no one is watching."

Jessica swivels her head to me, beckoning me to follow her out. Her lips are tightened in a thin line.

Keep her safe.

Love her for me, Morgan.

This woman, Nicole, knew I'd be at Grand/State. She chose me. I don't know why, but I'm going to find out. I'm not going to make the same mistake twice. I'm not going to sit here doing nothing while the whole world decides I'm a terrible person.

Jessica takes me by the arm. "Let's go," she says.

I step over the threshold and out the door. I never want to be in that room again. I'm tired of detectives and police and the leading stories they tell when they don't know a thing about me. This time, I'm not going to take it. This time, I'm going to clear my name once and for all.

CHAPTER SIX

NICOLE

Before

Sweat pooled between Nicole's breasts and dripped down the back of her neck. The early-morning sun blazed through the buttercream silk curtains, its brilliant rays stabbing her sore, grainy eyes. She'd never understood what sleepless nights meant until she had a baby. Not only did Quinn seem hungry every hour, but Nicole was up all night obsessively watching her, making sure she was still breathing. Every time her daughter shut her beautiful eyes, the color of the deepest ocean, Nicole kept vigil. Sometimes she even gently shook Quinn awake to make sure she was still alive.

Horrible things happened when no one was watching.

As a teenager, she'd never understood why Donna was so anxious and uptight all the time. The shelves in her living room were full of her dog-eared parenting books. She kept charts and notes on sleep and diaper schedules. Nicole had thought it was all over the top. Amanda was the sweetest, most content baby. But now that she had Quinn, she suddenly understood Donna's worries. All she could think about were disaster scenarios. What if Quinn choked on her formula? If Nicole dropped her? Held her too tightly?

The transition from hyperefficient, confident CEO to nervous, insecure new mother was overwhelming. Nicole wasn't quite sure who she was anymore.

She squeezed her eyes shut, leaning against the white lattice headboard, trying to hold herself steady against waves of dizziness. Quinn cried in her bassinet, wanting to be snuggled. Nicole opened her eyes to look at Quinn, and all she saw was Amanda.

Suddenly, she was a seventeen-year-old nanny once again, walking slowly down the narrow hall to Amanda's nursery. Nicole had just meant to close her eyes on the sofa for a second, but somehow she'd fallen asleep for longer. Nap time was over, but Amanda was still sleeping, which was strange. She had never slept this long before—a full three hours. Nicole pushed open the door to the nursery. Spinning above the crib was the butterfly mobile that always put Amanda to sleep. The soft, slow pings of "Rock-a-Bye Baby" still played on a continuous loop.

Nicole edged closer to the crib. Amanda looked so peaceful. "Never wake a sleeping baby," Donna had told her over and over. Inexperienced Nicole did what she was told. That was her job.

But something was terribly wrong. The baby was too still. She leaned down to pick up Amanda, and when her long dark curls brushed the baby's cheek, it didn't make her open her eyes and giggle as it usually did. Those little arms didn't reach for her. Amanda didn't move.

Nicole lifted her out of the crib and felt her forehead. The baby was cold to the touch. Heart pounding, Nicole fell to her knees. She gently laid the tiny, limp body on the floor, pressing her mouth to the baby's and pushing the tips of her fingers into her fragile, narrow chest. *Please, please, please*, she said out loud.

Her chest pinched so hard that she thought she was having a heart attack. She crawled to the phone to call 911, and the next thing she remembered was an oxygen mask covering her mouth and nose.

"What have you done?" Donna howled when she showed up to find Nicole on a stretcher. Donna's long red hair curtained Nicole as she screamed, "You're a murderer!"

It was then Nicole learned Amanda was dead.

And it was her fault.

She could never tell Greg any of it. Yes, some of the worry and panic she'd experienced since Quinn's birth was normal. But he would never understand the depth of her terror, its true source. Never for a moment could she forget that something awful could happen to Quinn. And because of that, Nicole never let her out of her sight. She would be the perfect mother. That was her goal. But when she expressed any concern, all Greg could say was "Follow your maternal instincts." How could she when she wasn't even able to breastfeed her baby? No matter how hard she tried, she didn't have enough milk. She was so disappointed in herself; in turn, Greg had been frustrated, distant, and short with her. And when she raised her concerns with him, he dismissed her.

"You don't understand, Greg," she told him, tears streaming down her face. "Breast milk contains antibodies to fight infections. It lowers her risk of asthma. It keeps her safe, and I can't do it!"

"I wasn't breastfed, and I turned out okay." He'd wrapped her in his arms, but she couldn't stop crying. "Nic, you have to calm down. You're a great mother, and Quinn is healthy. So she gets a few more colds? It's going to be fine."

It wasn't fine, though. Amanda had been healthy, too.

Now Nicole could hear Greg banging around downstairs, getting ready for work. She considered asking him to come up and hold the baby so she could shower and get dressed, but she decided she could manage on her own.

She placed a hand on her still-tender stomach, trying to draw in a breath and let it out slowly, but it hurt her incision. And deep breathing was no longer a match for her incessant panic attacks. Those attacks weren't just because of Quinn. No, not at all. She could deal with her daughter's cries. Those were the sign of a healthy, lively baby. But what still had her rattled was that name on the bassinet: Amanda. She couldn't shake the feeling that she was being watched. Or that she was seeing things that weren't really there. Had Donna been right outside her hospital room? Was she in Chicago now? If so, what did she want? Payback? Revenge? And if so, how far was she willing to go to get it?

For two weeks, Tessa had come over almost daily, bringing oil samples from Breathe and trying every mindfulness technique she could to help Nicole, but nothing worked. Finally, a few days ago when Greg was at work, they were sitting on the couch in the living room, Tess holding Quinn because Nicole couldn't breathe. Sweat dripped down her face, and she had a hand jammed against her chest to relieve the crushing pain.

"Nic, I think you might need to see a doctor. I know you don't want to go on medication again, but you're really struggling."

"I hate meds, Tess. I need to be alert," she choked out.

"You're not alert, though. And medication has changed a lot in the last few years. Please. For Quinn. Just talk to your doctor."

Desperate, Nicole did as Tessa instructed. Her doctor prescribed Xanax immediately, assuring her it was the safest option. Nicole had taken the pills as prescribed for four days already. Now, Nicole was sure she'd never make it through the day without drugs. Frantically, she raked her bedside table, a gorgeous hand-rubbed mahogany that their decorator had picked up from a beautiful shop on North Clybourn Avenue. But she couldn't find the omnipresent orange bottle of white tablets she always kept by her bed.

She got up, holding on to the edge of the table so she wouldn't pass out. Had the bottle somehow rolled onto the floor? Nothing. She was so tired she couldn't think straight. Had she moved the bottle and forgotten?

She opened the drawer of her bedside table to see if she'd put the bottle inside by mistake. No pills. But there was a crumpled ball of paper next to a hardcover book. Nicole pulled it out. Donna's last letter. The letter Nicole was sure she'd left in her desk at Breathe.

You don't deserve a baby girl. You're a murderer. You can't keep her safe.

How did it get in her house? Had she brought it home herself and forgotten? Or had someone put it in there?

Quinn cried out again. Nicole put the paper back in the drawer and slammed it shut.

"Mommy's here. I'm here," she said, her breath ragged. She reached into the bassinet to cradle her baby. Her stomach pulled. She'd had no idea recovering from a C-section would be so painful. No idea that the love she felt for Quinn would completely overtake her.

With Quinn tucked against her, Nicole managed to make it to her en suite. She flipped open the glass cabinet while still holding her baby. There was her bottle of medication. Relief washed over her. Was this what motherhood felt like for everyone? A constant state of fear and panic? Transforming overnight from a fully confident adult into a terrified, anxious, forgetful mess? She had no friends with children, and though some of her staff had kids, it wasn't like she had a personal relationship with them, so she couldn't ask. And she couldn't ask her mother. The thought made her feel a spear of grief in her heart.

Quinn was still sobbing. She brought her back to the bassinet in the bedroom and dry-swallowed the tablets, knowing it would take only a short time before her head was clearer. Greg's cell trilled from downstairs. His *Mission: Impossible* ringtone used to make her roll her eyes and giggle. Nothing made her giggle lately.

From downstairs, she heard him answering the call. Greg chuckled; she could tell he was talking to a woman. He never laughed like that with her these days. Not since the baby was born. Nicole was simply no fun since she'd become a mother.

She picked up her daughter and curled her fingers around Quinn's fragile head. Then she made it to the top stair, carefully descending to the main floor on her bottom. It was humiliating to have to do this, and every step shot pain through her stomach, but it was better than crashing headfirst to the marble and Quinn's skull splitting open.

"Calm," she said out loud to remove the intrusive thought.

She thought about her misplaced pills. When she'd dropped the white prescription bag on the kitchen counter after seeing her doctor, Greg had said, "You wouldn't get an epidural, but you're going to take Xanax?"

"I've always had a bit of an issue with anxiety, but it was manageable for a long time," Nicole had replied, the most she'd ever admitted to him. "It started after my parents were killed. Then I went on Zoloft in college but stopped taking it years ago. It made me drowsy and unfocused. My doctor said Xanax is better and totally safe for me to be on while I take care of Quinn."

"You never told me you took antianxiety meds." He'd rubbed his forehead, then gently caressed the back of her neck. "Nic, I know you're a workaholic, but never once have I seen you so on edge. I worry about you."

"Don't worry, I'm fine," Nicole had said as she popped the cap and took two tablets.

Now she made it to the bottom step, tucking Quinn firmly in the crook of her arm so she could use her other to lift herself. Getting to the main floor was exhausting, but it was also good to move. How she loved this house. Their three-story graystone on East Bellevue Place was a masterpiece, prime Gold Coast real estate. Paid for in cash, and a far cry from the two-story brick house in North Kenwood she and her brother, Ben, had struggled to maintain after their parents died. Their inheritance ultimately couldn't keep up with the leaking roof, busted boiler, and flooded basement. They'd sold their family home after Nicole returned from Kenosha. She'd moved into the dorms at Columbia College, and Ben got a small apartment near his medical school.

Nicole passed the pure-white living room, decorated with chrome and glass—all clean lines and no clutter—and saw that the purple tulips she always kept fresh in Lalique vases were dead, their petals falling to the floor in a sad heap. She had postponed the cleaning crew that used to keep her home spotless. She wasn't comfortable with strangers in the house right now.

Greg was in the kitchen drinking a cup of coffee, phone to his ear. He flushed and ended the call when he saw her looking at him. Why was it that lately he hung up quickly whenever she walked into the room?

"Who was that?" she asked.

"My assistant, calling about a client's portfolio."

Greg stroked his hands up and down his suit-clad thighs, a habit that was endearing to her. It was a small crack in his confident facade, and it made her feel like she wasn't the only one with flaws. "She has a big learning curve and needs help."

She was a new mother who needed help, too, Nicole thought to herself. But she didn't say it. Greg's eyes scanned her up and down. She could just imagine what he saw—the bluish-red smudges under her eyes; limp, lank hair; and the same black Breathe yoga pants and white T-shirt that she'd worn for days. How could she have created a multimillion-dollar empire yet not have the energy to shower and change her clothes?

"Is Tessa coming over at some point today?"

Nicole shrugged. "I'm not sure. Why?"

"It would be good for you to have some female company. Actually, I was thinking we should get some real help, paid help in, so you have more time for yourself. Even a spa day. We could go together, like we used to."

Her chest pinched. Greg just didn't get it. She didn't want to leave Quinn for a second. In his eyes, she saw a sadness she'd never seen from him before, as though the spark had dimmed. She remembered how his face had lit up when she'd surprised him with first-class tickets to Paris for their first anniversary. How they'd barely made it to their hotel room before ripping each other's clothes off, and he'd held her hand on every cobblestone street they'd strolled.

He'd proposed only six months after they'd started dating. On one knee in the Breathe lobby, in front of all her employees, he'd said, "I've never known anyone who embraces life with the confidence and passion you do. I want to share my life with you."

Where was her confidence now? When Breathe's fourth international storefront opened in Singapore, Greg made a reservation, under Nicole's name, at Everest, her favorite restaurant. He'd waited there, on the fortieth floor of Chicago's Mercantile Exchange, for an hour by himself because she was on a conference call. Greg didn't mind. He would have waited for her forever back then. Now she felt so disconnected from him. But she didn't know if it was only coming from her.

"You're so tired, Nic. I really think we should get a nanny."

"No nannies," she said quickly, and dug the heel of her hand into her forehead where a headache drilled into her temples. "Do you know what happened to my pills? They weren't beside my bed."

Greg frowned. "You left them down here in the pantry next to the formula, and I put them in the medicine chest in the bathroom."

Nicole racked her memory. Is that where she'd left them? She could barely remember to brush her teeth anymore.

He brought her a warmed bottle of formula and tears sprung to her eyes. Just this small kindness made her want to fall apart in his arms. But she didn't want to seem weak. She had to keep it together.

Quinn was sobbing. Nicole slipped the bottle between her rosy lips, and the kitchen became so quiet that Nicole almost wept at the respite. Every time her child let out that heartbreaking cry, she felt like it was her fault.

Her phone buzzed in the pocket of her yoga pants. It had been Tessa's brilliant idea to add pockets to the spring line last year.

Greg took Quinn from her arms and smiled down at his daughter. For that brief moment, Nicole reveled in her little family. Everything would be okay. This was a massive adjustment. But they would get through it. He'd always put her career first because he knew how much Breathe meant to her—to them and their dreams of success. Together they could do anything.

She pulled her phone out of her pocket. It was a text from Tessa, the only person she could talk to these days.

Can I come by later? We could go for a walk. I bought a dress for Quinn.

Nicole wrote back: Not sure I can manage a walk just yet. But come by after work. Please.

She looked up from her phone. Greg and Quinn were no longer in the kitchen.

Suddenly, a high-pitched, tinny sound broke the silence— "Rock-a-Bye Baby," a lullaby she never played for her daughter be- cause it reminded her of Amanda and that harrowing summer day. Nicole froze.

Where was it coming from? She and Greg hadn't yet opened any of the musical toys they'd received.

The eerie melody stopped.

"Honey," she called out to Greg. "Did you hear that?"

"Hear what?" he called back from the living room.

Had she imagined it?

Her hands shook violently. It had sounded like it was coming from upstairs.

Rather than have Greg look at her yet again like she was crazy, she decided to investigate herself. Her pelvis throbbing, she went to the stairs and started climbing. She approached each step like it was a mountain. She made it to the top, triumphant.

Upstairs, silence. She was just about to go back downstairs when the slow, sinister timbre of the lullaby started up again. It was coming from the nursery. Nicole pushed open the door.

Cherry blossom decals climbed the dove-gray walls, bracketing a white shelf filled with plush stuffed animals. It was a dream room, perfect for her baby girl. But spinning in lazy circles above the crib was a mobile of pastel-colored butterflies, one that Nicole hadn't seen in almost twenty years. It was the exact same spinning toy that had hung above Amanda's crib all those years ago, the mobile Donna had changed the batteries in on a weekly basis.

"*When the bough breaks, the cradle will fall . . .*"

The lullaby stopped. Nicole scanned every corner of the room. Who had done this? Was someone in here still? But the room was empty, and the mobile went silent.

Eventually, she found her voice. "Greg! Come here!"

She heard his thundering footfalls rush up the stairs. He appeared, panting at the door with Quinn in his arms. "What?"

"This." Shakily, she nodded to the mobile.

"What's the problem, Nic?" he asked. "It's just the mobile."

"Did someone give that to us?" she asked. Quinn started to cry again, and Nicole was desperate to hold her. But she was trembling so much she was afraid to. "Why is it here? Where is it from?"

Greg gawked at her. "Are you kidding?"

She pressed her hand to her stomach as a cramp seized her. "What do you mean?"

He walked over to the crib, then placed Quinn in it. Nicole backed herself against a wall and slid down it so she could rest on the floor.

"Hey," Greg said when he saw the terror in her face. He came down to her level, sat beside her. "It's okay." He laid a gentle hand on her knee. He was being overly kind, as if she were on the verge of a breakdown. "Nic, *you* bought that mobile."

Nicole pushed herself away from him. "I didn't!"

"Honey, you did. You left a printout from eBay on the living-room table a few days ago. You ordered it. I put it up for you, so you'd have one less thing to do. What did I do wrong?" His shoulders fell.

She felt a crawling sensation, a thousand insects skittering down her arms. Nicole had never bought anything from eBay in her life. And even if she did, she would never have bought *that* mobile. Never.

Nicole's throat felt like she'd swallowed broken glass. The name card, the redhead outside her room at the hospital, the missing pills, and now, the mobile. Was she losing her mind?

She could see that Greg was trying to stay calm, but there was impatience on his face.

"Nicole, it's not a big deal. I forget stuff, too." He got up carefully and went to the crib, sniffing at Quinn. "She needs a change. I'm really sorry, but I have to go to work." He came back to her and wrapped his arms around her freezing body. "You need more sleep, babe. How about I come home a bit earlier and take Quinn for a walk so you can nap?"

"No, don't worry. Tessa's coming." Then she squinted at him, re-membering his voice laughing on the phone. "Greg, I know you're here, so why does it feel like you're not? Like you're not really present."

He massaged his temples hard. "Nic, I've offered to give her a bath. To change diapers. Let you nap on the weekends. You always say no or just ignore me."

What was he talking about? She couldn't remember a single time he'd offered anything like that.

He looked at her sadly and got up from the floor. "Tessa says you haven't once checked in with your office, and you're walking around like a zombie. Please see if she can come over earlier so you're not here by yourself. I'm just worried about you. I want you to feel happy and safe with Quinn."

You can't keep her safe.

"She's safer with me than anyone!" Nicole cried out.

But she wasn't sure anymore if this were true.

CHAPTER SEVEN

MORGAN

Jessica and I are in her white Mercedes. She's driving me home, after rushing me past the throng of reporters outside the police station. They were already scouting for information about the well-known CEO's suicide. Even through the glass, I could hear them shouting out questions. "Were you on the platform?" "Was she pushed?" "Where's the baby?"

As their cameras furiously clicked, I wondered if my photo would get published. Would my colleagues and former friends see my picture in the press? Would my mother? I'm already a pariah, but now this? The last thing I need is to find myself back in the limelight.

We exit the lot and sail through a green light to turn onto West Division Street. Jessica is focused on driving me safely to my home, the brown-brick apartment building where I live on North Sheridan

Road. "How could this happen?" I ask. "I was just going home. And does Martinez really think I could have grabbed the baby and pushed Nicole Markham off that platform? For what reason?"

"Right now you're only a person of interest. Martinez will try to figure out the connection between you and Nicole. Which is exactly what I'm going to do, too, as soon as I get back to the office. If reporters contact you, do not comment."

"I have nothing to say to them. I don't know anything." I curl up in my seat, wishing I could disappear.

When we pull up to my building, I point out the back parking lot. "Go that way. I'll enter from the rear entrance."

Jessica navigates the dark, narrow driveway. Her phone rings on the console between us, startling me. She takes one hand off the wheel to pick up. "Hi, Barry."

Barry is Jessica's investigator. Her face changes as she listens to him. At one point, she glances at me, but I can't tell if her look is nervous or confident.

She hangs up and parks the car. "You were on YouTube. A dad taking his son to his first baseball game was recording his kid on the platform at Grand/State. He caught what happened between you and Nicole. The cops have taken the video down, but Barry managed to copy it beforehand. He's emailing it to me now."

I sit up straighter. "This is great news, right? It's proof that she handed that baby over to me just like I said."

Jessica doesn't answer. Fear zips up my rib cage. She flicks on the car light, then loads up the video and turns her phone toward me so we can both see the screen. I prepare myself to watch Nicole jump. But I am not prepared at all for what it is I see.

The footage is grainy, but I recognize the subway platform. A blond boy of about seven is grinning at the camera, a baseball glove clutched in his raised hand. In the far-right corner of the screen I see Nicole, and I can see myself, too. Nicole is heading straight for me, her blue bag over her shoulder, daughter clamped against her. I'm a figure in white, frozen in bewilderment, my purse dangling from my shoulder.

Nicole presses close to me, too close to the platform's edge. We're side by side. Her left hand moves to my hip. Is that when she slipped the note onto my purse?

It's amazing what you can get caught doing when you think no one is watching.

Is this what Martinez meant? Did she know about the video when she questioned me at the station?

Nicole steps in front of me, her back to the tracks. There's a moment when my figure is partially covered by hers. She takes a small step back and I'm visible again, holding the baby. I know I didn't grab for the child, but our arms move at almost the same time and it's hard to see exactly what happened. To anyone else, it might seem like I did take that child. On the screen, I look down at Quinn in my arms and Nicole retreats another step, right to the lip of the platform. Some commuters walk in front of the camera, obscuring us both for a moment before we appear again. Nicole looks startled and then her arms are flailing in the air, but I'm eclipsed by people. She falls backward off the platform and off the edge of the video screen. The train barrels into the station.

Watching her fall is like a punch to my stomach. The video comes to an end, and Jessica takes a sharp breath. I shake my head so hard and fast that blood rushes painfully through my skull.

"No, no, no. That video, it's not showing what really happened! She *gave* me her baby, but you can't see that part. And I didn't push her. I swear I didn't push her. There were so many people. There must be a witness who saw what really happened." I grab the door handle, wanting more than anything to get out of this confined space. To escape the horror Nicole Markham has put me in.

Jessica puts her phone on her lap. "So you see now why Martinez was grilling you? It's not clear how Nicole went over. She moves away from you. Not far enough that you couldn't reach her, but enough for me to possibly use this as exculpatory evidence that she jumped. But, Morgan, none of this explains why she knew your name, and that's not good."

I can't breathe. Watching this has made me so scared. Even my own mother thinks I'm guilty of helping Ryan bilk innocent victims out of their savings. So why wouldn't total strangers think I pushed a woman to her death?

Jessica observes me. "Is there anything you're not telling me? I need to know everything so I can help you."

"Nothing. I didn't know her at all." I press a hand over my eyes, wishing this were all a nightmare.

But it's not, and I have to deal with it. I remember the baby. I can't forget Nicole's eyes, drilling into mine. This was a mother who was desperate to protect her child. And from what? What if the person who has her baby is the person Nicole was so afraid of? "I need to know where Quinn is."

Jessica scratches the bridge of her nose. "No, you don't. If you insist that you don't know Nicole, then her baby can't matter that much to you, right?" She puts her hand on my arm. "All you need to do is help me build a defense, because I think you're going to need it. You have no motive to want the CEO of Breathe dead. But think. Are you *sure* you've never met Nicole? There has to be some reason she approached you."

I wish the answer were that easy. I wish I knew the answer.

My heart thunders. "Jessica, if I really am tied up in this thing, or if Ryan is, what kind of danger could I be in?" The back of the building is pitch-black. Jessica has turned off the car, turned off the lights. I can barely see the door from here. Anyone could hide behind the dumpster and not be seen. They might be ready to jump out at us the second we leave the car.

Jessica purses her lips. "Let's just say you should be extra vigilant until we figure things out. In the meantime, I'll start investigating Nicole's background and any link she might have to you."

A thought occurs to me. "Jessica . . ."

"What?"

"Do you think this Nicole woman somehow knew how much I want a baby?"

Jessica looks at me like I'm either crazy or dangerous, or both.

"I don't know," she says, her voice flat and cold.

But the truth is Nicole *did* know how badly I want a baby. I could see that in her eyes.

I know what you want. Don't let anyone hurt her.

And no matter how much I lie to myself now, saying that I'll never have a child after everything that happened with Ryan, the truth is, I think about it every time I see a mother with a baby. I feel a stab of envy right in my soul. I think about it every time I hear the giggles and splashes of children at Foster Beach, close to my home. I think about it every time I go to bed and wake up all alone.

Love her for me, Morgan.

Why me?

Jessica clicks on her high beams. She must be wondering why I'm just sitting there, staring out the window. She cocks her chin at the back door. "Do you want me to come up with you?"

I shake my head. I trust Jessica even if she doesn't fully trust me. Twice, I've left the same police station a free person because of her. But I haven't really been free. And now, what will happen? What will people think? I wish I didn't care. But of course I do. I feel very alone.

We say good night, and I head inside. The elevator dings open to my floor and I step off, my sandals sliding a bit on the cheap oatmeal-colored carpet of the hallway. I open my door and almost fall to the hardwood floor in gratitude. I'm finally home, greeted by my familiar sage walls and silence.

I make little more than minimum wage at Haven House, and a suicide clause voided the insurance policies Ryan and I maintained during our six-year marriage. Our joint accounts were drained in restitution to all the people he stole from. I sold all my jewelry, except a few pieces that belonged to my grandmother, and all my designer clothes, but it will never be enough to repay the people Ryan destroyed. My mother refused to take any money from me. "The damage is done, Morgan," she'd said.

My father taught me to keep a private account, where I socked away half my paychecks for years. I offered as much of my savings as I could to the victims Ryan swindled, with only enough left to afford Jessica's legal fees, rent, and basic needs. It's enough for me. I never wanted to be rich. I just wanted a family.

I look around my small apartment—two cramped bedrooms, a postage-stamp-size kitchen, and a bathroom with a shower and tub. I have a secondhand fuchsia couch. Bright colors help lift the dark sadness that weighs me down inside. I collapse on my couch and rest for a moment. Then I have an idea. I dump out the contents of my purse. Maybe Nicole left other clues in there, anything that might lead me closer to knowing what really happened at Grand/State and why.

But once my wallet, phone, car keys, lipstick, gum, pepper spray, purple note, and lint are strewn over the couch, my bag is empty. So that one Post-it is all I have to go on. The name "Amanda," which means nothing to me. Is she Nicole's sister? A friend? If not her baby, then who?

I shove everything back in. On my skin, I smell sweat and sadness and fear, the smell of a trapped animal.

I need to feel clean. I head to my very basic bathroom and turn the water as hot as I can take it. I strip down and hop in the shower. I scrub myself raw. I can't stop tearing apart the dry, rough skin on my neck. I feel my sharp collarbone and bony hips. I miss my roundness, even the small belly I once bemoaned, which is now concave and laced with stretch marks from sudden and extreme weight loss. I was never thin until Ryan died. It pains me that I still miss him.

I miss my father, too. I miss his bellowing laugh at stupid jokes, his hard hugs. He always made me feel like the most beautiful and interesting woman in the room. I hate that I will never feel his comfort again.

The tears come fast and furious. I crouch in the shower, the scalding water sending needles of pain down my back. I wail like I haven't since my father's casket was lowered into the ground. I give in, to all my losses and regrets. I accept it all. But there are two things I can't accept: I didn't take that baby, and I didn't push her mother off the platform.

Finally, shivering and soaking and emotionally drained, I turn off the shower and stop sobbing. I dry and cover myself in a scratchy towel. In my bedroom, I open my dresser drawer to find leggings and a T-shirt to sleep in. Quickly throwing them on, I go to close the drawer when I see a pair of rose-colored Breathe pants. A sob builds again, but I force it down. *Enough*, I tell myself. *You have to get yourself together*.

I grab my phone from my purse and my computer from the coffee table. I mostly avoid going online, since social media and blogs ruined my reputation after Ryan was exposed. But the Internet seems like the place to search for any reason Nicole might have sought me out.

I head to my room and lie back on my bed, in the middle, though by the morning, I'll end up on the left like I always do, as though Ryan still sleeps beside me on the right.

I take a deep breath and turn on my computer. The ticker tape at the top of my search engine reads: "CEO of Breathe Athleisure-Wear Dead at Thirty-Six Under Suspicious Circumstances."

It's real and it's out there. I read the first five posts. The video is mentioned, but it's been taken down, so the link is broken. There are scant details, but what's concerning is that they haven't confirmed suicide—it's as though there's doubt that she jumped. There is one line about the police questioning a person of interest who spoke to the victim before she died, someone who was holding Nicole's baby after she landed on the tracks. My name isn't mentioned. Yet. How long do I have before it's splashed across a lurid headline?

To know they're talking about me exhausts me. I shut down my computer. I won't learn anything else right now because I can't stop my eyes from closing. I can't think straight. I'll just take a quick nap to restore myself, then I'll continue researching.

When my phone rings, I don't know why my cheeks are damp with tears or why my eyes feel puffy and sore. Birds chirp, and the sun streams in through my small window where I've hung sheer peach curtains. I realize that for the first time in a long while, I've slept through the night and, for a second, all seems right with the world. Then I remember. Grand/State. Nicole. Amanda. Quinn. The video.

I grope for my phone on the bed and put it to my ear. "Hello," I croak, my eyes still closed.

"Ms. Kincaid, this is Rick Looms."

I run a hand through my tangled hair, barely awake when he says, "I'm Nicole Markham's attorney."

Anticipation and apprehension twine together into a ball in my throat, preventing me from responding. Why is Nicole's attorney contacting me?

I should never have answered the phone.

"I was Ms. Markham's attorney for many years. I'm sorry to inform you that she passed away unexpectedly last night."

The ball in my throat expands, and I say nothing.

"It's a shock, I'm sure. Because there's a child involved, I had to contact you immediately should you wish to begin the process."

What process? What is he talking about? All I can hear is the blood roaring in my ears.

"Ms. Kincaid?"

I cough into the phone. My throat has gone completely dry. "Sorry," I say. "I'm trying to understand what you just said. I'm not sure why you've contacted me."

"Ms. Markham left very clear instructions for you in her will."

I bolt up. "Her will?" I ask incredulously.

Mr. Looms clears his throat. "Ms. Kincaid, Nicole left you custody of her daughter."

CHAPTER EIGHT

NICOLE

Before

Nicole was reaching for a bottle from the kitchen cupboard when she heard the piercing crash of glass shattering. She jumped in fright, bashing her head into the sharp corner of the cabinet. Then she froze. Was someone in her house? Greg was at work. Quinn was in her arms. Nicole's head was spinning. She was so woozy that she put Quinn on the floor and curled into a small ball beside her.

Then she heard the front door open and close quietly. Footsteps echoed on the marble through her house. Nicole whimpered, starting to crawl toward the pantry, which had a door she could shut.

The footsteps got closer. She wasn't going to make it.

"Nic! What are you doing?"

Tessa's dainty sandaled feet appeared in front of her. Nicole touched her forehead where a cut oozed blood. Trembling, she explained. "I heard a noise. Something breaking, and I banged my head on the cupboard. Was the glass on the front door smashed? Is that how you got in?"

Tessa glanced toward the front hall. "No, the door is fine." Her brow wrinkled. "I knocked, but you weren't answering, so I tried the knob and it was open." She inspected the cut, her eyes clouded with worry. "That looks like a hard bang. You okay?"

"What do you mean the door was open? That's impossible!" Her voice rose shrilly, and Quinn screamed. "Shush, honey. Mommy's here. I'm here," she soothed.

The door was locked. Nicole knew it was. She had checked it five times after Greg left that morning, like she did every day since the mobile had appeared in Quinn's room a week ago, the mobile she'd ripped from the crib and tossed in the garbage and never wanted to see again.

Tessa gently took Quinn from the floor, quieting and cradling her as though she were her own child. "I think she's sensing your stress. Just take a minute. I'm here now."

Nicole blew out a breath. She touched her forehead. The bleeding had stopped. The silence was so nice. But seeing how calm and efficient her best friend was made her feel inadequate and worthless. She was so obsessed with watching Quinn every second that daily tasks had become insurmountable. Who was she? She barely recognized herself.

She hadn't sent any photos of her daughter to anyone at Breathe to show her off, like her staff did when they had a baby. She hadn't felt this untethered, this useless, in decades. She had hundreds of unanswered emails in her in-box, unreturned phone calls. Yes, she was on maternity leave, but she'd fully intended to work from home and pop in to Breathe at least every few days. She hadn't stepped foot into her company in three weeks. She couldn't hear a noise in the house without thinking someone was after her and the baby.

She hadn't confided in Tessa about the odd occurrences since Quinn was born. It would sound deranged. She couldn't tell her she was paranoid that Donna was watching them. And she couldn't tell Tessa she was terrified Donna was going to hurt them. Nicole didn't know what Donna was capable of. Or what she could be planning.

Still holding the baby, Tessa handed her a towel for her face.

"Thank you, Tessa," Nicole said, wiping away the sticky blood on her forehead. "I swear I heard something. I was just so scared that someone broke in." Tessa had always been the person she vented to. She needed to explain how she felt, without mentioning Donna. She tried to form the right words. "I'm not myself at all right now. I'm so anxious all the time. I don't know what's going on with me or how to fix it."

She'd also gotten more forgetful since the mobile had shown up in the nursery. More panicked. She put her head on her knees. "Tess, I think something's wrong with me."

She lifted her head and watched Tessa put Quinn in the vibrating chair—Nicole had one in almost every room, even though she rarely let Quinn out of her arms. Tessa was at her side. She helped Nicole to her feet. She was so dizzy. She made it to a chair, and the wooziness faded.

Tessa sat across from her. "I think your hormones are out of whack and you're exhausted. And, legally, you're on maternity leave. Lucinda, the other board members, they can't do anything about that. When you're back in three weeks, it will be like you never left. I've taken over every project I can, including the brochure launch. All you have to do right now is be a mom."

"Being a mom is harder than being a CEO."

Tessa laughed. "That's only one of the reasons I don't want kids. I think you're too hard on yourself."

Now that she was talking to Tessa about how she felt, the band around her chest loosened. "Lucinda was a bit cold when I called and told her I can't even work from home right now."

Tessa snorted. "I'll bet. She's a bit of a bitch," she said, then glanced at the dishes piled next to the sink, crusted with food, the counters stained with coffee, and the dirty bottles lying all over the place. "I'm always here for you, Nicki. Anytime, okay? This is just a bad patch. Things are going to get better."

Tessa was the only person allowed to call her "Nicki," the term of endearment her mother used to call her before she died.

Nicole nodded. "Thank you. I know you're working overtime. And you're always here. You must have better things to do."

Tessa waved her off. "I love you, Nic. I'm working at night as much as possible, and I'm happy to help in any way I can. You'd do the same for me."

Nicole was so grateful to have Tessa. So glad she'd hired the twenty-two-year-old straight out of college. At the time Nicole had been twenty-nine, the same age Tessa was now. She'd never expected to be so close to such a young woman, but Tessa was an old soul.

Quinn reminded them both that she was there. "That girl's got lungs, huh? Fierce like her mom." Tessa rocked the vibrating chair with her foot until Quinn calmed down. Then she wet sheets of paper towels, brushed Nicole's hair away from her forehead, and held them to her temple. "She's still crying a lot. Have you asked your doctor about it?"

"She said it was probably colic and that the first three months are sometimes hell."

Tessa giggled. "And there's reason two I'm happily remaining childless." Then her face became serious. "Look, it's really hard to go from a life of work to staying home with a baby all day. You could get a babysitter once in a while. Not a live-in or anything like that, but just during the day."

Nicole looked into Tessa's eyes. "You know I can't do that."

Tessa nodded sympathetically and knew not to say Donna's or Amanda's names. She clearly understood how Quinn's birth had brought that horrendous summer to the forefront of Nicole's mind.

There was so much Nicole wasn't saying. Her panic attacks were getting worse, despite the medication. She was scared to sleep. Scared to be without her daughter for a minute. She also couldn't rid herself of her apathy toward everything that wasn't Quinn—Greg, yoga, and Breathe, the company that used to be her whole life.

Tessa dabbed at the cut on Nicole's forehead, and each pat made Nicole feel taken care of. "Come on. Let's go see what that noise was. One step at a time."

Nicole nodded and waited for Tessa to pick up Quinn. Then she followed Tessa out of the kitchen to search the main floor.

As they passed the front door of the house, Nicole paused. "You said the door was unlocked when you got here?"

Five days before, Greg had arranged for a new dead-bolt lock to be installed. It made her feel safer. Had she really left it unlocked? She'd taken her Xanax a few hours earlier, but that wouldn't make her forget locking the door.

"Maybe Greg forgot to lock it when he left. He must be wrecked, too."

Nicole extracted Quinn from Tessa's arms so she could feel her baby's warmth on her body.

"He's not . . . He's been staying late at work and sleeping in the guest room the past week. He can't get enough sleep with Quinn in the same room."

Tessa's face softened with sympathy. "Could you put Quinn to bed in the crib in the nursery? Give you guys a little space?"

Nicole fought the irritation that quickly rose inside her. Greg had suggested the same thing, and when she'd said no, that was when he'd given up offering to come home early. Tessa and Greg just didn't understand what it was like to be a mother. She felt a deep plunge of loneliness.

"Maybe soon," she said as they continued to scan the main floor, finding nothing broken.

Yet as they mounted the spiral steps, Nicole's skin pricked with needles of dread.

At the top of the stairs, Nicole gasped. "What the hell?"

The nursery door that had been tightly closed was now open. Tiny pieces of crystal glinted in the crib, the chandelier smashed to bits on the pink polka-dotted sheets. A large crevice marred the tray ceiling, the exact spot where the pretty, pink-beaded light fixture from Petit Trésor used to hang above the crib.

Nicole's eyes swept over the destruction. Lights didn't just fall for no reason. "You can see what I see, right?"

"Yes." Tessa paused, as though weighing her words. "Were you actually afraid I couldn't?"

"Oh my God," Nicole said. She kissed her daughter's silky hair over and over. "Quinn could have been killed."

You can't keep her safe.

"Nicki?"

Nicole's vision blurred. It was all too much. "My pills. Please, I need my pills. They're in my medicine cabinet." On shaky legs, she eased herself to the nursery floor and sat.

She couldn't hear Tessa's sandals pad along the expensive cream carpet, but she heard the rattle of the bottle and water rushing out of the tap in the en suite.

"How many?" Tessa called out.

"Two. Now. Please." Pressure thumped in her throat. She was about to hyperventilate. Tessa appeared. She exchanged Quinn for the pills and a glass of water. "Thank you," Nicole croaked.

The only sounds were Tessa's gentle inhales and exhales as she sat down beside Nicole. Then Tessa laid Quinn comfortably across her lap.

"Nicki, it was an accident. That's all. I know this is hard. Listen, postpartum depression can cause these feelings. Paranoia. Fear. Panic. It's going to be okay."

Nicole's shoulders shook, and tears poured from her eyes. "It's not okay, Tess. I think Greg's working late to avoid me. I don't blame him. I'm a mess." She sniffed her shirt. She caught the unpleasant odor of her own sweat.

"It's never been bad like this between us. He looks at me like . . . like

I'm glass that can shatter at any moment. I . . . I can't tell him about that summer, and it feels like he's hiding things from me, too."

Tessa rocked Quinn and got up. "Greg never expected to be a father. It's hard on him, too, you know." She smiled. "Go easy on him. He'll come around. If he doesn't, he'll have to answer to me."

Nicole had to smile. Only five foot two, but Tessa had so much inner strength.

"You'll keep my secret, right?" Nicole begged Tessa with her eyes.

Tessa looked right back at her and said, "Always. You're not alone, Nic. I'm here for you. The future is going to be so bright that all this will fade away into the past and won't even matter anymore."

You don't know, Nicole thought. *And I can never tell you the whole truth.*

CHAPTER NINE

MORGAN

August 8

Nicole Markham left me custody of her child? My phone clatters to the floor, and my body chills like ice water was poured down my back. This is insane.

I'm still half-asleep, and it suddenly occurs to me that this might not be real. I grab my phone and ask, "Is this a cruel prank? Who are you really?"

"Ms. Kincaid, as I've said, I'm Nicole's attorney, and I realize this is a shock, but it's no joke. You can easily look me up. I called you from my office number." There's a pause.

"It's not that." How much do I tell this man? I have to tread carefully. Does he know I'm the woman from the platform, the last person to talk to Nicole before she jumped?

"There must be a mistake," I say. My voice is strangled.

He coughs. "There's no mistake, Ms. Kincaid. I assumed you knew about Nicole's plans. When I saw Nicole on Thursday, she was adamant that I arrange a legal petition granting you custody of her child. Soon, I'll file the will into public record, but I needed to alert you immediately because this now concerns a child's physical and financial security. You need to sign and file the guardianship form within thirty days."

I hold the phone so tightly I hear a crack. "Wait, Nicole changed her will on Thursday?"

On Thursday, I was at Haven House all day. Little did I know that at the same time, a complete stranger was writing my name on a petition giving me custody of her baby.

"Ms. Kincaid, I'm confused. Are you saying you weren't aware you'd been named guardian?"

"No, I was not."

I'm as confused as he is, but there's something else I feel—a tiny spark of hope, so ridiculous, so crazed, that I shouldn't pay any attention to it. It's that same bud of promise I let bloom when, a year after Ryan's death, I printed off an application from an adoption agency. I started filling it out but stalled when I got to the section asking for personal references. I'd lost my entire network. I'd even tried finding some solace in a web forum for childless women like me. None of my friends had been in touch, so who would vouch for me? And if the agency searched online, they'd soon find out about Ryan and everything that had happened. Has Nicole's attorney checked me out, too? It doesn't sound like he has.

I know how dangerous hope can be. Quinn Markham doesn't belong to me. It's absurd.

I pull my duvet closer. "Where's Quinn's father?"

"Mr. Markham abandoned the family home some time ago and seems unwilling—or perhaps unable—to carry out day-to-day care for Quinn. That's why Nicole named an alternate guardian."

"Mr. Looms, do you know why she chose me?"

He pauses for a few seconds before answering. "Nicole led me to believe that you and she were close friends and that you are the best person to raise her daughter. You were close friends with her, right?"

I blink. How can this be? How scared and desperate must this woman have been to trust a total stranger over anyone else in her life? I rack my brain for what I'm missing, for clues about what I should say. I have to tell her attorney the truth. There's a baby's life at stake. "We weren't friends. I—I actually didn't know her at all."

There's silence on the other end of the phone. Did he hang up?

"Mr. Looms?"

"I'm a bit confused by this news, Ms. Kincaid. She told me you were willing to retain custody of her daughter should the need arise. And—" He stops.

"And what? Please, Mr. Looms. I don't understand what's happening."

"Ms. Kincaid, if you're not a friend of Nicole's, what exactly is your connection to her?"

"I don't know," I whisper. "Until she spoke to me last night on the Grand/State platform, I'd never met her before in my life."

There's another long pause. "So you were there when it happened? When she . . . jumped?" I hear him shuffle papers. "Look, I need to figure this out, Ms. Kincaid. I assume you're also not aware Nicole named you executrix of her daughter's estate? I'm obliged to inform you as soon as possible because Nicole has considerable shares in Breathe, and those will need to be managed right away."

"But . . . what about her husband?"

"Mr. Markham is currently in control of the shares and dividends from the stocks Nicole owned in trust for Quinn. But if he loses or severs his parental rights, and you retain guardianship, those will be your responsibility as well. There's a lot of money at stake here, and a child. That's a lot of responsibility for someone who didn't know Nicole at all."

He sounds accusatory, like this is part of my nefarious plan. My vision gets blurry, and I rub my eyes. Quinn has a father, and

Nicole granted *me* custody? And why would she leave me in control of Quinn's money, likely a fortune? And who is Quinn's father, Mr. Markham? Is that who Nicole was running from?

Something else occurs to me. If anyone finds out that Nicole left me in charge of Quinn's money, how much danger could I be in? Suddenly I feel very vulnerable and alone in my apartment.

"Who else knows about her will?" I ask as I scoot closer to the headboard. "Is there anyone in her family I can talk to about this?" My heart squeezes when I remember the soft warmth of her child. "Is Quinn okay?" I know I'm rambling, but I can't stop myself from asking all the questions swirling in my mind.

The attorney clears his throat. "Quinn is fine. I can't give you any contact information for her family members." There's a beat of silence before I hear him take a breath. "Look, I'm not sure what's going on here. I don't like what I'm hearing, but I'm obligated to send you the form for standby guardianship." His voice sounds clipped. "If you can give me your email address, please?"

I care not a tiny bit about the money. I care that I'm exonerated and that the little girl that mother passed to me is safe.

Don't let anyone hurt her.

"Is Quinn with her father now?"

"I can't answer that."

I try a different tack. "Do you know Amanda?"

"Who?"

"Forget it. I . . . I'd like to see the will."

"I can't send the entire will, but I'll send you the petition of guardianship."

"Thank you," I say.

After I give him my email address, he abruptly hangs up.

Part of me wants to burrow under my cozy covers and avoid all of this, but I can't. I pull my computer onto my lap. My in-box lights up with a new message, the subject: PETITION FOR GUARDIANSHIP. I open the file. This is real.

Petitioner Nicole Markham, under the penalties of perjury: Quinn Markham, whose date of birth is June 27, 2017, and whose place of residence is 327 East Bellevue Place, Chicago, Illinois, is a minor.

It is in the best interest of the minor that a guardian of the estate and person of the minor be appointed for the following reasons:

Morgan Kincaid is a loving, warm, compassionate, dedicated person who will serve in the best interests of Quinn Markham's emotional and physical needs.

The person having custody of the minor will be Morgan Kincaid, friend of Nicole Markham, at the address of 5450 North Sheridan Road, Suite 802, Chicago, Illinois.

My skin crawls. Nicole knew where I *live*. East Bellevue Place. She lived in the Gold Coast. My old neighborhood. After I found Ryan dead, I never went back to our beautiful, showstopping home. I never belonged there in the first place. Am I going crazy and can't remember her?

I check the time. I have to be at work soon, but I pull my computer closer and type in Nicole's company, Breathe. A sob catches in my throat: link after link directs me to articles about its commitment to wellness and healing for women and girls who are victims of trauma. Maybe we're connected through Haven House?

I gaze at a photo of Nicole Markham, beaming behind a podium as she holds a glass award in her hand. She looks healthy, happy, and successful. She looks like she has it all.

I trace her bright blue eyes and full lips with my fingertip. "What happened to you, Nicole? And who is Amanda?" I whisper.

An article in *Page Six* catches my eye.

An anonymous source confirms that Markham is housebound and unwell, struggling to care for her newborn daughter. She has not been seen in public since she left on a six-week, unpaid leave, negotiated with the board of directors. Should Markham not return

to Breathe as CEO on July 31, she is at risk of being ousted from the company she founded.

I try to connect the dots. It's clear Nicole suffered after the birth of her daughter. Back when I was in charge of the cases at Haven House, I had many clients who experienced postpartum depression. Maybe she was mentally unstable. Maybe there was no one coming after her on the platform at all. She could have seen my picture or name anywhere and convinced herself we were close. On that platform, her eyes were wild, her cheeks sunken. She was disheveled, unhinged. She might have been suffering a psychotic break. If not, then someone drove her to the edge. Could it be this anonymous source?

But none of that explains what led Nicole to me. I keep scrolling, trying to find the missing link, but there's nothing. Frustrated, I type in "Husband of Nicole Markham," and press on a link to a splashy photo in the *Chicago Tribune* of a charity gala a year earlier. The caption reads: "Breathe CEO Nicole Markham with husband, stockbroker Greg Markham."

Quinn's father is handsome, maybe in his late thirties, with wavy brown hair and a cleft chin. A stockbroker. I click another link, to the website for his brokerage firm, Blythe & Brown. I don't recognize him, but could he have been involved with Ryan somehow? Did Nicole know my husband?

Greg left Nicole and her newborn baby. Why? How on earth could any father do that? But I shouldn't jump to conclusions. Should I try to find him? Talk to him?

I spot a brief article in the *Chicago Reader* with a report on Nicole's death. In it, Greg is mentioned. It says he was in New York yesterday, the day she died. Is he back in Chicago now?

I type in "Nicole Markham; family." I skim the first ten links, my heart aching when I find an interview in which she talks about losing her parents in a car accident as a teenager. It mentions an older brother, Ben Layton, an emergency room doctor at Mount Zion hospital.

Mount Zion Funds Flatlining. Low-Income Hospital Slated for Closing.

I click through the images until I get to a recent one from a medical conference. A tall, lean man stands on a stage, long brown hair flopping in his eyes.

There's a slew of glowing five-star reports on RateMDs: "Understanding and kind." "He saved my son's life." "He helps people in need, even if they can't afford insurance."

He sounds like a decent man and a true professional. Then again, that's exactly how people used to describe Ryan. People hide their darkness under a facade of light and goodness. Nicole didn't give her brother custody of Quinn, either, and there must have been a reason for that.

I type in Ben Layton's name, and for $14.95, I can access all his public records. Bingo. Benjamin Layton, with an address in Wicker Park.

It's been less than twenty-four hours since Nicole fell to her death. Jumped. I have no solid information about her. But I have her address and her brother's address. And I know she has a husband who's here or in New York. I'll go to work first, then drive to her brother's place after. I'll ask him if he knows why she stuck that note on my purse, why she chose me, where his niece is now, and if he's seen her.

I close my laptop. My neck is itchy, and I think I've been scratching it without noticing. The stress is making my eczema act up. I reach for the tube of steroid cream on my yellow-painted bedside table. On top of my pile of self-help books is my wedding photo.

I clap my hand across my mouth, suppressing a scream. Since the day I moved in here, that photo of me and Ryan—laughing in a clinch on the steps of the Keith House where we got married—has been facedown in the top drawer of my nightstand. I couldn't bear to look at it, couldn't bear to see the man who had betrayed me so deeply. But I also couldn't quite get rid of the photo, either. So why is it face-up, right in front of me now? Someone must have taken it out of my drawer.

Someone who might still be in my apartment.

CHAPTER TEN

NICOLE

Before

Nicole's eyes flew open at the sound of the door slamming. Where was she? It took a moment for her to realize she'd fallen asleep on the sofa with Quinn in her arms. After Tessa had left, she'd meant to close her eyes for only a minute. What was she thinking? She knew better than to sleep with her baby—what if Quinn had fallen off the sofa as she dozed? Or she was smothered in the cushions?

Greg called from the entry, "Nicole, are you here?"

She glanced at the silver clock on the living room wall above the flat-screen TV. It was too early for Greg to be home. He appeared in the doorframe.

"What are you doing here?" she asked.

"I've been calling and calling. Why didn't you answer?" His jaw was hard.

She carefully sat up, trying not to wake Quinn. "Quinn and I were napping. If you were ever around these days, you'd know that's what babies and mothers do." She hated her tone, but she was furious that he was angry with her for missing his calls. Her job was to take care of Quinn, even if it meant not being available for him.

Greg exhaled. It was the sigh of a very frustrated man. "We need to talk." He sat down beside her. He looked miserable. "This isn't working, Nicole. We're not working."

Before she could say anything, Quinn awoke. Her beautiful face screwed up unhappily, and she wailed. A foul odor filled the room.

"No, not now!" Greg said, as though a baby could control its bodily functions.

Nicole got up from the couch, placed Quinn on the change mat on the floor, and grabbed one of the organic diapers from the side table.

She waved the diaper in Greg's face. "Want to take over with this? Can you see how caring for our child means I'm not always checking my phone?"

Quinn squirmed and kicked so much that she hit Nicole hard in the nose. "Stop it!" she snapped, then felt deep shame for losing her patience. She stroked Quinn's tiny face over and over. "I'm so sorry. Mommy's just upset. This isn't how it's supposed to be."

Greg crouched beside her. "Please, let me change her." He smelled musky, his Straight to Heaven cologne evoking the man she'd loved so many years ago. She enjoyed his flirtatious bravado and the way he looked at her back then. How impressed he'd been when he discovered she was in fact *that* Nicole Layton, the CEO of Breathe. Now she watched him struggle to put on the diaper until she gritted her teeth and couldn't take it anymore.

"It leaks if it's too loose." Nicole leaned in and took over, tightening the tabs. "But thank you for helping." She turned to smile at him, hoping to ease the thick tension that hung between them. But when she looked at his suit, she saw a long red hair on the lapel.

She backed away from him. A long red hair. A woman's hair.

She pulled it off his jacket and dangled it in front of his face. "Whose hair is this, Greg?" She whispered it, hissed it almost. She was petrified of the answer.

Greg looked at her wearily. "My new assistant is a redhead. Her hair gets on everything." Greg stared at her so hard she thought she might turn to stone. "I can't live with you like this. I'm trying my best. I really am. But I can't keep going. You're paranoid. You're sick, Nicole. You've become a different person. I barely recognize you."

Sick? Paranoid? Was she? Or was she being stalked by a figure from her past? Was her husband cheating on her right under her nose?

A notion occurred to her. "Did your assistant come to the hospital after Quinn was born?" *Please say yes*, she thought. Paranoia would be easier to handle than the thought that Donna was back to get revenge.

Greg's brow furrowed. "No. Why would she come to the hospital?"

Nicole struggled to stop the panic threatening to swallow her whole. But something else was needling at her. "What's your assistant's name?"

Greg blew out a breath. "Melissa."

"Are you sleeping with Melissa?" It made sense. All the nights he spent at the office since Quinn was born. Though he'd come to every sonogram and set the crib up for her, he'd been working more right before Quinn was born. The sudden errands he said he had to run late evenings. She'd assumed he was trying to help out because she was heavily pregnant. Had he been lying to her? Did she care if he was having an affair? She wasn't sure.

Greg rolled his eyes. "You're asking ridiculous questions."

You can't keep her safe.

"I just want you to be a loving father and husband. We need you." She had no energy to speak anymore, and her voice faded.

Greg's voice dipped low, full of self-pity. "That's just it, Nic. I . . . I can't do this anymore. I don't want to be your husband. And I don't want to be a father to this child, either, not like this," he said, glancing at Quinn, who lay on her change mat, watching them. "This isn't normal. This isn't who we are. I'm so unhappy."

Nicole took in the full force of what he'd just said. She couldn't stop the tears that burned her tired eyes. "But you *are* my husband. And you *are* a father." She gazed at her innocent daughter, hopefully oblivious to the angry words between her parents, who were supposed to make her feel secure.

Greg stood and rubbed his thighs, the scratchy sound making Nicole want to break his hands. "I know. But you're not letting me be a husband and father." He adjusted his blue silk tie, one she'd chosen for him. "I think we need some time apart."

Nicole stood, too. She heard the crack of her palm against Greg's face before she realized she'd slapped him. He stared at her with enormous tear-filled eyes. Her palm had imprinted an angry red mark. She dropped to the floor beside Quinn.

Greg put his hand to his cheek. Then he just shook his head and went upstairs.

Nicole remained on the floor, unable to believe what was happening. Her husband was leaving them. The man who'd proudly framed every article in which she'd been mentioned. Who'd missed his brokerage's Christmas parties to accompany her to the ones at Breathe. She wasn't sure how long she'd been looking at the cream wall when he came back. In his hand, he held the charcoal Prada carry-on she'd given him for their fifth anniversary.

He dropped the bag beside her and Quinn. "I'll help with Quinn financially. But—" He stuck his finger into the small cleft in his chin, one Nicole loved to kiss. "I can't live like this any longer. You need help, Nic, and you won't accept it. This is for the best." He shrugged. "At least I know you'll take care of her. You're obsessed." He leaned down and kissed his daughter on the head. Then he dragged his suitcase to the door, and she watched him walk right out, shutting it behind him.

Quinn batted at her mouth with her tiny thumb, which made Nicole cry harder.

Greg was gone. Nicole huddled on the floor with her child. She reached for her phone on the coffee table to call Tessa.

Things were so bad. But how much worse were they going to get?

CHAPTER ELEVEN

MORGAN

I stare at my wedding photo that I didn't put on the nightstand, my heart racing. Is someone in my apartment right now? Have they been in here, hiding, waiting, overnight? I fly out of bed and furiously scan the room. I need something to defend myself. The only thing I find is a pewter candle holder on my dresser. Wielding the candlestick overhead, prepared to smash an intruder in the face, I drop to my knees to check under the bed. Nothing.

I back myself against the wall and tiptoe out of my room, waiting for someone to jump at me. The walls between units are thick, and if I can't hear my neighbors, they won't hear me cry out. I whimper, then hold my breath. I'm completely vulnerable and totally defenseless. And if I call 911, I'll sound like a lunatic—*a photo was turned face-up in my apartment, which means someone's either in my apartment or was in my apartment.*

With my heart slamming against my rib cage, I enter the living room. It's empty. It doesn't look like anything has been taken: my TV is still mounted on the wall.

I whip open the closet door. No one's there. But in the bathroom, when I look in the drawers, I can tell they've been opened, and my cosmetics have been rummaged through. A roiling, sickening sensation slithers through my stomach. Did someone break in while I was at the police station? While I slept? I know my door was locked last night. But I was so drained I could barely see straight.

The more important question is: Why would anyone break in? I don't have anything of value. There's only one plausible answer to why: Nicole or Quinn.

I shudder so hard it hurts. I dart my eyes around. The glass door to the fire escape is slightly ajar. I think it was shut before I went to work yesterday morning. Was it just yesterday that I was at Haven House, content to go home at the end of a productive day, nestle under my soft magenta throw on the couch, and watch TV?

I'm the sole person who's been here since I moved in. I only open that back door if I've cooked something and there's smoke I need to clear. There's a staircase leading from the ground floor, no cameras, no security whatsoever. I never realized how unprotected I am here.

I run to the fire exit and lock it, then check the front door, which is already shut and locked. I move into the second bedroom, which I use as an office and storage space. No one there, either. My apartment usually smells of lemon furniture polish. It's only now that I notice it smells different, like the undertones of sweat.

My papers are still neatly stacked on my desk next to my blue-and-white vintage lamp I found in a thrift shop. I step closer to my desk and bang my shin hard against it because the bottom drawer is sticking out. I had only one piece of paper in there—my unfinished application for the Adoption Center of Illinois. And it's gone. What importance could it have to anyone but me?

"Why?" I yell into the empty room, the green walls no longer soothing but suffocating. I think of what Nicole said to me on the platform.

I've been watching you.

I have to get out of here. Now. I race to my room, snatch my laptop and phone off the bed, and hurry to the front door, still wearing my clothes from last night. I grab my purse, shove my feet into sandals, and bolt, taking the stairs down eight floors. The idea of being confined in the elevator right now petrifies me. I'm going down the steps so quickly I trip over one, and my heart flies to my throat. I slow down.

I never use my car for work, but after what happened at Grand/State, I can't imagine taking the L today. Moving through the underground lot to my silver Honda, I feel the hair on my arms stand at attention. I remember the method for self-defense my dad taught me and jam the sharp end of my key with my thumb through my index and middle fingers. As I approach my car, I hear a door slam, but I don't see anyone else in the garage.

I jump into my used Civic. After three tries, because I can't stop the tremors in my hands, I finally shove the key into the ignition and back out so fast I almost crash into the Toyota parked behind me.

My hands are slippery on the wheel as I ascend the ramp out of the dark garage. I make it to the street and drive toward Haven House. I hit my Bluetooth to call Jessica.

"Someone broke into my apartment." I tell her about the wedding photo and missing adoption application, my voice pitched in fear.

"Nothing of value was taken?"

"I don't th-think so," I stammer.

"Morgan, take a breath. You suffered a trauma last night. You're not thinking clearly, that's all." Then she asks, "You applied to an adoption agency? When?"

"A while ago. I never completed the form. I couldn't. I had no one left to stand up for me. So I shoved it in the drawer and never looked at it again." I sob into the phone.

"Okay, try to calm down. You're fine. Do you have a house cleaner? There has to be an explanation for this."

I want her to understand the gravity of the situation, but it's clear to me she doesn't. "You think I can afford a cleaner? I'm telling you, Jessica, someone broke in. And they weren't there as petty thieves. Someone's after me."

I merge onto the packed 41, feeling like every driver around is watching me.

"First, if your apartment really was broken into, it could be connected to Ryan. This could all be connected to Ryan. Second, it could just be a random break-in and the thieves heard a noise and ran away before they could take anything important."

Right, I think to myself. Except they took one form, just that.

When I go quiet, Jessica changes the subject. "Listen, I found out that Nicole was briefly hospitalized before her first semester in college for severe panic disorder. Mental instability seems to be part of her past."

Do I tell her about my call with the attorney, about Nicole's will? I know what she'll say, so I put it off for a while, telling myself I'll inform her soon. I know Jessica's job is to help me, but how do you trust someone who doesn't believe you?

"Morgan?"

"I'm close to the shelter, and I'm late for work. I have to go."

"Get in touch if anything else happens. I really think you're just overtired and looking for connections that aren't there."

"Connections like why Nicole knew my name?" I say, my sarcasm thick.

"Look, that one I can't explain. I'll keep digging. There has to be a clear answer."

She ends the call. I wish I believed that exhaustion is affecting my ability to be rational. But it just doesn't add up.

As I turn onto West Illinois my phone rings. It's my boss, Kate. I accelerate past the brick warehouse to my left and the gleaming glass building to my right. "I'm sorry I'm late. I'm on my way. My apartment was broken into and . . . something happened last night on my way home."

Some instinct makes me glance in the rearview mirror. There's a dark blue car that I remember seeing merge behind me as I left my apartment. I'm not even focusing on Kate. I missed what she just said.

"Can you repeat that?"

She heaves a loud sigh. "I said I don't think you should come in, Morgan. I'm sorry. You've been late so many times. You've missed important deadlines. I understood it was because you were grieving. But this morning a detective was here asking about you, and if I know anything about your relationship with Nicole Markham. It's just too much. I have to let you go."

Tears roll down my cheeks. I hate how weak I'm being, but to lose the place I get to go every day, the only people who talk to me at all, undoes me. Kate is quiet on the other end of the phone.

I change lanes, then wipe my face and square my shoulders. I don't want to beg for my job, but I don't know what I'll do without it. "I've tried to stay under the radar. Please. I've done nothing wrong. It's possible that Nicole Markham knew me from Haven House. Did we ever ask her or Breathe for a donation?"

Kate's voice is hard. "Goddamn it, Morgan. I just told you you're fired. Are you even listening to me? I depended on you. I kept you on because you wanted to help so much, and I wanted to help you. You used to be really good at your job. But you're just not as dedicated as you once were."

"That's not true!" I hit the horn by mistake and swerve a little. I have to calm down. I'm barely paying attention to the road in front of me.

And Kate's right. I'm not the same person I was before Ryan's death. Before he left me to suffer for his mistakes. I'm wary, jumpy, and unsure of myself. I'm afraid to get close to people and really let them in. I'm not the best advocate for women who want to restart their lives.

"I didn't want any of this to happen, Kate. I appreciate everything you've done for me." Heartbroken, my voice cracks. I'll never again be able to help, even in a small way, the women at the shelter who were brave enough to escape their abusers. Just one more thing that's been taken away from me.

She hangs up. So do I.

I pull up to the curb under the shade of an elm tree and park. I'm hot and upset. Now that I'm fired, I can go over to Ben Layton's house right away. At least I can try to sort out that other piece of my life that's a mess. I pull the purple note out of my purse, trying to find a clue in the loopy handwriting. Of course there's nothing.

I think about Ben Layton. He's just lost his sister. He might have heard I was on the platform with Nicole. He might think I'm involved. He might not be willing to speak to me. But what if Nicole's brother holds all the answers about my connection to her? I can just ask him if Nicole ever mentioned me. If he knows who Amanda is or if there's someone who might have wanted his sister dead. Or if she was unstable and suicidal. Right now, he's the only lead I have.

I put his address in my GPS. By the time I get to the end of the block, the same dark blue car I noticed earlier is right behind me again. I'm sure of it now.

In the rearview mirror, I see the three interlocking ovals of the Toyota emblem: it's a Prius, although the sun is shining on the windshield and I can't see the driver inside. Would a detective drive a Prius? I doubt it. I signal to merge onto I-90 W/I-94 W, and the Prius does, too. *Focus*, I tell myself, and tighten my hands on the wheel. I'm stuck between the Infinity in front of me and a Kia on my right. I'm blocked in. My anger vanishes. I'm now so scared I can barely breathe.

Traffic is moving at such a fast clip. I want to keep a car-length behind the Infinity, but I need to get away from the Prius. I speed ahead.

The Prius speeds up, too. I try to get a clear look at the license plate, but it's caked in dirt and unreadable from my mirror.

I could slam on my brakes and cause an accident, forcing the person out of the car. But we're on a busy highway. It's far too dangerous. All I wanted was a simple life with a loyal husband and a baby. Why has it all gone wrong?

Tentacles of fear climb up the back of my neck as I watch the car come closer and closer. It's practically on top of my bumper. In the rearview I manage to make out a woman with long red hair driving, but huge sunglasses obscure her face. Then she bangs into me with enough force that I fly forward, bracing my hands on the steering wheel.

Who the fuck is this woman? And why is she trying to run me off the road?

CHAPTER TWELVE

NICOLE

Before

It had been a week since Greg left, and no calls from him. Nothing. Nicole had no idea where he was. She missed his comforting presence in the house, but she wasn't sure she missed him. He never did answer her question about sleeping with his assistant. He was probably with her now. Melissa. Why did it take her so long to figure it all out? How could she have been so blind? She'd stopped trusting her instincts. Those gut feelings that had made Breathe a top company in the competitive athleisure space had all but disappeared since having a child. She was a shell of her former self.

She hadn't left the house all week. She'd ventured out only to the backyard so Quinn could get some vitamin D. But the incessant buzz of mowers, even the sound of leaves rustling in the breeze, rattled her nerves. She was constantly listening for Donna, waiting for her appearance. When would it ever end?

Nicole told Tessa right away that Greg had left. And almost every day since, Tessa had come by after work, bringing groceries or dinner. Their last conversation worried Nicole. They'd been sitting in the living room a few evenings before, Quinn in Tessa's arms while Nicole folded the laundry. Quinn's tiny sleeper was inside out, and she couldn't pull the legs free. She threw the sleeper to the ground in frustration.

Tessa said, "I've been doing a lot of reading on postpartum reactions. It's completely normal to be scared and anxious." She'd looked at Quinn, then back at Nicole. "It's common to feel like you can't take care of yourself or your baby."

Nicole stiffened. "What are you trying to say?"

"You're not getting dressed anymore. You're not taking Quinn out of the house. You're getting frustrated by simple tasks. Why don't I stay here with you for a bit? Just so you can get some more sleep and get outside."

Nicole considered it. She was afraid to be alone in the house. But she resented the suggestion that she wasn't taking care of Quinn. Her baby was well-fed, well-rested, and clean. She resented the implication she wasn't a good mother. Then she instantly felt guilty. Tessa was only trying to help.

"I'll be fine," she said. And Tessa had relented.

Now, Nicole looked at the clock: 11:00 a.m. Tessa would be at the office. She picked up her phone.

Tessa answered on the first ring. "Hey, what's up?"

Nicole could hear the hustle and bustle of Breathe in the background. She couldn't imagine being there anymore. It felt so improbable that she was ever in charge of a company when she now struggled to leave the house.

"I'm . . ." She grasped for the right words. "Could you come over and help me move a table? It's not safe for Quinn where it is."

"Sure. I just have a quick meeting with Lucinda. The launch for the Aromatherapy for Exhaustion line is this week."

Nicole didn't know what launch Tessa was talking about. "Sounds like you're busy. It's fine."

"No, it's okay. I'll be there later. Have you heard from Greg?"

"Not a word."

"I really hope he's not sleeping with his assistant. He'd be a walking cliché."

"Ha!" she said, though inside she wasn't laughing. "He has no problem using our joint account, though. He's been taking a lot of money out recently. I tried to check the portfolio he manages for us, but it's in his name only."

Tessa paused on the other end of the line before asking, "Do you know where he is? Do you want me to talk to him? It's just so strange that he hasn't even been in touch."

Nicole didn't care where he was, or who he was with. But she did have an idea.

"Thank you, Tess, but I don't think you talking to him will help. Maybe we could stay with you, though, Quinn and me? Just for a bit?" Moving in with Tessa for a while might be the answer. Her colorful condo was warm and soothing. More important, Donna wouldn't be able to find them there.

"Oh, sweetie, I don't think that would work. I'm sorry. You know I'd do anything for you, but my place just isn't suitable for a baby. I'm not even sure the condo board would allow it." She was quiet for a moment. "But I'll come over later. And like I said, I can always stay with you."

Nicole felt her cheeks flame with embarrassment. She wished she'd never asked. "It was a dumb idea. Sorry. Come for dinner. Maybe I'll even make us something."

She wouldn't and couldn't, but she could at least pretend. They hung up, and Nicole had a sudden burst of energy. With Quinn wrapped around her, she tucked her phone in her pocket and went to the entryway for her sneakers. She and Quinn could go to the park and watch the older kids play. She stopped in the front hall, confused. On the bench by the door was a photo album, her flower-covered family album that she hadn't looked at in years. It always rested on the bookshelf. She called Tessa back.

"Did you take the photo album from my bookshelf for some reason?"

"No. Why would I?"

"I don't know. Sorry. Forget it."

"Are you sure you don't have mommy brain?"

Nicole laughed, but it was thin. "Yeah, that must be it."

She hung up. Nicole picked up the album, then lay Quinn on her back on the animal play mat in the living room. Nicole laughed as she sat beside her daughter, who cooed and swiped at the lion above her head.

"If my mom were here, she would spend hours playing with you. She was so patient." Nicole opened the album to a photo of her and her older brother on Halloween. She was five, skinny arms crossed over her chest, scowling in her princess dress; he was eight, a lanky vampire with a gap-toothed grin. She quickly flipped to the next photo. "There's your grandma." Nicole pointed to a photo of her mother crouching beside a three-year-old Nicole in her stroller. She was so young and beautiful, her long, thick cocoa-colored curls tied in a low ponytail, her hand on Nicole's pink snowsuit-clad leg. "Her maiden name was Quinn. That's how you got your name."

She wiped the tears from her eyes. Then she turned the page. And her heart stopped.

In the middle was a single loose Polaroid. Nicole's hands shook uncontrollably as she picked it up by the corner, as though it were a snake about to strike.

Little Amanda sat on the green shag carpet Nicole remembered so well. She was wearing a pale yellow dress with a ruffled bodice and tulle skirt tied with a pretty bow. Her face beamed with glee at the Playskool popper in front of her.

How alive and healthy Amanda looked in this picture. How cold and still she'd been when Nicole last held her.

Nicole didn't remember ever having a copy of this photo. She wouldn't have saved it. She would have been too scared Greg would ask who it was.

Her head spinning, she removed the photo from the album before putting it back on the bookshelf where she'd last left it. She needed more pills. She didn't know how many she'd taken today, but they weren't working. She slipped the photo into the waistband of her yoga pants, the sharp edges digging into her skin. Then she picked Quinn up from the play mat and tucked her into the carrier, holding her close so she could feel her breathe against her.

She took Quinn to her bathroom, swallowed two more tablets. Her baby gnawed on Nicole's shoulder. She was hungry and would need a bottle soon. Nicole opened the bathroom drawer to hide the photo, the photo she was sure that Donna had brought into her house. How and when, she didn't know, but it was the only explanation.

And it terrified her.

The danger was getting closer.

CHAPTER THIRTEEN

MORGAN

The Prius is still right behind me. My exit is just up ahead, so I yank the wheel, screeching over to the shoulder, rocks spraying from under the tires, then pinging off my window. I lurch onto the ramp, my knuckles white with the force of my hands clamping the wheel.

The woman follows.

"What do you want?" I shout, a fireball of alarm shooting through my veins. "Please, please go away."

I hear the roar of an engine revving, and the Prius speeds past me. Then it's gone.

I drive to a quiet block where I can pull to the curb. My seat belt is cutting into me, and I wrestle to undo it and lock my doors just in case the redhead in the Prius finds me again. I could have been killed just now.

I grapple in my purse for my phone. I dial Jessica. I've kept her in the dark about a few things, but this is more serious than I thought. I need to tell her that someone is after me. I make the call, but she doesn't pick up.

"Damn it," I say, pressing end and slamming the phone back into my purse. I'll call her later, after I try to get some answers myself. I should also file a police report, but right now, I just want to get away from here.

I pull my hair back from my face, start the car, and drive to West Evergreen Avenue, Ben Layton's house. I roll up to a beautiful yet imposing two-story Victorian. I park right across the street. I wipe my palms on my leggings. Butterflies flit in my stomach. I know I'm acting rashly, but I can't stop myself. My gut tells me this is the right thing to do.

The thin beige curtains covering the bay windows are closed, but there's a car in the driveway, so I reason Ben might be home. I look down at myself and cringe. I look like hell and feel even worse. I didn't even brush my teeth this morning. I pop a stick of gum from my purse into my mouth. My skin is wan, deep purple grooves are etched under my usually bright green eyes, and the skin on my collarbone is so inflamed I worry it might be infected.

I take a deep breath. "You can do it," I tell myself. I'm about to step out of my car as a very tall, slim man in a white V-neck T-shirt and gray board shorts emerges from the front door. He's carelessly handsome, as though he's not aware how good-looking he is. This is Ben Layton. I recognize him from his photo. He pushes his wavy brown hair off his forehead as he heads toward the black Altima. In his arms is a baby. Quinn.

I can't help but gasp, my relief springing out of my throat. She's in a pale pink onesie, and she's crying, the sound punctuating the lack of noise on the street. But she looks secure in his arms. I feel a physical pull toward the baby girl I held for such a short time. I have to stop thinking about the fact that I've been entrusted to protect her. It can't be. It's too much to hope for. It doesn't make any sense.

I stay right where I am, watching him. Even from far away, I can see how red and puffy his face is. His sister just died. What right do I have to intrude on his life?

He pops into the Altima and pulls out of the driveway. On impulse, I decide to follow.

"Okay, Ben Layton, where are we going?" I ask out loud as I start my car and follow a safe distance behind. I'm tailing Nicole's brother around Chicago and ignoring every piece of Jessica's advice. Clearly, I'm out of my mind.

I've followed him for about fifteen minutes when he turns onto North State Street.

I slow as the Altima pulls up to a row of gorgeous three-story homes on East Bellevue Place. I park a few houses back. The address is familiar. Then I realize why. I saw it on Nicole's petition for guardianship. This is her street.

He parks in the driveway of a stunning graystone and gets out of the car. I've pulled over a safe distance back, behind a parked car, but I have a good view. I watch as he takes Quinn out of her car seat. I wonder if he had it on hand or if he just bought it. She's quiet, so I surmise she's asleep. So much turmoil for this little baby. I wait while he walks not to Nicole's house but to the home beside hers, up to the front door. He knocks. An elderly woman opens the door slowly. They talk for a minute, and she puts something in his hand. Then he heads out, walks to Nicole's house, with its limestone facade and elegant, bowed windows. He climbs the wide steps set between two intricately carved columns. Quinn looks so comfortable in his big arms. Protected.

I can't wait any longer. I pull my ponytail tighter and exit the car. Then I step to the edge of the driveway.

Ben must have heard my footsteps because he spins around and looks right at me, his blue eyes widening. They're lined with exhaustion, lighter but no less piercing than his sister's.

As he draws closer, I step back a little. I think of how so few people expressed their condolences to me when Ryan killed himself. No one knows what to say after a suicide.

"Dr. Layton?" I say quietly.

"Yes. Who are you?" he asks warily, shifting Quinn into the crook of his arm and adjusting the strap of the red backpack slung over his shoulder.

"I'm so sorry about your sister."

Sorrow is etched into his face. Quinn opens her eyes and shrieks in his arms, and it's all I can do not to rush forward, reach out, and try to soothe her.

"What do you want? Jesus, can't you reporters just leave me alone?"

He looks so lost and confused, so unbearably sad, that I feel bad I've come at all. "I'm not a reporter," I say. "I swear, I'm not."

"Then who are you?"

I swallow hard. "I—I was there. With Nicole. I mean I was with her right before she . . . jumped."

"It's okay," he says. "How could you have known what . . . what she was about to do?" His blue eyes darken. "Wait. Are you the woman on the platform? The one who took Quinn? You talked to Nicole?"

I hesitate. I don't want to set him off.

"Nicole pushed Quinn into my arms. I didn't know what was going on or what she was about to do. If I'd known, I would have . . ." My eyes fill with tears. I can't help it. "Your sister begged me to keep Quinn safe. To watch out for her, take care of her. Those were the last words she said. I didn't know who she was. I had to tell you that."

He walks toward me until we're face-to-face in the driveway. His eyes scan me, and I recoil from his scrutiny. Grief and doubt start to cloud his face. "Morgan Kincaid, right?"

I nod.

"Detective Martinez wanted to know if I knew a woman named

Morgan Kincaid. And I said no. And now you're here. You know, you actually look a bit like my sister."

"I didn't know your sister before yesterday. Do you think she chose me because we look alike?"

"*Chose* you? That detective told me to let her know if you tried to contact me. Said she can't figure out how you knew my sister. That your husband also committed suicide and he was all mixed up in stealing millions of dollars. That you were a 'person of interest' in relation to my sister." Quinn screams, and he flinches, pushing his unruly hair off his forehead, a muscle ticking in his sharp, angular jaw.

Instinctively, my hands go out to quiet the child. He pulls Quinn away. "Whoa. What are you doing? What is it you want from me? I'm going to call Detective Martinez."

He must be around six foot three because he looms over my five-foot-seven frame. But I don't shrink back. I'm banking on my gut instinct that he wants to hear me out. He hasn't gone inside, and he hasn't actually dialed Martinez, so there must be something he's looking for from me.

I have nothing to lose. "Amanda," I say.

His face drains of color, and my heart speeds up.

"What did you just say?" His eyes are huge, his face set in an expression of shock and disbelief.

I reach into my purse for the Post-it. I uncrumple it and put it right in front of his face.

Just then, there's an ear-piercing screech of tires. We both turn to see a car speeding down the street, going faster and faster.

It's a dark blue Prius. And it's racing straight for us.

CHAPTER FOURTEEN

NICOLE

Before

In between bathing and feeding Quinn, all Nicole had done for days was stare at the Polaroid of Amanda. She couldn't look at it anymore without seeing Quinn's face transposed in the picture. Without checking every closet and corner of her house for evidence Donna had been inside. She felt nothing except a staggering sense of doom. Now she finally put the photo in the back of the bathroom drawer, promising herself not to look at it again.

Quinn babbled in the bassinet. Nicole removed her pills from the medicine chest. From now on, she'd keep them on the main floor, where she spent the most time. She went to her bedroom, picked up Quinn, and slid her into the wrap, nuzzling her nose into her baby's sweet-smelling neck. Next, she went downstairs, where she leaned her forehead on the stainless steel Sub-Zero, the cold door a balm to her hot, debilitated body.

Her eyes caught something purple sticking out from under the fridge. Lowering herself as slowly and carefully as possible, Nicole found a purple Post-it. "Staying late at the office," read the old note in Greg's messy handwriting. She had no clue when he'd written it.

Something about the Post-it gave her an idea. She went to the junk drawer and pulled out the pack of purple Post-its at the bottom. Sitting on the floor, Quinn cozy in the carrier, she stuck the papers to the natural stone tiles. With a Sharpie, she wrote each idea on a separate Post-it:

Letter. Name card. Redhead. Missing pills. Mobile. Door. Shattered chandelier. Photo.

She stuck them in a line, then a circle, trying to make sense of every frightening incident. The clues were in the words in front of her, and if she put all of them together the right way, she'd know exactly what Donna was planning to do to her. And how she could stop it.

But what if it wasn't just Donna? Maybe Greg was right, and she was coming unhinged. He'd been so insistent that she needed help, and she'd ignored him. It was odd, though, that he hadn't even called once since he'd left two weeks before. How long had he been unhappy with her? Did he just not want to be a father? Or was she even more off-kilter than she thought and he wanted to be as far from her as he could? Was it possible, as he had suggested, that she herself had bought the mobile? Had she unscrewed the light fixture and unlocked the door? Had she kept that photo of Amanda for all these years and forgotten? What if she was simply dealing with a very bad case of postpartum depression, like Tessa had suggested?

Stupid purple Post-its. It was all meaningless.

She put them back in the drawer. She looked down at Quinn, who rested peacefully on her chest. She'd fed and changed her earlier. Her baby was content but needed fresh air. And Nicole needed exercise. She could manage a short walk. They couldn't stay in the house a minute longer.

She didn't bother switching clothes or showering. She packed Quinn in her fancy red Bugaboo stroller, toting the gorgeous Tiffany-blue diaper bag Tessa had given her. "Let's take a walk, sweetheart."

Nicole closed the door behind her, set the alarm, and turned the dead bolt. Even though she heard it click shut, she pushed at the door five times to make sure it wouldn't open. She snapped a photo of herself and Quinn, then texted it to Tessa.

I'm going out!

Tessa texted back: Proud of you! Call me when you're home.

The air was dense with heavy storm clouds, but a little rain never hurt anyone. Quinn was quiet, completely awestruck by the colorful rings dangling from the stroller's sun canopy. Nicole told herself she was just a mother off for a stroll with her daughter. As she eased the Bugaboo down the four wide steps, Mary, her eightysomething-year-old next-door neighbor, came running out of her house.

"Nicole, sweetheart. Do you have a second?"

She didn't want to chat with Mary, who could keep her on the sidewalk for an hour talking about her grandchildren and her bad hip. But Mary didn't give her a chance to refuse.

"I wanted to tell you something. I saw someone peering in your front window late last night. At first, I thought maybe it was a friend of yours, but whoever it was, they didn't stay long. I thought I should mention it. I get those twinges, you know? When something is funny? I didn't want to ring the bell in case you and the cherub were sleeping."

Nicole's blood ran cold and she moved the stroller closer to Mary. "A man or a woman? What did they look like? What time was it?" Spittle flew as she fired the questions.

Mary stepped back. "My eyes aren't so good anymore, dear. I couldn't see if it was a man or woman, but it was around ten. I was watching my soaps that my son taped on that DVR. So it wasn't a friend of yours? Oh my. Should you call the police? If there's a prowler around here, we have to be on alert."

"No police!" Nicole said, too loudly.

"Pardon me?"

"Don't call the police!" she screeched. If Mary called the police, everything could fall apart. She didn't want anyone snooping about. She wanted to keep her past in the past. Also, what if the police thought she was an unfit mother? What if they took Quinn away? The thought terrified her. She breathed in through her nose and exhaled slowly. "Thank you for watching out for me," she said in a perfectly measured tone. "It must have been my friend Tessa. I'll give her a call."

Mary peered at Nicole. "Are you sure you're okay, love? You seem really rattled."

She assured the older woman she was fine, though she wasn't, and pushed the stroller down North Rush Street toward East Oak, her eyes drinking in the professionals in tight pencil skirts and lightweight suits, going to and from meetings, to lunches. The sky darkened to the color of silt, but the air was scented with the smell of fresh-cut grass. It made her want to stay out just a little longer, despite the threat of rain.

She walked and walked until she saw the one person from Breathe she never wanted to run into. She stopped the stroller suddenly, making Quinn cry out in surprise. *Please don't see me. Please go away.*

"Nicole, is that you?" a bemused voice asked. Lucinda Nestles was standing in front of her on the sidewalk.

Nicole looked up, shame making her face burn. "Hi, Lucinda. How are you?" She covered her mouth with her hand. Had she even brushed her teeth today?

"You look . . . Is this your baby?"

Nicole nodded and couldn't speak.

"Well, she's gorgeous. Congrats!" She leaned in to kiss Nicole's cheek, her eyes running up and down Nicole's stained T-shirt and

Breathe pants. "I'm on my way to meet with the board, actually." Lucinda smiled, but it was icy. "I was very surprised when you said you couldn't do some work at home. I don't expect you to be at Breathe full-time during your maternity leave, of course, but you are CEO. There's been some concern about the forecasted share earnings and then that piece in *Page Six* . . . I've called you quite a few times this week. You are returning to work on the thirty-first, right?"

Before she could ask Lucinda what *Page Six* piece she was talking about, she felt someone else's eyes on her. Standing in the small alley between the Barneys and Hermès stores was a redhead in large sunglasses, staring right at her.

Nicole squeaked, tightening her grip on the stroller handles.

"I have to go," she said.

"Are you all right?" Lucinda touched her arm.

She flinched. "Do you see her?" she asked, and pointed to the redhead. "Is she watching us?"

Lucinda's eyes widened. "Is who watching us?"

Nicole cocked her head toward the alley, but the woman was gone.

"I'm . . . I'm sorry," Lucinda managed. "I don't see anyone."

The woman was there a second ago. Nicole was sure of it. But she wasn't there now. Nicole faked a smile. "Forget it. I haven't been sleeping much. I'm—I'm a little overtired. You know how it is in the newborn days." Her smile felt warped.

Lucinda watched her cautiously. "Is there something you need help with? Are you sure you're okay?"

Nicole didn't answer Lucinda's questions. "See you!" she said, too loudly. She swung the stroller around and took off, her unused muscles straining and knotting, her incision burning. She ran down the sidewalk, shoving past startled pedestrians and cars furiously honking horns as she hurtled through a crosswalk.

She turned onto East Bellevue Place, her hands shaking so forcefully she dropped her keys on the pebbled walkway leading to her front steps. The sky cracked with a thunderous boom, and rain poured down on her, soaking her hair and blinding her. On her knees, scrabbling among the stones, she finally got ahold of the keys. With tiny rocks now embedded in her skin, she made it up the steps and moved to unlock the door, tripping over an unseen object as she did.

Sitting on her doorstep was a white box with "Nicole" written on it in pink Sharpie.

CHAPTER FIFTEEN

MORGAN

There's no time to think.

"Move!" I scream, pushing Ben and Quinn onto the driveway before I jump out of the way, inches from the Prius hell-bent on crashing into us.

His backpack goes flying, and my ankle slams on the curb. I land hard on the grass as the car spins around and peels off in a cloud of dust.

I moan from the white-hot pain, my heart boxing my rib cage. I frantically look over to where Ben is standing with Quinn—are they safe? His mouth hangs open, and the baby screams against his chest.

"Are you okay?" I yell from where I'm lying on the lawn.

Ben races over to me, Quinn still shrieking. He presses her against his shoulder and kneels beside me, his face creased in concern and shock. "We're fine. Are you okay? Can you walk?"

That's when I feel the pain blasting down my leg. "I banged my ankle, but I'm okay." The terror of watching the car aim straight for us is sinking in. Hot tears spill out of my eyes. So it's real. My fears are real. Someone really does want to harm that baby. Or me. Or both of us.

Ben runs a hand over his stubbled face as he stares down the road where the car took off. Then he looks at me. "You pushed us out of the way," he says, with wonder. "You didn't even think twice."

"Of course I pushed you out of the way."

He looks at me with new eyes. I'm no longer a threat but someone who can help him. I try to stand, but a burst of fire shoots through my ankle. "Did you see the driver? Was it a redhead? A redhead in a Prius followed me on the highway and rear-ended me, on purpose, but I thought I lost her."

"To be honest, I didn't see. It happened so fast." He stands and stares down the road, then at me, his expression inscrutable. Cupping his hand around the back of Quinn's neck, he heaves a sigh. "Look, this is Nicole's house, and I need to get some clothes and things for Quinn. I don't know how long she's going to be with me." Ben shifts from foot to foot. "Do you want to come inside, and we can call the police? Also, you can explain what the hell you're doing here and why someone just tried to kill us."

I consider my options, knowing I have none. I just hope he's not a threat. I hope he's not the one who Nicole was running from.

He awkwardly grabs his backpack from the ground and hoists it over his shoulder. He looks at me for a beat and then reaches his hand down. I hesitate, then take it. Ben is the lesser of two evils right now. He hauls me to my feet and lets me rest on him, so I can hobble up the driveway and the four steep steps to Nicole's house. I stare at Quinn, who's calm again and gazing right back at me. She's so perfect. So innocent. How could anyone want to hurt her?

Ben opens the door, and I limp in behind him to the foyer, leaning against the ivory wall for support.

I'm immediately bowled over by the sheer size and whiteness of the house. "Wow," I blurt out.

He nods. "I know." He sniffs the air. "But it smells rotten in here."

I detect stale air, and decaying food. Being in Nicole's home scares me. To the right of the foyer is a magnificent living room, where black silk sheets cover every window.

Why was she living in the dark? What was life like for Nicole here?

He shuts the door, drops his backpack on the floor, and adjusts Quinn so she's tucked in the crook of his arm. Then he pulls out his phone.

I don't want Martinez to know I'm here. "Wait. Please. Can we just talk for a minute before you call the police? I think we both have things about Nicole to tell each other, and once the police come, there won't be a chance to talk."

His gaze sweeps over me, then he leans against the wall next to a silver deco table. "Can you tell me why you think that car is after you—or . . . us?"

I exhale a long stream of air. "I don't know why. And I really am so sorry about your sister. I'm a social worker. When I saw how anxious she was on that subway platform, I wanted to help, but just like with that car tearing down the street, everything happened so fast. I am so, so sorry. I wish I could have stopped her." I stutter on a sob and pause to get myself together.

He watches while I wipe my tears. "Will you walk me through it? Will you help me understand what happened?" There's profound pain in his eyes that's hard to ignore.

I take a deep breath. "So yesterday, I was on my way home from work at the same time I always head out. Your sister was beside me on the platform. She dug her nails in my arm and begged me to take her baby. That's the first thing she said to me—*Take my baby*. I was startled, and I pulled away. Then she moved right in front of me, close to the edge. She was looking everywhere, like she was scared of someone.

Then she told me not to let anyone hurt Quinn and shoved her in my arms. I looked down and when I lifted my head, Nicole was . . . The train was in the station."

He winces, then looks down at the table in front of him. "I saw Nicole a couple of weeks ago, but the house wasn't quite as bad as it is now. I was concerned with how awful she looked."

"So you were worried about her?"

He nods but gives no further information.

He glances at my foot, which I'm holding in the air above the marble entryway, so I won't put pressure on my ankle. Then he shifts Quinn so she's resting on his shoulder and slides his phone back in his pocket. "Let's go to the kitchen and get you sitting down," Ben says.

I don't know how much time I have before he calls Martinez. I need him to trust me enough to tell me who Amanda is, but I don't know what else to say to gain his trust.

He leads me to the left of the foyer into a large and airy snow-white space, save for the stainless-steel Viking range and Sub-Zero fridge. Every surface is covered with the detritus of newborn care—bottles, washcloths, cans of formula, even balled-up diapers I can smell from here.

It suddenly occurs to me I shouldn't be touching anything. I don't want to leave any indication that I've been here.

Ben notices my hesitation. "I'll tell Martinez I let you in, okay? I'll tell her everything that just happened. It's obvious you're not out to get us. You just saved our lives."

I look down at my feet. I'm relieved he believes that I've done nothing to hurt his sister. He pulls out a tall, white leather kitchen chair, and I gingerly sit down, careful not to bang my throbbing ankle against the chrome base of the sleek marble table.

Ben places Quinn in a vibrating chair in front of another black silk sheet covering what I assume are the doors to the backyard.

Nicole's home is beautifully decorated but as disheveled and grimy as the distraught, bedraggled woman I met on the platform. I desperately hope there are clues here to prove I wasn't involved in her downfall.

Quinn's tiny fists bat at the air. Her cries are so painful to hear. I want to take her away and hold her myself.

"Ben, Nicole said my name. On the platform. She said Morgan, like she knew me. But I swear to you that I'd never seen her before in my life. I didn't know she was the CEO of Breathe. She seemed scared for Quinn's life."

Ben sits next to me and kneads the back of his neck. "So she knew you, but you don't know her? How is that possible?"

"I don't know. I'm racking my brain trying to figure out what the connection is. Did she make a donation to the shelter I work for—worked at before—or is she connected to my husband? I'm sure Martinez already told you about him. I must sound like a complete idiot, but I was in the dark about my husband, too. The fraud part, I mean."

Jabbering, I fidget uncomfortably and watch Ben's Adam's apple bob as he swallows. He doesn't say anything.

"I'm hoping you can tell me something, or we can find something in the house that connects me to your sister, because things are looking bad for me. Martinez seems to think I might have had a hand in what happened to Nicole. But as you can see, I don't. And I'm worried for Quinn and myself. And now, for you, too. Someone wants to hurt us." I swallow, hoping I'm not pushing too far.

"I—" He pulls at the neck of his shirt. "I don't know what might be here to help you. Us. I've been here only a few times."

"Have the police searched the house?" I ask.

"No. My attorney told me this morning that a warrant for Nicole's residence hasn't been granted. Her husband, Greg, won't give consent. Apparently, his attorney has been trying to hold off the Crime Scene Unit until Nicole's will is released because Greg has a legal right to the house. Fourth Amendment at work. Nicole's will won't be made public for a while yet, I don't think."

My stomach turns. I'm hiding the fact that part of Nicole's will is in my in-box. That his sister has given me, not him, custody of Quinn. But how can I tell him when I don't know what kind of man he really is? I didn't know what kind of man Ryan was until he died. Why wasn't Nicole closer to her brother? I need more information before I can trust Ben. And I need to look around here for clues linking me to Nicole—fast, before Martinez finds out I'm here.

Ben looks over at Quinn, then observes me. He's looking for the truth, trying to see if he can find it in my eyes.

I assess him right back, and pretend I'm not crushed when he doesn't say a word.

Suddenly, he gets up and paces across the sand-colored stone floor. Every time he walks toward me, I see the raw grief and bewilderment all over him. They're the same emotions that slammed me after Ryan's suicide.

His hair flops in his face and he sighs. "I should call Martinez and I will, but you're the last person to talk to my sister, and I have no clue what the hell is going on here. Just a couple of weeks ago, Nicole was fine. Stressed and exhausted, but not what I would have called desperate or terrified. Nicole was—she was a force. I never imagined . . . But then yesterday, I get the call that tells me what she did. Then Greg's assistant called and asked me to take Quinn. He didn't even call me himself. The assistant said he was on his way to New York and that he and Nicole weren't even living together anymore. I was stunned. I had no idea they were having troubles. I could barely process what I was hearing. I still can't. I don't even know where Greg is—here or in New York. He hasn't answered my calls or emails. What kind of a man leaves his daughter just like that? What kind of a man doesn't rush back when his wife is . . . gone?"

My stomach clenches. "I don't know."

Ben shakes his head. "Anyway, I raced to the police station, where a detective told me they were investigating Nicole's death. Martinez thinks you pushed her. But there's more going on, right?" He narrows his eyes at me. "So who the hell are you really? Please explain that. And how you know about Amanda."

He looks so baffled that my heart aches. Ben is her family. Nicole's family. I'm no one to them.

I reach into my purse and show him the purple note.

"I found this stuck to my bag after Nicole jumped. She must have given it to me for a reason. I don't want to cause you any more pain, but it's clear to me we're in this together, whether we want to be or not. The sooner we figure out how Nicole knew me and why she gave me Quinn, the sooner we can figure out what the hell is going on. And part of the answer has got to be this."

Ben's shoulders start to shake. He's crying. "Amanda is dead. She died almost twenty years ago."

I wait. I don't press for more.

He sticks his hand in his pocket, and I'm sure he's about to call Martinez, but then he says, "I'm going to show you something because I don't know what the hell else to do. I've never talked to anyone about this."

From his shorts, he retrieves a black wallet. Then he pulls out a yellowed newspaper clipping, holding it tightly in his fingers.

"Before I show you this, you have to understand that I became Nicole's legal guardian when I was twenty and she was seventeen. We had no one else. Our parents died in an accident. And then I fucked everything up." He stares at his sneakers. "I found this on Nicole's floor when I was last here. She asked me to take it, so I did. I should have stayed with her, realized this was a call for help. But she was always so proud and always pushed me away."

As he passes me the newspaper clipping, our fingers touch. I unfold and gently smooth out the paper. It's an obituary from the *Kenosha News* for Amanda Taylor, who died at only six months old in 1998. Time stops, and I look from the paper to Ben.

"Telling anyone is very hard. Nicole was Amanda's nanny. Amanda died in Nicole's care."

"I'm so sorry," I say. Ben's face has aged in seconds.

"When I became responsible for Nicole, I tried to be like my dad, firm and tough, but she had no respect for me as an authority figure. She ran away, all the way to Wisconsin, where she became a nanny. And then this happened. I thought she'd gotten past it, though. We never talked about it. But she kept the clipping. And gave it to me that day, the last day I saw her."

He sits down and pinches the bridge of his nose.

I feel for him, this man who has lost not only his sister but also his entire family. "How did this happen, Ben?" I gesture to the article I hold in my hand. I'm hoping it contains the answers that link me to Nicole.

"Nicole was alone looking after Amanda while her parents were at work. She put her down for a nap in her crib, then Nicole fell asleep on the couch. When she woke up and went to check on the baby, she was dead." He sighs with his whole body. "It wasn't Nicole's fault, but Amanda's mother made her feel like it was. She blamed Nicole from the beginning. She went as far as to suggest that Nicole strangled the baby. When the medical examiner's report came in saying it was sudden infant death syndrome, Amanda's mother still didn't believe it. She came to our door, tried to attack Nicole. Said she was going to choke her the way Nicole had choked Amanda. I was so shocked I just stood there. It was horrible."

Poor, poor Nicole. To go through that at seventeen, I can't even imagine.

I look at the obituary again. My pulse speeds up. "Ben, Nicole was nervous on that platform, like she was looking around because someone was after her. And Martinez said it's odd for someone to commit suicide by jumping backward."

He leans forward, listening intently. "Donna," he says.

"Donna?"

"Amanda's mother."

"And this Donna woman, what happened to her?"

"Like I said, she harassed Nicole for a long time. She used to send threatening letters to my sister every year. I think they stopped years ago, though. Nicole never talked about it. I should have done more to make sure she was okay. But I didn't. And I guess she buried it, all that pain. Until Quinn was born."

I yearn to comfort him and tell him it wasn't his fault. But I don't know that for sure.

"If Donna was on that platform, maybe that's why Nicole was so scared," I say.

Ben stares at the paper in my hand. He reaches out for it and studies it closely. Then he looks up at me, eyes wide. "Holy shit," he says. "I didn't make the connection before."

"What?" I say.

"Amanda died on August seventh."

And it's then I realize what he's saying. That was yesterday, the same date Nicole landed on the tracks.

CHAPTER SIXTEEN

NICOLE

Before

Nicole dragged the box inside her house. Then she wheeled Quinn, asleep in the stroller, to the middle of the living room, as far from the box as possible. She lifted the lid slowly. On top was a pink piece of paper with the words "For Quinn" in a Comic Sans font. Underneath the paper was the soft white blanket she had never forgotten—Amanda's baby blanket.

Nicole felt as though she were being smothered.

You don't deserve a baby girl. You're a murderer. You can't keep her safe.

She dropped the blanket as if it had singed her. Leaving Quinn in the stroller, Nicole crawled to the kitchen to get her pills and swallowed two. The tight wrench of panic in her chest loosened and she could breathe again. This panic attack was as extreme as the one she'd had when Ben had brought her home to Chicago, two days after

Amanda died and Donna showed up at her door. Nicole was glad to see her. She wanted to express her anguish and her condolences. She wanted to say how much she, too, had loved Amanda. But before she could say anything, Donna launched herself at Nicole and grabbed her throat, wailing with the raw agony of an animal snared in a trap. "You were supposed to keep her safe!"

Nicole sobbed, barely managing to free herself from Donna's strong fingers. Ben just stood there. Something inside her cracked then. How could she rely on her brother, the only family she had left, if he wouldn't come to her side when she was in need? Ben told her later he was shocked and regretted not acting. But to Nicole, it felt like he wanted Donna to hurt her.

She'd been admitted to the psych ward, diagnosed with severe panic disorder, and kept under observation for three days. Because she was a minor, they would only release her, with a prescription for Zoloft, to Ben. And it didn't matter that Donna's hands weren't circling Nicole's throat anymore. The feeling of someone squeezing the life out of her was a sensation that never left her.

She jolted herself back to the present. It was no help to dwell on the past. She returned to the front hall, where Quinn was awake and alert. She couldn't bring Amanda back. But Quinn was alive. She had to keep her safe.

Nicole stuffed the blanket back in the box, then took her daughter out of the stroller, holding her close to her heart. She paced with her around the foyer. "I'll never let anything happen to you, I promise."

Was Donna playing with Nicole's mind? Or was she planning something too horrendous to even imagine?

The doorbell rang. Nicole's greatest fears raged through her body. Then she remembered that Tessa was going to come over, so maybe it was just her.

She cradled Quinn in one arm, moving to the front door. Her head was foggy, and she was having trouble walking steadily. She kicked the box into the closet, then peered through the frosted glass rectangle on the door. The figure outside was much too tall to be her best friend. When she realized who it was, her insides curdled.

Her brother. Ben.

Why was he here?

He banged on the glass. "Nic, I can see you. Open up."

Everything was okay. She could do this. She was good at pretending.

So she opened the door.

CHAPTER SEVENTEEN

MORGAN

I take the obituary back from Ben, and it crinkles in my hand. I can't stop looking at the date: August 7.

"It never occurred to me that the date was the same." Ben digs his fingers into his forehead. "Could Donna have had a hand in all of this?" He gets up again and walks circles around the kitchen, tugging at his dark waves. "Or do you think Nicole just chose to end her life on the seventh?"

It's making me dizzy watching him. "What do you know about Donna?" I ask. "Did she have any recent contact with Nicole?"

"No clue. I left it all behind. Nicole obviously gave me this obituary for a reason. She hadn't said Donna's or Amanda's names to me for years."

"Maybe Donna was on the platform. If we can find her photo, I can see if I remember anyone who looked like her at Grand/State. But I have to be honest, the whole event is a bit blurry."

Ben stands still and wrings his hands. "It's worth a shot."

If I can find the truth, Martinez will be forced to admit I was just an innocent bystander. And if we get to the bottom of this, Quinn will be safe, and I can get my life back.

I take my phone out of my bag, type in: "Donna Taylor; Kenosha, Wisconsin," and hand it to Ben.

Quinn's arms and legs jut out suddenly like a starfish, but she doesn't wake up.

He takes my phone and taps then holds it out to me. "Here she is. She still lives at the same address and works from there. Recognize her?"

The thumbnail is of a thin, pale redhead, wearing a pained smile that doesn't reach her empty blue eyes. She runs an online consignment shop from her home in Kenosha.

I squeeze my eyes shut to try to recall everything I saw on the platform, but all my attention was on Nicole and Quinn. Donna has red hair, like the woman in the Prius. But it's not enough to know for sure that was her. And in this photo, her hair is more auburn. The color isn't quite the same. "I don't think I saw her on the platform. And I didn't get a good look at the redhead in the Prius."

I take my phone back, suddenly exhausted. I wish I could sleep the day, the year, away, until all of this is over. But I did that after Ryan died, and it didn't help me at all.

My stomach growls loudly, and heat creeps up my neck.

He smiles weakly, and for a moment he looks younger. "I haven't eaten, either. I might have some granola bars in my backpack, if you're hungry."

"Thank you," I say softly.

"It's just a granola bar," he says, and leaves the kitchen.

Ben's awkward joke is almost childlike. He seems like such a genuine person, but I've learned the hard way I can't rely on my intuition anymore. I have to remain guarded.

Only a moment later, I hear his low voice from the front hall. He mentions Donna Taylor, a redhead, a Prius. Then I hear my name. And I know he must be talking to Martinez. If I could run, I would. Why did I think for a second that he trusted me? My skin prickles with anger, and using the table as leverage, I stand up just as Ben walks back into the room.

We look at each other. His cheeks are flushed, and mine feel hot.

"You think I'm lying," I say coldly, though really I want to cry.

"No. I don't. But I had to call Martinez. We almost got run over by a car, and Nicole died the same day as Amanda. She has to know."

I say nothing. Just because Donna is in the picture doesn't mean I'm safe.

"Martinez took all the information down, and she's going to check into Donna, the make of her car and license plate. It's fine, Morgan."

Fine. He has no idea what can happen, what can go wrong. I should get out of here and call Jessica. But then I notice a set of double doors next to the fridge. One of the doors is ajar. I want to scour the house for clues that will set me free, but I know I have to tread carefully.

"What's in there?" I ask.

"The pantry, I think. Why?"

"Do you think we should look around a bit before we leave?"

He nods. "I'll go. You can barely walk. And . . ."

"And she was your sister."

Ben walks toward the doors and disappears inside. Then I hear a sharp intake of breath.

"Morgan." His voice is low. "Come in here."

I hobble slowly to the pantry. It's a vast walk-in with shelves upon shelves filled with cans and boxes. Instantly, I see why Ben is shocked. Scores of purple Post-its cover the wall. Post-its like the one I found on my purse.

Name card. Redhead. Missing pills. Letter. Mobile. Door. Shattered chandelier. Photo. Box. Text. Exhaustion. Help me. Shelter. Widow. Morgan Kincaid. Mother.

"My name!" I whisper, unable to tear my eyes from the tiny papers. Seeing my name is like a fist to my solar plexus. The words swim in front of me, and I reach to steady myself against the wall.

Ben touches my shoulder. "You all right?"

I pull myself together. I have to think fast. It's clear something horrible happened to Nicole that made her write these notes. Something or someone caused her to track me down. I stare at the wall.

Ben's face is ashen. "What does all this mean?"

"I don't know. I still have no idea how she knew me, but we'll find out, Ben. And we have to figure out if Donna is somehow responsible. Or someone else." I dig at the rash on my collarbone. "I just want this to end."

Ben looks at me, and I see his struggle to believe me.

He helps me out of the pantry. My ankle is killing me, and my head is whirling. I can't make sense of any of this.

We go to the vibrating chair where Quinn is sleeping.

"I don't know what I feel. Confused. Definitely confused and really awful. I'm trying to believe everything you told me, but right now, I just can't believe any of this has happened. That my sister is really gone. I never told her how amazed I was by what she did with Breathe, how she pieced her life together again after such a terrible thing happened. I never helped my little sister." His eyes film, but tears don't fall. He looks away from me, as though he doesn't want me to witness any more of his pain.

I always longed for a sibling. It's a shame Ben and Nicole never had a chance to make amends. If Nicole had really known the adult Ben, the doctor, the caring man he seems to be, maybe she would have entrusted Quinn to him. Maybe she would have felt safer about sharing her concerns with him. Or maybe she knew something about her brother that I don't.

We stand awkwardly for a moment. I glance at Quinn, fast asleep. Her eyes flutter. Do babies this young dream? If they do, I hope hers are sweet.

It's then I hear the front door open. Ben pushes his hair from his face, a gesture I'm learning is his nervous tic.

Heels clack along the marble floor until they stop. I turn around.

It's Martinez.

CHAPTER EIGHTEEN

NICOLE

Before

Ben was standing on her stoop. Nicole watched his eyes widen as he took in the sight of her. In one hand, he held a white paper bag; in the other, a small brown teddy bear.

"What are you doing here?"

Ben looked at her strangely. "You asked me to come."

She gaped at him. "No, I didn't."

Nicole was surprised by the crow's-feet at the corners of his eyes and the sharp edges of his jaw. They were so much like their father's, it was like going back in time. She hadn't seen her brother in more than a year, since he'd bought his house and invited her for a tour. She'd gone, but she usually put off his attempts at reconciliation. He was always a reminder of her past.

"You texted me last night." He pulled his phone from the pocket of his scrubs. "Look."

Nicole viewed the screen. It was true. There was a message from her.

Could you pick up my prescription refill and bring it over tomorrow? I'm in a bind.

Nicole couldn't speak. She would never have asked her brother to do anything for her. She had enough pills to last two more weeks, and she'd certainly never invite him over. Ben walked inside, the legs of his scrubs making an irritating swishing sound as he closed the door behind him. "You don't look so good."

She bristled and ignored him, taking Quinn to the living room. She dropped the pharmacy bag on the table and picked up her phone, opened her text messages. There it was: a text from her to Ben, sent at 11:00 p.m. the night before. A text she had no memory of writing.

She slid her phone into her pocket and turned to look at her brother. She had to keep it together for long enough to let him visit, then she'd get him out of her life for good.

"Can I get you something? Coffee?" Her head spun, but she could manage an espresso.

"Sure. Thanks. Can I . . . ? I'd like to hold Quinn."

Nicole didn't want Quinn anywhere near her brother. He'd failed at protecting her, so how would he protect Quinn?

"She doesn't like to be away from me," Nicole said. She turned and walked toward the kitchen, where she'd make Ben a coffee and take another pill.

Except there were no coffee beans in the kitchen, not even a jar of instant coffee. She couldn't remember when she or Tessa had last ordered groceries. The fridge was bare, save for a carton of orange juice, a bruised apple, and a couple of shriveled peaches.

She tapped out a pill, then squinted at the bottle. It was half-empty. How could she not have noticed that before? And how many pills had she taken the night before? Enough to text Ben and forget about it?

Her phone rang. She took it out of her pocket. Tessa. Thank God.

"Hi," she whispered.

"Is Quinn asleep?"

"Ben is here."

"Ben as in your brother? Wow. What's he doing there?"

"He brought me a prescription refill. . . ." She stopped herself from saying more. "He wanted to meet Quinn."

"Well, that's kind of nice, I guess. You okay with it?"

"Not really."

"So tell him to leave. Do you want me to come as backup?"

Nicole laughed. "I'm fine. I'd better go."

"Okay, but I just wanted to give you the heads-up. I told Lucinda you approved the final designs for the cuffed trench coat line for spring. I hope that's fine. I can come over tonight to talk about all this."

She hadn't told Tessa she'd run into Lucinda. She didn't have time now. She had to deal with Ben, get him out of her house as quickly as possible.

"I'll call you after Ben leaves, okay?"

"Do you promise you will?"

"Sure," Nicole said. She hung up and crouched with Quinn against her chest. Her throat felt tight, and she dry-swallowed the tablet, hoping it would take effect immediately. She knew she was taking too many pills, but she couldn't let Ben see her have a panic attack. What would Tessa do if she were here? Nicole sat down and laid her hand on her belly. Five deep breaths in. Five slow exhales out.

She calmed herself enough to stand up and walk back into the living room, as steadily as she could. "I've run out of coffee."

Ben pushed his too-long hair back from his forehead, worry crossing his boyish face. It hit her suddenly that her brother, at thirty-nine, was a year younger than their father had been when he died.

"How's Greg?" he asked.

Nicole decided she wouldn't tell him Greg had left them. "Greg's fine."

"But you're not," he replied.

All her past misery and resentment bubbled to the surface. "You're not responsible for me anymore!" Nicole blazed with anger. She leaped off the couch, Quinn's head banging hard against her chest. Her daughter wailed.

"Nicole! Her neck!"

"Ben! Do you think I don't know how to take care of my daughter? Is that why you came? To criticize me?"

She felt sick. Their relationship hadn't always been fraught. She missed the boy who'd walked her home from school every day, carrying Band-Aids in his pocket because she'd always run ahead of him, trip, and scrape her knees.

"You asked me to come, and I came! Jesus, I never get it right with you, do I? You'll never forgive me no matter what."

Her insides were on fire. She steeled herself, just in case he said her name. Amanda. She waited, but he didn't say it. Not that it mattered— it was there between them forever. "Just leave. We don't need you."

Ben tugged at his hair. "Nic, I'm here because you asked me to be. And now that I see you, I'm concerned. You look thin. And that Xanax you had me pick up? Just know that lorazepam might be better for you right now, given that you have a newborn."

"You're not my doctor, Ben."

"You're right. Have you seen your doctor recently?" He stood and moved closer to her. "Look, Nicole, we see this all the time at the hospital. It's not uncommon for new mothers to experience difficulties after they give birth. I can easily get you in to see someone in my hospital, maybe a pediatrician. Or a psychotherapist? I can get you an appointment today."

She backed away and spit out a dark laugh. "Fuck you."

His face fell, like the little boy who cried and cried when their father had given away his Star Wars action figures because he said Ben was too old for them. Nicole refused to feel bad.

He stood. "Okay. Okay. I'm sorry. I'll leave you be, but if you need anything, I'm here." He looked at Quinn, and his eyes softened. "I'd like to be in her life. Your life. We're all the family we've got."

She gestured to the door. He walked toward it but stopped suddenly. He bent down and picked something up from the marble floor. Then he turned around, and on his face, she saw horror and fear.

"Why do you have this?" He held out a yellowed newspaper clipping.

Nicole didn't know what he was talking about. She took the clipping, and her stomach flipped. Amanda's obituary. Had it been in the box with the blanket?

They locked eyes. In his Nicole saw disappointment and blame.

"Nic. You're not well. I can help. I understand more than anyone what you went through."

"No, you don't." She held the obituary out to him. "I don't need this. Take it."

He looked at the obituary being waved in his face, then at Quinn. Was he afraid to leave Nicole alone with her?

"The past is the past. It's over, Nicole. It was a tragedy. An awful tragedy, but it's been almost twenty years. It's time to let it go."

"Take this. Get it out of my house. Do this one thing for me."

He nodded and accepted the clipping. With his hand on the doorknob, he said, "I love you, Nic. I always have. I always mess it up with you, but it's not because I don't love you."

He opened the door, turned for a last look at her and then the baby, and walked out. She twisted the dead bolt and pulled the doorknob five times to make sure it was really locked.

She cradled her daughter's small body and looked in her eyes. "You don't need anyone else to fulfill you. You'll do that all by yourself."

Her eyes landed on the peg by the door where she kept the extra keys to Ben's house, the keys she'd never once used, the keys he insisted she keep, in case anything happened.

And now the keys were gone.

CHAPTER NINETEEN

MORGAN

I'm furious when Martinez adjusts the jacket of her black pantsuit and strides into the kitchen toward me. I whip my head at Ben and hiss, "How dare you try to trap me?"

Ben holds up his hands. "Look, I don't think you did anything, and that's why I called Martinez. So she can hear all of this herself, from you. If I told you, you would have left and been in danger."

I refuse to answer him. I snatch my phone from my purse and bang out a text to Jessica, telling her to come to Nicole's.

On my way. Do NOT say a word.

I can't just stand here wobbling like an idiot on my throbbing ankle, so I sit in a chair. Ben and Martinez take seats, too.

"Morgan, I have a few questions for you." Her intense expression is eager, almost excited.

Frightened, but trying to hide it, I make my expression as blank as possible. "You can't speak to me without my attorney present." My tone is firm, but my voice betrays my nervousness.

She scoffs.

Ben puts his hands on the table and looks at Martinez. "I told you everything already about the blue Prius, Amanda, and Donna Taylor. And that Morgan was rear-ended by a redhead in a Prius on the highway. But just now we, I, found this in Nicole's pantry." He leads Martinez to the open doors, and they disappear inside.

I strain to hear their hushed voices. I know they're talking about me. I can't defend myself until Jessica gets here. Anything I say to Martinez she will use against me.

They're in the pantry for about fifteen minutes when there's a loud knock on the door. Martinez leaves the kitchen, coming back seconds later with Jessica, resplendent in a fitted red dress. She marches over to me. She puts a hand on my back. "What's this about, Detective?"

"Are you aware your client was named guardian and executor of Quinn Markham's significant shares of Breathe? That Nicole Markham changed her will mere days before she fell onto the tracks at Grand/State?"

My mouth drops open before I can stop it. She knows. Rick Looms must have called her. And I haven't yet informed Jessica. Damn it, how much trouble am I in now? I'm afraid to look at Ben, but I can feel his shocked glare.

Jessica swivels her head to look at me. I nod, almost imperceptibly.

"I'm not sure what your point is," she says to Martinez.

I marvel at her cool, calm tone, because I'm a raging inferno inside.

"I think you know my point, Ms. Clark. It serves your client's best interests to just be honest about how she knew Nicole. Why she's harassing Ben Layton. Gaining custody of Quinn and her fortune is, of course, motive."

I sneak a glance at Ben, whose face has paled. He walks to the vibrating chair, lifts Quinn out, and holds her close. He averts his eyes from mine.

"My client has no statement to make at this time. Is that all?" Jessica puts a hand on my shoulder, turning me slightly so I'm facing her and not Martinez.

"That's all for now. But we will find out the truth. It's beneficial for Morgan to come to us before we come back to her." She gestures toward the front hall. "You need to leave the premises. The Crime Scene Unit are on their way. You can file a report about the accident." She spins on her heel.

Jessica raises an eyebrow, but follows, and I'm about to limp after her, leaving Ben and Quinn. I feel his eyes on my back, and if I turn around, I'm sure they'll drill his mistrust and disbelief right into me.

I tap Jessica. "Can you give me one minute to talk to Ben?"

She turns around to face me and sighs. "I'm staying right here."

I nod and meet Ben's gaze. "Nicole's attorney contacted me this morning. I swear that everything I've told you is true. I didn't know your sister. But she wrote a legal petition making me Quinn's guardian and executrix of her shares of Breathe. It doesn't make sense to me at all."

Ben's face reddens. "Why did you hide that from me? And why would she do that when she had me? Why would she choose a total stranger to raise my niece rather than her own brother?"

Everything he's saying is tinged not just with his lack of trust in me but with his own guilt. I can hear it. His raw pain is almost visceral.

"I'm sorry I didn't tell you about the petition sooner. I didn't want to hurt you more than you've been hurt already. I haven't filed, obviously. I don't even know what to do about it. You seem like a great person, and I've seen with my own eyes that you care about Quinn. All I can say is that something awful happened to your sister inside this house. And she wasn't herself when she drew up those papers." I look into his sad, weary eyes. "You didn't do anything wrong. And I certainly didn't, either."

He sighs. "You don't seem like a criminal."

"That's because I'm not," I reply. "Look, I just want to make sure we're all safe, okay? Can we exchange numbers just in case?"

He hesitates for a moment, then agrees.

After I add him to my contacts, Jessica and I leave the house immediately. As we're making our way to the driveway, Martinez comes out onto the stoop, watching us. She says, "Whoever gets custody of Quinn has access to her money. Someone is lying here."

When we get to my car, Jessica stands in front of me, hazel eyes blazing with anger. "Let's go to your apartment and talk." She points to my foot. "Can you drive?"

"I'll manage."

My ankle throbs as I navigate back to my building, Jessica's white Mercedes right behind me. We arrive and park. Jessica silently follows me to my apartment and takes a seat on my fuchsia couch. I sit on the other end, my nerves crackling with fear.

"Why are you limping?" she asks.

"Funny story."

"Morgan."

I scratch my neck so hard it burns and take a deep breath. Then I finally spit it out. I tell her about the redhead in the Prius who followed me and tried to kill Ben, Quinn, and me.

"What? You need to call me immediately if you think you're in danger!" Then Jessica just stares at me, tapping her palm slowly on her thigh.

"Say something, please."

She sighs. "Is there more?"

I nod. "Quinn's father, Greg, abandoned her and Nicole, then basically handed his daughter to Ben like he doesn't give a shit about her. What kind of father does that? Maybe he's involved."

She throws her hands in the air. "Maybe he is, but you are not an investigator. You're a person of interest. And you shouldn't be doing anything but staying out of Martinez's way right now. All of this only makes you look guilty of something."

"Why didn't you tell Martinez about the break-in and my stolen adoption application?"

"Because if she knows you wanted to adopt a baby, it will look like getting Quinn *is* your motive."

My stomach sinks. I tell her everything Ben told me about Donna and Amanda Taylor. And everything we found at Nicole's.

After I'm through speaking, she clicks her tongue. "Barry can definitely search DMV records to see if a Prius is registered in Donna's name. We'll file a police report about the accident on the highway." She takes her phone out of her coral Prada handbag and taps. "I've emailed you the footage at Grand/State that Barry saved so you can take a better look at the people there and see if you spot her. This might actually help us, but for now lie low. And next time, tell me right away before you take matters into your own hands, Morgan. Leave a message if I don't pick up. We don't know why your name is on a wall of Post-its. Taking it upon yourself to try to find out only hurts you. You do realize I'm trying to protect you, right? And you're making it close to impossible." She catches her own impatience and her voice suddenly softens. "You can trust me, you know. You're not in this alone."

But I feel very alone. It's not like she could protect me last time, with Ryan. I know all Jessica wants is to help me, but no one truly understands how lonely I am, how hard it is to trust anyone after all that's happened. How hard it is not to have a single friend to call, or to come over and be with me. Who can tell me I couldn't have known what Ryan was doing because he hid it so well, and I shouldn't blame myself for not being able to stop him.

She emits a frustrated grumble. "You're not actually thinking of filing for guardianship, are you?"

I swallow hard. "I don't know. Will you stop representing me if I do?"

"Have you lost your mind? I strongly advise against filing. Morgan, you're not responsible for raising her child. That's her family's job. You're too focused on saving a baby who already has people to take care of her. That gives you a clear motive for murdering her mother. Don't you see that?"

I take a pillow from the couch and put it on my lap. "But I didn't know the baby before yesterday. I didn't know Nicole had any intention of giving her to me."

"And how exactly are you going to prove that, Morgan? I'm working on it but coming up dry." Her fingers fly over the screen on her phone. "I need to get to court, but take a look at that video and call me if you recognize anyone, okay? Martinez made a good point. There's someone out there who might want Quinn's money. Be careful who you trust. In the meantime, ice that ankle and stay here. Got it?" She pats my leg, then stands up. "Lock up after I leave."

We say goodbye at the door, and I do as she said. I realize Jessica is the only person apart from me who's been in my home since I moved in, besides whoever broke in and stole my adoption application. Tears threaten to burst, but I shake them away and limp to the kitchen for an ice pack.

Then alone on my couch, I take my phone from my purse, exhaling long and loud before viewing the video again. Watching it is excruciating. It's incredible to me that it's the same moment I lived through, and yet, viewed from this perspective, it raises doubt about me rather than quells it. I try to look with new eyes, focus instead on what I didn't see at the time—who was around me and who Nicole was looking at on the platform. The video is grainy and opaque. I see not one person who might be Donna Taylor. What I do see is Nicole going over the edge. And even watching this for the second time, it makes me double over with pain. If I'd only realized what she was about to do.

There are just too many people to spot anyone she might have been scared of. Any redhead who might be watching me. A mother who blamed Nicole for her daughter's death.

What do I do now? I know I should step back and leave Quinn to be raised by her father or her uncle, leave the system to sort it all out.

But Nicole didn't want her to be with them, and something about that nags at me. And I don't trust the system anymore.

Life isn't fair. It's short, hard to navigate, and full of pitfalls and unforeseen dangers. And the truth of it?

I want a baby.

I want Quinn.

———

Blythe & Brown, where Greg works, is about a fifteen-minute drive from my apartment. My ankle is still very sore, but I can limp. I quickly change into a long, blue cotton dress and sneakers, and get in my car before I can change my mind. I haven't told Jessica what I'm doing, and that makes me a little nervous. But this is something I must do on my own. I'm too impatient to wait for answers, to wait for all the fingers to twist and turn and eventually point at me. Too worried Martinez will find out something about me before I do. I've been in the dark about my own life for too long.

I head down North LaSalle, my eyes peeled for a redhead in a dark blue Prius. By the time I park, I haven't seen any sign of her. I hope Quinn and Ben are okay and she's not following them.

The strap of my bag cuts into my shoulder, and sweat collects on my upper lip as I trek on my still-aching ankle toward the six-story, redbrick building that houses Greg's brokerage firm. The earlier coolness has faded, and it's a steamy afternoon. I already feel damp. I hover at the door. Maybe I should use my social work credentials instead of my connection to Nicole to get in. But if anyone calls Haven House to check, I'm screwed.

The brunette at the reception desk looks up and smiles at me. It's now or never, so I approach, watching her face for any sign of recognition. She doesn't glare, and her eyes don't widen. I'm always wary, always prepared, for that wounding look of apprehension to cross someone's face. Though that might be all in my mind.

"May I help you?"

I glance around the large open-concept office, where a conference room is set to the left of the front desk and row upon row of cubicles fill every available space. Everyone is either on the phone or hectically tapping keyboards. The tension is high, and it reminds me of Ryan. Late at night, his head in his hands, as he furiously made calls and yelled at his laptop. No one is looking at me, like he never looked at me at the end of his life.

"I'd like to see Greg Markham, please." My voice squeaks, and heat floods my cheeks.

She narrows her eyes slightly, and I realize she might think I'm a reporter. "May I have your name?"

"Morgan Kincaid."

I watch her eyes drop to a newspaper on her desk.

She leans away from me. "You're the woman who was with Nicole when she jumped."

I feel my polite smile fall from my face. I peer over her desk to see a photo of me on the front page of the day's paper, taken when I was leaving the police station Monday night. My face is chalk-white, my eyelet dress is wrinkled and grimy, and the camera caught my panic, which could certainly be construed by an outside observer as an expression of guilt.

"What a tragedy. We didn't get to see her much except for the year-end summer barbecue, but she was lovely." Then her cheeks go pink. "Do you know why she did it?"

I'm at once disgusted and horrified. This is exactly how I imagine people talked about me and Ryan after he died. With obvious titillation over a juicy story, as though I wasn't real, wasn't suffering and mourning his loss and his unconscionable deceit.

I tell myself it doesn't matter. I straighten and look the woman in the eyes. "I'd like to speak to Greg."

In a colder voice now, she says, "Sorry, but he's out of the office today, and I'm not sure when he's returning. If you leave your contact information, his assistant will be in touch." She shrugs, then looks down.

I've been dismissed. I worry she'll call Martinez, who will then call Jessica. What am I doing? Jessica's right. I'm making everything worse for myself. I should just go home and stay put. Dejected, I leave the building. My neck tingles, but it's not the stifling heat, or my eczema. It's the dark blue Prius parked at the curb in front of me.

My instinct is to run, but instead I head straight toward the Prius. I'm sick of being scared. I'm sick of being stalked, being a passive victim. I have every right to walk the streets of Chicago without fearing for my life. With my fists pumping and ankle throbbing, I march up to the car and bang on the driver's-side window.

"Who are you?" My voice is loud, shocking passersby into moving quickly away from me. "What do you want from me?"

The window lowers, and I come face-to-face with a redhead. It's not Donna Taylor, or, at least, this woman looks nothing like the one in the photo Ben showed me. I've never seen this woman before, but if she tried to run us down, it's time to know why. "Why are you following me?" I spit at her.

She looks shocked and terrified. She presses a button and the window starts to close. Without thinking, I shove my hand into the small space left. The window stops.

"I could have sliced off your hand!" she cries, rolling the window back down an inch.

I put my face as close to the window as I can. "Tell me who you are!"

"Why are you yelling at me?!"

"I'm the woman Nicole was with when she died. Now tell me why you're after me!"

"Please don't hurt me." She holds her hands up like I have a gun.

"Hurt you? You tried to run me over!"

"I don't know what you're talking about. This is my office. I have no reason to follow you. Why are you even here?"

"Did you follow Nicole, too, like you've been following me? Did you break into my apartment?"

"You're crazy! Greg Markham is my boss. I never even met Nicole. Now get away from my car." Her words are firm, but her voice is tremulous.

She's scared of me or she's an excellent actress, either one. I have to stop myself from reaching in and shaking her until her teeth rattle. "I'm not leaving until you tell me the truth. How can a man just leave his child like that? Her mother died, and Greg's nowhere to be found!" I stick my head right into the window this time. "What kind of person does that? What did he do to Nicole?"

She revs the engine, and the tires squeal as she jams on the gas and peels away. I fly onto the road, feeling a searing burn along my leg where the car scraped my skin.

I push myself to standing, blood dripping down my shin. I try to memorize the license plate. H57 3306. I repeat it over and over as I stumble to my car, my ankle throbbing and leg on fire. I weave in and out of temporary construction zones set up all down the street, and the head-pounding sound of the jackhammers only adds to my frenzy.

I think back to the video from Grand/State. Maybe *she* was there. And now, she's getting away.

CHAPTER TWENTY

NICOLE

Before

Nicole wrapped a hand over Quinn's back in the Moby and with her other pushed the orange Breathe folder off the kitchen table. The glossy design pages for the trench coat line flew all over the floor. She couldn't even do one simple task anymore. Tessa had begged her to at least look at them and Skype with Lucinda. That was four days ago.

"I'll take Quinn for a walk while you meet with the board. I'll make sure she falls asleep and gets fresh air. Please," Tessa implored as she pressed the folder into Nicole's hands. "Lucinda said she ran into you and you looked terrible. 'Unrecognizable' was the word she used. She said you freaked out and took off."

Nicole could not leave the house, and she certainly couldn't let Tessa walk the streets with Quinn when Donna could be anywhere. But she'd promised Tessa she would think about it.

Now, though, she was ignoring Tessa's texts and the incessant calls from Lucinda and the other board members. From the cupboard above the farmhouse sink, she got her bottle of pills and the refill Ben had brought. As she extracted a couple of pills, Quinn grabbed for them. The pills flew out of Nicole's hands and scattered all over the floor.

"No!" Nicole quickly unwound the wrap and put Quinn in her chair. On her hands and knees, she gathered all the tablets she could find. She couldn't afford to lose any of them. She couldn't order another prescription online, and there was no way she was seeing a doctor, not a chance.

Desperate for relief, she leaned against the cupboard and swallowed a pill covered with dirt and dust. She was so dehydrated that the pill got stuck in her throat and she choked. Quinn gurgled, watching her mother intently as Nicole finally got the tablet down.

Everything was wrong, and she didn't know how to make it right. This was not how she wanted her daughter to see her. Nicole got up, stumbled to the drawer, and smoothed out the Post-its she'd shoved in there. She needed to see them lined up again, but somewhere Tessa wouldn't find them the next time she came over. She opened the pantry door and stuck them inside, on the white wall to the left. Tessa never went in there. Then Nicole retethered her daughter to her and stroked her silky tufts of hair until her own breathing slowed.

She pointed up at the wall of purple.

"We can fix this, Quinnie. Visualize a red light and ground yourself in the here and now."

She added more notes, new words.

Quinn's back was wet, and she needed to be changed. "You deserve the best mommy. The strongest mommy." Her breath stuttered.

Maybe she should ask Tessa to stay with them for a while, to help out a bit, just until she could get herself together.

But she realized, with intense sadness, that she couldn't ask that of her friend, even though she'd offered. Tessa was too good to her.

How much more could she expect her to do? Tessa had her own life. More than that, she now carried a significant burden at Breathe. She was doing Nicole's job, and she was also keeping Nicole's struggles a secret from the board. Nicole felt such gratitude for that. She wasn't sure she deserved it.

Quinn needed a bath. She took her to the en suite and knelt on the bath steps, turning the brushed nickel taps to full stream. She stripped off the baby's soiled clothes, and her own dirty, wrinkled ones, then poured a glass of water and gulped it down. Her mouth felt like it was stuffed with cotton. She drank another glass and then another, while Quinn babbled in her arms. No matter how unstable she felt, her daughter was happy. Nothing mattered more than that.

"We have to get clean, Quinn. Cleanliness is next to godliness." Maybe she and Quinn both needed to be baptized. Reborn.

With Quinn lying on her stomach on top of her, Nicole lay back in the bath, sinking lower and lower into the soothing warmth of the water. It was so quiet and peaceful. Here they were safe, even from Nicole's own thoughts. She wanted to stay under the water forever. She closed her eyes.

Suddenly she bolted up, clutching tightly to Quinn's slippery skin, splashing water over the sides of the tub as Quinn sputtered and cried.

"I'm sorry, baby. I'm so sorry. Mommy fell asleep. I didn't mean to. I'd never hurt you!" she sobbed as the water kept running.

It had been only for a moment, but her baby could have drowned.

Gasping, she turned off the water and rocked her daughter back and forth. Her stomach twisted with the sick realization of what could have happened. In the softest tone she could, she whispered over and over to her precious girl, "I'll keep you safe. I'll always keep you safe."

She got out of the bath and gently wrapped Quinn in a fluffy towel, as guilt, shame, and self-loathing crawled up her throat. She laid her daughter on the floor, knelt, and vomited in the toilet. Then Nicole wiped her mouth, and with no towel for herself, she took Quinn to the bedroom. She managed to get her daughter into a fresh diaper and a pretty denim dress. Then she brought her downstairs and put her in the vibrating chair in the living room, where she promptly fell asleep.

Nicole stroked her beautiful girl's cheeks. Quinn's tiny hands were curled, and she looked so pure. So perfect that love flooded Nicole's entire being.

She had to do something to stop her never-ending guilt and fear. She could call Donna and beg for her forgiveness. Open Donna's second chakra. Then they'd both be free. Her phone lay on the coffee table. She grabbed it and dialed the number that was etched in her memory. Disappointment flooded her when there was no answer and no voice mail.

Wet and shivering, she wrapped herself in a purple fleece throw from the sofa and slapped her head over and over. "Think. How can we find her?" She closed her eyes, remembering those warm summer evenings when Amanda's father came home from work. He'd toss the baby in the air over Donna's shrieking protests. Nicole had always laughed along with Amanda's giggles. She couldn't recall where he worked, but she knew he was an accountant. She googled "Flynn Taylor" until the links blurred together. She rubbed her eyes and finally she found him. Then she dialed.

"Flynn speaking."

She recognized his husky voice.

"Hello? Can I help you?"

"It's Nicole," she whispered.

"Who?"

"Nicole Layton."

No sound came from the other end of the phone.

"Does Donna still hate me?" she asked.

There was a long pause. "I don't know what you want, Nicole. Why are you calling me?" His voice was cold and flat.

She felt as though she'd swallowed a rock, but she spoke through her pain. "I had a baby, and now horrible things are happening. Please tell Donna to stop. I want it all to stop."

There was some rustling on the other end of the line, the sound of a door being closed. "Look, I don't know why you would call me after all this time, but I don't want to hear from you. Donna's in a good place now. She's got her life back, and we're not together anymore. I'm married to someone else. I have two children. And I don't need you to remind me of the child I lost. Leave us alone, Nicole."

"You and Donna are divorced?"

"Not that it's any of your business, but yes, we are."

"Donna sent me Amanda's baby blanket." Nicole burst into tears.

His sigh was filled with suffering. "Donna did no such thing. And I gave all of Amanda's things away nineteen years ago, Nicole."

Nicole nearly dropped the phone. The white blanket in the box was Amanda's. It *was*.

"Hello? Hello?"

She heard him hang up, and the call went dead.

She ran to the front hall closet where she'd left the box and the blanket.

But they were gone.

CHAPTER TWENTY-ONE

MORGAN

I sit in my car and wipe the blood from my leg, where there's a nasty three-inch gash. It's not deep enough to require stitches, and I don't want to go anywhere but home. There are two redheads—Donna and Greg's employee—who might have torn Nicole's life apart and who might want Quinn and me dead. I still don't know my connection to Nicole. The adrenaline has worn off, and terror has taken its place. My hands are damp, and I keep dropping my keys every time I try to start the car. I have no solid evidence to bring to Martinez. I'm at the same place as when I started. I finally call Jessica.

"I really think I'm in danger, Jessica. I think I found the Prius that was following me before. I talked to the woman driving it, who says Greg is her boss. She drove off really fast and hit me! What should I do?" I ramble the license plate number, speaking so quickly I'm almost hyperventilating.

"Wait, slow down a minute. Are you badly hurt?"

Jessica is so calm that it makes me feel a little better. "I'm okay. But please find out exactly who this woman is. I'm so scared."

I'm more than scared. I'm hysterical with fear.

"Morgan, where are you exactly?"

"I'm—" Shit. Biting my thumbnail, I mumble, "I'm at Blythe and Brown. Greg Markham's brokerage firm."

"Tell me you did not talk to him."

Her tone is cold. But this is my life, my choice. And I don't regret it.

"He wasn't there."

"This is *motive*, Morgan. How am I supposed to disprove that you and Nicole never met if you first go to her brother's house, then try to track down her husband? Basically, what I'm saying here is: Are you trying to get yourself arrested?"

"I need to know why she chose me, Jessica. I need to clear my name!"

"I get that you feel vulnerable and scared. I'm doing everything I can to find the link between you and Nicole. I do have information about Donna Taylor's car. She owns a 2010 black Chevy Impala. Which means she probably wasn't the one in the Prius that chased you down. Barry's checking on that, and I'll give him the update about the redhead you met at Greg's workplace."

Good. She's on it. Which is all I really wanted. I need help. There are too many missing pieces to know what to do.

"Please go home, Morgan," Jessica says. "We'll look into this new redhead, okay? Just go home." Her stern tone brooks no argument.

"Yes," I say. "I will. I promise."

My hands still and I finally get the key in the ignition. I'm suddenly filled with despair. I feel like an idiot chasing down impossible leads and trying to fit pieces together in a puzzle beyond my comprehension. For once, I follow Jessica's advice and keep my promise to her.

No one follows me home, and for that I'm grateful. In my apartment, I clean and disinfect my leg, change into black leggings and a hot pink T-shirt, order a greasy burger and fries, and eat it on the couch, the blinds drawn. My ankle and shin throb. I know I shouldn't, but I go online and scroll through the staff list at Blythe & Brown until I find the photo of the woman in the Prius. Melissa Jenkins. Greg's assistant. She's young, maybe mid-to-late twenties, with shoulder-length, wavy red hair. She's only been at the company for three months.

From the articles I read about Nicole, it seems that until Quinn was born, she was a strong, powerful woman in control. Could Melissa's recent hiring have contributed to her downfall? I'm too bone-weary to do any more searching or look at the video from Grand/State again, so I lie on my couch. It's only 7:00 p.m., but all I want to do is sleep.

A noise wakes me up. I shoot up on the couch and yell at the pain in my ankle and leg. It's pitch-black, and I scramble for my phone. It's 3:00 a.m. I was out for eight hours.

My eyes adjust to the darkness. Gingerly, I stand up, flicking on the hall light.

A manila envelope has been pushed under my door. It lies on the floor. There's no address or postmarks. I look through the peephole on the door, but the hallway outside is empty. I pick up the envelope and bring it back to the couch. I'm afraid to look inside.

I gather my courage and pull out a sheaf of papers. It's the adoption application that was stolen from my desk drawer. Scrawled in red pen on the bottom of the last stapled page is a message.

Stay away from Quinn. You can't keep her safe.

Paralyzed, I drop the envelope. I pull the door open and scan the hallway outside, but it's too late. Whoever dropped this off is gone. I go back inside, locking the door behind me. I keep myself so still, moving only my eyes around the room.

"There's no one here," I whisper, reminding myself. "I'm safe."

My phone rings. I slide my eyes to the screen. It's Ben. My hand is shaking so much I almost miss the call.

"What's wrong?" I ask the second it connects.

"You need to come over right now. Quinn's in trouble."

CHAPTER TWENTY-TWO

NICOLE

Before

"Nic, open this door, or I will break it down! I might be small, but you know how mighty I am!" Tessa yelled through the mail slot.

At any other time in her life, Nicole would have laughed. Now she almost bawled with relief. Tessa would take care of them.

She grasped the arm of the couch and heaved herself up, dropping her chin to her chest until the wooziness passed. She lifted Quinn from the vibrating chair, her arms aching. She couldn't carry her daughter everywhere, even in the Moby. Nicole barely had the energy to make it up the stairs at all. She'd draped black silk sheets over all the first-floor windows, so her house felt as dark as she did inside.

It was July thirtieth. She was due back at Breathe tomorrow.

She opened the door.

"Thank you." Tessa frowned when she saw Nicole. "You're white as a sheet."

Nicole nodded. "I don't feel well."

Tessa walked past her and into the kitchen. Nicole followed as her friend wordlessly picked up the dirty dishes on the counter, put them in the dishwasher, then ran it. She took milk, a loaf of bread, and some apples and oranges out of her bag. When she opened the fridge, her head reeled back.

"Nic, when did you last eat? I've been calling and texting for days. I would have brought more groceries." She sniffed at the milk and immediately poured it out into the sink. The sour stench filled the room.

Nicole didn't know when she'd last ordered groceries for herself. She kept forgetting to eat, and most of the time she wasn't hungry. All she cared about was making sure Quinn was healthy. The baby's chubby legs kicked at the air, making Nicole smile. Her daughter was her only source of happiness.

Tessa dropped some bread into the toaster. From her Breathe tote she brought out two packs of organic diapers, and a bouquet of gorgeous yellow roses that she placed in an empty vase and filled with water.

She walked over to Nicole and gently brushed her cheek, then wiped the corner of her mouth. "Have you been keeping hydrated? You need to."

Nicole touched her finger to her sore lips. "I try to eat, to drink, but nothing tastes good. I feed Quinn, though. She looks good, right? Healthy? I can't believe she's almost six weeks old."

Would her daughter make it to six months? Six years like Amanda never could?

Tessa reached out and tickled Quinn's tummy, making the baby's eyes twinkle with joy. "She looks wonderful. But you don't. Did you finally speak to Lucinda?"

I'm seeing things, Nicole wished she could say. *Things are appearing and disappearing, and I don't know how.* Instead she said, "I haven't talked to anyone but you, and Ben when he was here."

Tessa wrinkled her pert nose. Then she took Quinn from Nicole's arms and put her in the vibrating chair. "Just leave her there for a minute so you can really listen."

Nicole nodded and sat on one of the kitchen chairs, one eye on her daughter, who stared alertly at the monkey that hung from the handle above her.

Tessa sat next to her. "So how was it with Ben?"

"It was pretty bad. I don't want him back in my life, and I told him as much. But with Greg gone, I don't know if I'm doing the right thing. He's Quinn's only family." Even with her best friend beside her, Nicole had never felt lonelier. There were so many secrets to keep. She remembered seeing an article about Ben's hospital having financial trouble. "I think he wanted to ask me for money for his hospital. It might close." It was a total lie, and something in her burned as she said it.

Tessa curled her legs under her. "He came for a donation and not to see Quinn and you?"

"I don't know. Anyhow, I'm not going to see him again. We've never really gotten along. Don't see how it'll be different now."

"You're better off without men." She paused. "Greg still hasn't called?"

"Not once. I don't get it, Tess. I was everything to him, and now it's like he's cut me, cut us, out of his life completely." Nicole looked sharply at Tessa. "Have you spoken to him?"

"No. Of course not."

Nicole felt contrite. "Sorry. You're not the enemy. I didn't mean to snap."

"It's fine. You don't need him anyway. You have me." She took her phone out of her tote. "Nicki, I really need to talk to you about work."

The room was spinning, but Nicole managed to hang on.

"I have to fill you in on what's been going on. You need to come into the office tomorrow. I'm told there's been discussions behind closed doors. Key investors are selling. It's bad. I'm worried."

Nicole heard only white noise. Her personal attorney, Rick Looms, had called countless times, and so had all the board members, but she never answered those calls. She'd ignored every one of Lucinda's increasingly terse emails and messages. She massaged her head to clear the fuzz, but without enough food and sleep, she simply couldn't focus.

Tessa handed her phone to Nicole. She had pulled up an article from *Page Six*:

> **An anonymous source confirms that Markham is housebound and unwell, struggling to care for her newborn daughter. She has not been seen in public since she left on a six-week, unpaid leave, negotiated with the board of directors. Should Markham not return to Breathe as CEO on July 31, she is at risk of being ousted from the company she founded.**

So this was the piece Lucinda had referred to. "Did Lucinda do this?"

Tessa took a breath. "Do you think Lucinda would sell you out?"

"Why not? This way she can take what she's always wanted. She can hire her own CEO or become CEO herself."

She and Lucinda had butted heads for years. She'd tried to vote Nicole out just a year before, when Nicole had refused to launch a line of gingham leggings that looked far too similar to their biggest competitor's. Nicole would never be a follower. She was a leader. An innovator.

Tessa looked thoughtful. "It's bad, Nicki. The board will have legal grounds to force you out if you're not back at your desk tomorrow. We can't let that happen. They can't take Breathe from you."

Exhaustion and helplessness engulfed her. She closed her eyes. It drained her to even imagine getting dressed for work. She couldn't do it. She could not go into Breathe right now. But how could she sit back and let her company, the empire she had built from the ground up, be snatched from her and Quinn?

If Lucinda was spearheading her removal, Nicole had to fight back. She staved off her tears. She now regretted taking her company public. She'd let the prestige and the self-worth gained by going public control her logic. In exchange for remaining CEO of the company she'd founded, she'd signed a buyback clause for her 16 percent shares of Breathe. If the board fired her, Nicole could lose everything.

"The employees don't want to see you replaced. I don't want to see you replaced," Tessa said. "No one's ever going to be a better boss to me than you."

Nicole suddenly realized that her breakdown didn't just affect Quinn, herself, and Breathe. It affected Tessa, too. Tessa had no voting power. Like all Breathe employees, she was entitled only to 10 percent shares. Nicole had a single day to stop Lucinda, and the board, from terminating her.

She had to do something. She didn't want to live like this, straitjacketed by the terror, bone-crushing fatigue, and visions. And still she wondered if she was imagining all of it. She put the thought out of her mind. What women needed was balance. What Nicole needed was balance. She had reinvented herself once and she could do it again. She'd given that company her all. Surely, the board couldn't begrudge her some vacation days. It was her right.

"Tess, can you do something for me?"

"Anything," Tessa said, her voice sounding happier than a moment ago.

"Can you tell Lucinda I'm taking my accrued vacation time?"

Tessa was quiet. "How much time?"

"A week."

"You promise you'll be back in a week? On the Monday? August seventh?"

Of course. August 7. That date would always come back to haunt her. But Tessa wouldn't remember its significance.

Nicole gripped the edge of the table to hide her shaking hands.

"Yes," she said quietly. "On August seventh, I'll be back."

CHAPTER TWENTY-THREE

MORGAN

Quinn is in trouble.

I stuff the adoption application back into the manila envelope, grab my bag and phone, and run out the door, promising myself I'll call Jessica as soon as I can, as soon as I see Quinn.

I race down West Evergreen Avenue, empty except for the cars parked on the side of the road. I'm such a wreck of nerves I'm afraid I'll hit something.

I throw the car into park and tear up the driveway and Ben's front steps with my phone in my hand, ignoring the pain in my foot and shin. He must have heard me coming, because a light goes on outside and he whips open the door.

Ben is in a gray T-shirt and plaid pajama pants, and his eyes are wide with alarm.

"Is Quinn okay?" I ask in a frantic, high-pitched voice.

"Physically she's fine, but I need to show you something."

I'm shaking so much I have to lean against the brick wall next to his front door to balance myself.

He darts his eyes behind me. "Did anyone follow you here?"

"I don't think so."

He nods and leads me inside the house, locking and bolting the door behind me. "Quinn's asleep upstairs in my room. Let's sit on the sofa, so I can explain what's happened. I'm a mess right now."

As we enter the living room, I immediately notice how bland everything is. The paint, the hardwood floors, even the coffee table and TV console are all in shades of brown-beige. It's very neat and tidy, but also impersonal and drab. Lifeless, even. The only spot of color in the room is a pink bassinet under the large bay window.

I sit down, and so does he. Then he grabs his phone from the coffee table and holds it out to me. "Someone sent this to me tonight through Guerrilla Mail." With a jerking hand, he pushes his hair off his forehead. "It's some kind of untraceable email service."

It's a photo, taken in Ben's living room, of a baby facedown in the bassinet under the window. I gasp and jump up, crossing the room in a few strides. Inside the bassinet is a doll.

I turn to him. "Holy shit. This is horrifying. What . . . ? I don't understand."

He looks toward the kitchen then back at me. The fright in his eyes looks real. "I think someone broke into my house while Quinn and I were asleep upstairs. I heard my phone ding, and there was that creepy photo. I came downstairs, saw the doll, and called you right away. Then before you got here, I saw that the back door in the kitchen was open. Jesus."

"Get Quinn. Please. I need to see her."

He runs up the stairs. I take the doll and drop it with a *thunk* on the coffee table. Then I sit, cold with fear, on the sofa.

Ben returns with a sleeping Quinn in his arms and sits back down.

I can't help myself. I reach out and stroke her impossibly soft hair. A jittery sound comes out of me.

"Could I have a glass of water? It's been a really overwhelming night."

He sighs, gets up with Quinn, and walks through the black French doors that separate the living room and attached dining room to the back of the house, where I assume the kitchen is.

I take the opportunity to pull the manila envelope out of my purse. I remove the adoption application and look again at the threat scrawled on it.

Stay away from Quinn. You can't keep her safe.

I have to show it to Ben, so he understands someone is toying with both of us.

He comes back with a tall glass of water. He's even put two ice cubes in it for me. Then he takes a seat beside me, crosses a leg over his knee, and cradles a sleeping Quinn in his big arms.

I hand him the papers. "This was slid under my door tonight, right before you called me."

He takes it and tilts his head, his hair falling into his eyes. I can't see his expression.

I don't wait for him to stop reading. "I want to find out exactly who came to my place and knows where I live. Because I think someone is setting us up." I can see his chest rise and fall under his T-shirt. For a second, I want to put my hand to his heart and tell him I'm a good person. I'm genuine. "Ben, my apartment was broken into, and that adoption application was the only thing taken."

Ben looks down at the paper, not understanding.

"After Ryan died, I thought I might want to adopt a child on my own. But then my dad died, and he was the only person who could really vouch for me. And I didn't think I was worthy of a child anymore, so I never actually applied."

Saying that out loud, to someone else, should make me feel pathetic. But it's as though a burden I didn't know I was carrying has been taken from my shoulders. "Look at the last page."

He does, then trains those very blue eyes on me. His face pales. *"You can't keep her safe.* That's very similar to the threats Donna used to write in those letters she sent Nicole for years. 'You were supposed to keep her safe.'" He drops the application on the couch, lays Quinn across his lap, and puts his head in his hands. "This is insane."

He rubs his forehead hard. "I just don't understand how you're involved in any of this, Morgan."

"I wish I knew all the answers," I say. "Maybe someone wants to seed doubt between us. All I know is that I want Quinn to be safe."

He looks up at me with wide, tired eyes. "That's all I want, too."

I decide to tell him a little more. "My attorney sent me a YouTube video a man took at Grand/State, before Nicole . . ."

Ben's face turns a sickly shade of white. "Nicole's death is on YouTube?"

I realize too late how horrifying that information must be for him. "It was taken down. I'm sorry. I didn't mean to—"

"I don't want to watch it. Ever."

I don't want him to watch it, either. He might see what Martinez thinks she sees—the possibility that I pushed Nicole.

"I don't think she was on the platform, but Greg's assistant is a redhead who drives a dark blue Prius."

He frowns and looks down at Quinn protectively. "Greg's assistant? What does she have to do with this?"

I tell him about trying to talk to Greg at his office and Melissa Jenkins waiting in the dark blue Prius outside. I tug my leggings up to show him the three-inch cut along my shin.

"Are you saying Greg's assistant tried to run us down, stalked you, then broke into my house and put a creepy doll in my bassinet?" He says it as if the possibility is preposterous. And it does sound preposterous, but we have no other puzzle pieces to put together. It's clear something horrific happened to Nicole that made her write those notes we saw on her wall.

"Maybe someone's messing with us the same way they messed with Nicole."

"But why?" He strokes his hand over Quinn's head. "Look, it's late, and I need to get sleep if I'm going to function. I can't even try to make sense of this right now. I'm used to pulling all-nighters, but the last couple of nights have been . . . a lot. I can't deal with the police coming here right now again. It's not like they're going to offer us any security. They haven't done a thing for us, except pit us against each other."

"I know." I wonder for a second if Martinez suspects Ben, but I don't say it. We're on an even keel right now.

"I'll call Martinez first thing in the morning and tell her everything. I don't think she should find you here, and I don't think you should go home. You don't want to be followed again. You can crash here if you want." His cheeks flush.

Mine do, too. I don't want to go back to my apartment right now. I don't feel safe. But what will Martinez think if she finds me here tomorrow? It hits me that maybe that's exactly what the person who sent Ben the photo wants—for Martinez to catch me at Ben's. But it's equally possible that someone is out there in the dark, waiting for me to get in my car, waiting to attack. A wave of fatigue pummels me, and I make a decision, hoping it's the right one. "I'll stay over. I'll leave when I get up."

He nods, then heads to the hall and comes back with a plain white blanket and pillow. "This okay?"

"Thank you. That's perfect."

He tosses them on the couch and gives me a sad, crooked smile. "This is all so nuts. I'll bolt all the doors and set the alarm. Try to get some sleep."

"You too," I say, and wait until he and Quinn have gone upstairs. Only then do I collapse against the pillow. I pull the blanket up to my chin and fall into a heavy, dreamless sleep.

———

When I open my eyes, I'm unsure at first where I am. I glance around the beige living room. Ben's house. The threat slid under my door. The email to Ben. The doll.

I sit up and wipe the sleep from my eyes. My mouth feels furry, and I don't even have a toothbrush. I hear the rattle of plates and Quinn's babbles from the kitchen. I smell coffee. My stomach rumbles.

I fold the blanket neatly and place it at the end of the couch, then make a quick stop in the powder room I find next to the front door. I pee, then splash my face with cold water, tie my hair into a low ponytail, and am just about to emerge when I hear a knock on Ben's front door.

I freeze.

Silently, I push the door just a crack and see Ben open the door and let a man into the foyer.

It's Greg Markham.

He says, "I'd like my daughter back now."

And I watch helplessly as Quinn's father pulls her from Ben's arms.

CHAPTER TWENTY-FOUR

NICOLE

Before

Tessa finally left, happy with Nicole's promise to return to Breathe on August 7, and offered to come back later with dinner. After changing Quinn's diaper, Nicole caught her reflection in the foyer mirror. Her stomach sagged, and her cheeks had broken out into a rash of angry red pimples. She hated who she'd become. When she'd lain Amanda's cold body on the floor, Nicole wanted to die, too. But she realized during that very first panic attack in the baby's nursery that the fear she'd experienced when she couldn't breathe was proof of how much she wanted to live.

Now she lived for Quinn. But having a petrified, paranoid mother and living in this house—more like a dungeon—was no life for her daughter. She had a week to get back to Breathe. Something had to give.

Nicole slipped Quinn in the Moby, went to the living room, and picked up her computer from the coffee table. She set it on the large mahogany dining table, now covered in burp cloths and used Kleenexes. She sat on the plush ivory chair. Flipping the computer open, she pressed the power button. She prayed Google held the answer to everything.

She clicked on postpartum depression symptoms: hypersensitivity, constant crying, anxiety, worry, hopelessness, guilt. Yes, she suffered from every one of those. Maybe Tessa was right. Maybe there *was* help out there for her.

When she looked at Quinn, her baby girl smiled back. "I'm fixing it, sweetheart! Mommy's going to make it all better." Quinn stuffed her fist in her mouth and gazed at her. Nicole clicked and clicked through PPD forums. Almost all the women who posted mentioned not bonding with their babies and how hard it was to get a moment to themselves. But these weren't experiences she could relate to at all. She wanted Quinn with her all the time; she felt connected to her like no one else in the world.

She typed "paranoia" into the search bar. The first link to pop up was a different kind of postpartum issue: psychosis. Could it be? With a jittering hand, Nicole scrolled through the symptoms. It was possible, but also hopeless. How could she tell anyone if she was psychotic? Quinn would be taken from her. Nothing and no one could help her. She would never make it back to Breathe. She would lose everything.

She placed her finger on the power button, but before pressing it she saw a link to Maybe Mommy, a community forum for women who wanted kids and couldn't have them. Nicole's breath hitched. How awful to want something so much and not be able to get it. She began reading, caressing Quinn's soft wisps of hair.

> I've had three miscarriages. How can I go through that loss again?
>
> I've tried for seven years to have a baby of my own. After four failed IVF procedures, I'm ready to give up.

Baby dust and prayers, please! Just started Clomid again and gearing up for a second round of IVF!

Will I ever get what I want?

Nicole ached for these women. It had been so easy for her to get pregnant. She didn't even have to plan it.

There were hundreds of posts on Maybe Mommy. But one in particular stood out, from someone who called herself "Morose in Chicago."

Will I ever get what I want?

My 43rd birthday just passed and I'm still childless. Would an adoption agency actually give a single woman a baby? I know I could give a child everything: love, warmth, and security. I want a baby so badly. Will I ever have one?

Morose in Chicago deserved a baby. Who cared if there weren't two parents? Quinn had two parents, one who only cared about himself, and one who was not doing very well at all. Tears dripped onto the keyboard, and she wasn't sure if they were from pity for herself or this childless woman.

She scrolled back through some of Morose's other posts on the forum, all dated within the same three-day period, six months before. Something about her posts felt so sincere, so relatable. This woman was a widow whose husband had done something very wrong. She didn't explain what exactly, but it was clear she felt responsible for his wrongdoings and that all she wanted in the world was a chance to share her love with a child. And she lived here, right in Chicago.

Excitement, a feeling Nicole had almost forgotten existed, ran like warm water through her cold bones.

There was an icon you could press to send private messages to those who posted.

Nicole clicked "Morose in Chicago" and started to write to her.

CHAPTER TWENTY-FIVE

MORGAN

I'm shocked. I'm still watching this all happen through a crack in the door. I see Greg's clumsy embrace as Quinn cries out, and his face registers a flurry of different emotions—bewilderment, fear, and resignation. But the emotion I don't see is love. And it breaks my heart.

I step out of the powder room, and both men turn to me.

Greg looks surprised. "Sorry. I didn't realize you had someone here. I didn't know you were . . . dating someone."

"I'm not," Ben says.

"Okay. So who are you?" Greg asks, his tone arch.

"I'm . . . a friend. Morgan Kincaid." I reach out my hand to shake his.

He can't shake my hand because he's having trouble holding Quinn, as though he's not sure how to hold a baby at all. I'm not sure he'd want to shake anyway. I watch as recognition dawns in his eyes.

"Wait. Morgan Kincaid? The woman who was the last person to speak to my wife? The woman who took Quinn from her at Grand/State?"

"I didn't even know your wife. I don't know how we're connected."

He eyes me again, looking for someone he recognizes but coming up blank.

Greg turns to face Ben. "I didn't know Nicole could ever do something like this." He coughs and his eyes well up. But then that look is gone in a moment. Anger suddenly crosses his face. "The detective told me about your husband and all the money he stole. That you *both* stole. Did you mess with my wife to get her money?"

Then, like a LEGO set, the pieces begin to click into place. Martinez had pointed out that whoever has custody of Quinn has access to her money. Nicole didn't want that to be Greg or Ben.

I don't respond. Greg turns back to Ben. "Thank you for watching Quinn. I've been a wreck, as you can imagine. I can't believe Nicole's really gone."

His eyes have black circles beneath them, and a thin layer of stubble covers his jaw. Maybe I have it all wrong. He does seem to be grieving.

Ben must also see it because he says, "I'm sorry, Greg, about Nicole."

"I'm sorry, too." His voice cracks.

Both men are uncomfortable. They're family, but it's as if they don't know each other.

Ben reaches out and touches Quinn's back. "I took care of her the best I could."

Greg nods, holding Quinn slightly away from himself, as though he's afraid to get too close. I'm not sure he even notices that she's fallen asleep.

"I don't know how much you're aware of, Ben, about Nicole before . . ." He glances at his hand, which is bare of a wedding ring. "Nicole changed so much after Quinn was born that I didn't recognize her. She refused to let me get her some help. She fell apart, and I left.

I couldn't live with her paranoia. But I loved her, and I *never* wanted anything bad to happen to her."

Greg's mouth slackens as though he's weighed down by regret. I used to pride myself on being able to read between the lines with the families I counseled. When a child said he was good or fine and offered no information, I knew to dig deeper. But now, I have no idea what's real and what isn't. All I know is that now is my moment.

"Did you ask your assistant to follow me?" I ask. "She drives a Prius. Someone tried to kill us. Do you realize that?"

To my astonishment, Greg laughs. "Why would I ask Melissa to follow you? From what she tells me, *you* threatened her. And what exactly are you doing here shacked up with Nicole's brother if you're such a total stranger to all of this? Who are you, really? We don't even know you."

Ben crosses his arms over his chest. "Look, Greg. I really don't think Morgan had anything to do with this. We've been stalked and something really weird is going on. I love Quinn. I'm worried for her safety."

I look at Ben, hoping he can see how much it means to me that he would defend me.

Greg's face reddens. "Ben, are you blind?" He gestures at me with his chin. "What is this woman doing here? Focus your attention on that. Quinn will be fine. I'll make sure of it."

Ben's voice gets louder. "We think Nicole might have been in danger. Did she ever mention Donna and Amanda Taylor?"

Greg shakes his head. "I never heard her mention either of those names. Who are they?"

He continues as though he never asked the question. "Nicole used to be the most ambitious and relentless person I knew. But from the moment Quinn was born, she . . . lost it."

"How could you leave her like that? A new mother, suffering, and your own newborn?" Ben asks, moving right by my side.

"You're asking *me* how I could leave her? Where have you been all her life, Ben?"

Ben looks as though he's just been punched in the gut.

"I think we need to come to terms with the fact that Nicole jumped in front of that train. She was depressed and suicidal. And why on earth are you getting all friendly with a total stranger who happened to be on the platform at the same time? Why is she in your house with my daughter? What does she really want?"

Hot fury broils inside me, but for the sake of Quinn, I wrestle down my emotion. "Mr. Markham, you need to know that really strange things are happening." I watch him carefully. "Quinn is in danger. You might be, too."

Greg looms over me. "Are you threatening me?"

"No!" I yell, too forcefully. "I'm telling you that someone wants to hurt me, Ben, and Quinn."

Suddenly, Quinn wakes up. She's crying so hard she's almost choking, wriggling wildly in her father's arms. Greg fumbles with her. He has no clue how to soothe his child. It's awful to watch.

"I never want this woman near my daughter again. I'm Quinn's father. She belongs with me. I've rented a house on North Astor Street and that's where we'll be."

Ben's cheeks flame, but he says nothing. I know I can't step in. Doing so won't help either of us.

I stare at Quinn, trying to memorize her silky tufts of hair, blue eyes, and soft cheeks.

Greg opens the front door. Ben sees him out. I head to the large bay window in the living room and peek out to see Greg put Quinn in a red BMW.

It's then that I notice her. That red hair. It's Melissa Jenkins. In the passenger seat.

CHAPTER TWENTY-SIX

NICOLE

Before

Lost and Confused: I'm sorry for everything you've gone through.

Nicole pressed send.

A couple of minutes later, there was a *ding* indicating she had a new message.

Her stomach twisted with a mix of fear and elation. With shaking fingers, she clicked on the message.

Morose in Chicago: Thank you. I just wish I could erase the past. Do you ever feel that?

Nicole's breath caught in her throat. Yes, she felt that every minute of every day since Amanda died.

Lost and Confused: Always. I . . .

Nicole stopped typing. How much could she tell this stranger? She deleted what she'd written. Her fingers tapped again.

Lost and Confused: It's a horrible feeling when people blame you for something that you never intended or planned to happen. What happened with your husband? I'm sorry, by the way. Sorry for your loss.

Morose in Chicago: I don't want to talk about it. I'm trying to move forward. Make a new life for myself. Be happy again. I think a child would give me a sense of purpose.

Lost and Confused: I wish that's the way I felt. I'm afraid I'll never be happy again. I'm scared all the time. And there's no one I can really talk to about how I feel.

Morose in Chicago: I'm here if you need to talk. It's hard when you can't talk to the people in your life. And I know what it feels like to be scared all the time. I really do.

It took Nicole a moment to identify the feeling in her chest. It wasn't anxiety or fear. It was the release that came from an instant connection to another person. Already this nameless woman from Chicago was helping her feel more like herself. This wasn't psychosis. She just needed a little help.

There was a light knock at the door and her phone buzzed with a text from Tessa.

I'm back!

Shit. Nicole couldn't possibly tell her she was messaging with a complete stranger, who made her feel more understood than Tessa could right now. Nicole could never hurt her like that. She slammed the computer shut and went to answer the door.

Tessa held two bags in her hands and a big smile lit up her face. "I brought dinner and good news." She peered at Nicole. "You look a bit better. There's some color in your cheeks."

Nicole nodded, and Tessa closed the door behind her.

"I think asking for some more time before going back to Breathe eased a lot of my stress," Nicole said, and followed Tessa to the kitchen. Quinn was in the wrap, her tiny hand playing with her mother's face.

Tessa put the bags on the kitchen table, plugged in the kettle, and leaned against the counter. "So I asked Lucinda for your banked vacation time. She wasn't happy with the seventh as your return date."

Nicole bristled. Couldn't Tessa see she was trying to get better? And that adding more stress wouldn't help? "Thank you, Tess. I'll talk to her myself tomorrow. But you said you had good news."

Tessa pushed away from the counter and reached for Quinn. Nicole handed her over, though she didn't really want to. Having her in her arms was a comfort.

Tessa kissed Quinn's nose. "I do. I'm fiddling with a mix of oils right now for a postpartum line. I should have thought of it immediately, but with you gone, it's been really busy."

Nicole felt her face burn with shame. Her inability to function hurt everyone.

Tessa said, "I'm not blaming you. You have to take care of yourself, so you can take care of Quinn. Anyway, lavender, jasmine, ylang-ylang, sandalwood, bergamot, and rose can all ease symptoms of postpartum depression. It's such a common experience for new mothers, and I think it would sell very well. Lucinda loved the idea. Then something occurred to me."

If only a new oil could heal her. But now that she'd found Morose in Chicago, at least she had someone to talk to. If Nicole could return to the computer, she'd get better and make it back to Breathe. But Tessa had to leave first.

"Nicki, are you listening? This is important."

She focused on her friend, who had done so much for her. She wasn't being fair to Tessa. "Yes. Sorry."

Tessa shifted Quinn so she was facing her mother. "If you can get an official diagnosis of mental illness, everything will be fine. You could go on short-term disability under the federal Family and Medical Leave Act. And the board legally couldn't fire you or replace you permanently. If the board knows you're using yoga and aromatherapy to combat a mental illness, along with medication, and you come back better and stronger, it could even be great publicity for Breathe."

Admit mental illness? Was Tessa crazy? How could she not see the obvious—that such a diagnosis would put her custody of Quinn in danger. No, she was fine. She would handle this her way. Yes, she was a little mentally unsteady these days, but she had good cause—someone wanted Quinn dead.

She pulled her daughter away from Tessa. "I'm not going on disability and I'm *not* going to a doctor. I've given Breathe everything. All I'm asking for is a few more days. It's the least they can do."

"Nicole, there's no shame in having depression, right? We tell our followers that all the time. It's what Breathe is all about. Accepting when we need help and finding our way to wellness. What are you so afraid of?"

If only I could tell you, she thought. But she knew she wouldn't be believed.

"Greg, for one thing," she said. Which was true, or at least it was part of the truth. "I'm afraid that if I'm diagnosed with postpartum depression, Greg will use that to take Quinn away."

Tessa raised a brow. Clearly, she thought this was impossible. "He hasn't even seen Quinn in weeks." The kettle whistled, and she got up, pouring two mugs of hot eucalyptus tea. "Look, I don't want to push you to do anything you aren't comfortable with. I just want you to know that I care about you, and I'm worried."

Nicole was immediately remorseful. Tessa's concern was fair. "I just need a bit of time to get clarity, you know? I promise. Things will be better soon."

Tessa brought her a cup of tea. She took a sip half-heartedly. It was scalding, and she jumped back.

"You really do need to call Lucinda," she said, her tone oddly abrupt.

"I will," Nicole said. "Tomorrow."

Tessa brought her own cup to her lips and took a sip. Then she smiled at Nicole placidly.

———

Over the next few days, though, instead of calling Tessa or Lucinda, she messaged Morose. Besides when she bathed Quinn, who loved the water, and rocked her to sleep in her arms, Morose in Chicago was the highlight of Nicole's life.

They bonded over their shared losses, their guilt over their pasts. Nicole didn't tell her about Amanda and Donna, because she couldn't bring herself to write their names, but they talked about their parents. Morose's father had recently passed away, and she'd grown apart from her mother. Nicole didn't want to talk about how her own parents died, but she understood the pain of losing parents. Their conversations went deeper and deeper. Morose's mother shared many of the same traits Nicole's father had—judgment, blame, and a total lack of understanding of who their children really were. Eventually, Morose admitted that her husband had been a fraudster who'd bilked people out of money and had then committed suicide. She felt so much sympathy for this woman. Morose was a social worker at a shelter for abused women and their children. She did so much good for the world, and yet she was all alone.

Now she felt they were friends. Real friends who'd met in a virtual space. They accepted each other.

Morose in Chicago: I think you're the only person I can really talk to these days. Thank you.
Lost and Confused: I feel the same way.

And Nicole wanted more. With Quinn snug in the wrap, Nicole steepled her fingers under her chin and closed her eyes for a moment. Then she typed.

Lost and Confused: What's your real name?

She waited for the three dots to alert her that Morose in Chicago was typing a message. Nothing. She moved the mouse to the woman's user name. She was offline.

"Please come back," she whispered to the screen. She waited, anxiety chewing at her insides. But Morose didn't answer her.

Nicole yearned for the warm feeling the woman gave her. Her kindness and understanding. She wanted to find her and sit face-to-face. She wanted to know who she really was.

With the information Morose had given her, Nicole scoured the Internet for newspaper articles, editorials, anything that might lead her in the right direction. She searched shelters, and even tried adoption forums. She keyed in: "man; social worker wife; Chicago; fraud; suicide" and found something.

Hedge Fund Manager Ryan Galloway Found Dead of Suicide

The article outlined his embezzlement and sudden, tragic death a year and a half ago. The bottom line read:

He is survived by his wife, social worker Morgan Kincaid. They have no children.

Morgan Kincaid. Was she really the woman Nicole felt such a bond with? Such an instant, deep connection?

Now Nicole remembered the case. Some former board members of Breathe had invested their shares in Ryan Galloway's hedge fund and lost everything. She typed in "Morgan Kincaid; social worker." Nothing came up. She kept scrolling until she found a nasty headline in *Chicago-at-Large*.

Suspected Fraud Accomplice Morgan Kincaid Scales Down from Her Sprawling Gold Coast Home

There were photos of a run-down, brown building on North Sheridan Road, and one shot of Morgan, head bowed, as she headed inside the front doors. Her shoulders were hunched; her back curved like she was trying to make herself as small as possible.

Morgan really had lost everything. Nicole understood.

Quinn began to suck on her shoulder.

"Oh, honey, I'm sorry. I'll feed you right now. Then I'm going to make everything better for you. Mommy's going to make it all better."

She spilled the formula on the counter before finally getting enough into a bottle to satisfy her daughter, who gulped hungrily. Nicole held her close. "I love you, baby girl."

Voices rang in her ears.

What have you done?

You're so irresponsible.

She shook her head back and forth to get rid of them. She conjured up Morgan's posts in her mind. Serendipity. Kismet.

Nicole entered the pantry and added new Post-its to the wall, now a dizzying array of purple.

Shelter. Widow. Morgan Kincaid. Help me.

Morgan Kincaid was a social worker. She'd offered to listen if Nicole needed to talk. They'd connected on a deep level. If Nicole could actually speak to her face-to-face, unburden herself to the one person who might understand, she could clear her heart chakra and be the mother her daughter deserved.

Then Quinn would truly be safe. And Nicole might finally be free.

CHAPTER TWENTY-SEVEN

MORGAN

I can't believe we've lost Quinn. Why now? What does Greg really want? And how much can I trust Ben? These thoughts swirl through my mind as he goes to sit on the couch in the living room, his face a picture of misery.

I walk over and gingerly sit near him. "Ben?"

He looks over at me. "That's it then. I won't have a chance of getting Quinn back from Greg, and you certainly can't. You're a damn suspect." He pulls his phone from his pocket, and before I can ask who he's calling, I hear Martinez's raspy voice on the line.

"Greg just took Quinn. I think he might have done something to my sister. I never trusted him."

There's some back-and-forth between them. I can't make out

everything she says, but it's clear she's not happy when Ben tells her I'm there.

"I know he has every right to his daughter! You don't understand! She's receiving threats. We both are. And you're not even taking those seriously. We were sent—"

I can hear Martinez's voice droning on, but I can't make out her words. Ben tries to interrupt but he can't. Then, suddenly, he hangs up and draws the phone away from his ear.

His face is drained of color.

"What? What happened?" I ask.

He tosses the phone to the floor. "She just accused me of being mixed up in all of this. She was going on and on about how she finds it suspicious that I'd let you into my house, and then she accused me of being after my sister's money."

I stand up. I don't know what to say. "Ben, I'm so sorry."

His eyes drill into mine. "My sister's dead, and she thinks I want her money."

It all sounds familiar, the way Martinez jumps to conclusions, the way she hurls her suspicions around like knives.

"I know how you feel," I say.

"Yes, I guess you do." His fingers curl through his hair. "You know what the worst part is? I tried to tell her about the photo and the note, and she wouldn't listen. It's like she didn't want to hear it. Something's not right about this. Something's really, really wrong about this."

I look down at my lap. None of this surprises me. It's all like déjà vu, except this time, I'm watching it happen to someone else.

"Ben," I say. "Melissa was in Greg's car. And maybe she's the one behind this. But we just don't know. Nothing makes sense. But there's this note, too, and it points to Donna. There's not much we can do to track Melissa—we don't know where she lives. But we could talk to Donna. In person. Catch her off guard."

"And not tell Martinez? Morgan . . ."

"Look, what do we have to lose? Quinn's gone. I'm definitely a person of interest, and it sounds like you might be, too. Martinez is not on our side. We're the only ones looking out for us and Quinn."

I find the address for Donna's online consignment shop, which is also her home, and Ben plugs it into his GPS. Then we're off to Kenosha, Wisconsin, about an hour and a half away.

Ben and I decide to take his car because there might be less of a chance of anyone following. If Donna is truly behind everything, soon all of this could be over. It's either that, or it could be over for us.

He checks the rearview mirror constantly, and I check the side mirror for a redhead who might be behind us. As he focuses on the road, I have the chance to really look at him. He's lean rather than muscular. I imagine him as a string bean of a boy. I know he's carrying a lot of guilt about Nicole, but he won't talk about that. And he isn't talking about Quinn, either. Neither of us is. But we're both concerned for her.

He turns on the radio, and I let Coldplay's "Yellow" wash over me until he speaks.

"I still can't believe Martinez could ever think I'd hurt my sister for money."

I sigh. "It's a classic motive, Ben. I know firsthand how dangerous money can be. How far someone will go to get it."

He surprises me when he asks, "Why did you marry Ryan?"

I surprise myself by telling him. "I loved him. An easy answer for a very complex emotion." I remember the first time I saw his lopsided grin and how hard I fell. "My mom was set to retire in a couple of years, and my dad was a self-employed plumber. She had a nursing pension, but they needed to manage their money. Ryan was the financial adviser at our bank. He helped them, and he listened to me. He charmed me, like a good sociopath can. He pretended to be enthralled with my job as a social worker, with my love of lowbrow comedies. I helped him start the hedge fund and my charity. I was stupid."

"Or trusting."

"Same thing."

"Is it?" he asks.

I smile, and he smiles back. He is a very good-looking man. A bachelor, with no ex-wife or kids. No girlfriend or boyfriend. Alone, as I am.

I spin the conversation back to him. "Why are you single, Ben?"

He heads for I-90 W/I-94 W, keeping his eyes straight ahead. "I've put all my time into the hospital. There's nothing left for a social life, really."

"Do you want a family?"

He looks at me. "Do you still?"

"Answering a question with a question? Smooth." I pause, then decide to answer honestly. "Yes, I still want a family."

I like being in the car with Ben. I like how patiently he lets people into his lane and waits his turn without getting frustrated.

At a stoplight, he turns to me, holding my gaze, and I squirm under the intensity of it. "Do you promise me you did nothing to Nicole?"

I nod. "I promise you. Do you promise me you're not hiding anything from me that I need to know?"

"If I knew anything at all, you'd be the first to know."

Ben's words ring true, like he's starting to depend on me. And I realize that I'm starting to feel something for him, something I can't even put into words. But what if he's not who he seems? If I fall into another trap, I might never get out of it. *Please be as good as I think you are*, I silently pray.

We start to slow and get caught in a pocket of traffic. "Just when we were making good progress," he says. Then he looks at me, steadily, seriously. "I don't know you well, Morgan, but what I've seen is that you put everyone else before yourself. That's what my mom always did. She made everyone feel good, safe, and loved. You were there for Nicole when she needed you. It could have been anyone, but I'm glad it was you." He smiles at me. "Ryan was an idiot."

I laugh, but it's tinged with sadness. "So was I. I still wonder if I could have saved him, if I'd listened to my gut."

"You can't save someone who doesn't want to be saved." He shakes his head, dark waves falling into his eyes. "I should take my own advice. And yes, I always thought I'd have a wife and kids, but my schedule is all-consuming, and the women I've dated got tired of being woken in the middle of the night by my pager." He glances at me. "You miss him?"

I wrinkle my nose. "It's a hard question to answer. I miss the man I fell in love with. But I don't miss the man who left me to take the blame for his crimes." I feel flushed and awkward. "I can't believe I just told you all that."

"I'm surprised at how personal I've gotten with you, too." He scratches the stubble on his jaw. "I don't really get women."

He looks at me quickly then away. The traffic begins to ease, and we're on our way again.

I fold my hands in my lap because I don't know what to do with them. I'd like to touch his warm skin, and I can't. I won't. "Do you think Greg's taking care of Quinn? Properly, I mean. Feeding her enough? Holding her when she cries? Keeping her sleep schedule?"

He tightens his hands on the wheel. "I don't think he's the nurturing type. But he's her father. He must care for her, right?"

"I really hope so." I let out a sigh that carries a world of pain. "Could you call him maybe? See how Quinn's doing?"

"Yes, for sure. I've been thinking I would. I'll call when we're there." His face falls. "What are we going to do if we find Donna? What if she's dangerous?"

"I have pepper spray."

He laughs out loud, and it uncoils the cramp in my stomach. I close my eyes, unable to think anymore. I'm so tired from the lack of sleep, stress, and fear of the last few days that I don't realize I've fallen asleep until the car stops, and I lurch forward. I collect myself and take in a small, three-story house with white aluminum siding visible through a copse of pines a few feet ahead.

"Is this Donna's house?" I glance at the time on his dash. It's just after noon on a weekday. Donna might not be home. Now that we're here, I'm not sure I want her to be home. I'm scared.

Ben nods and rests his hand on the door handle. "I'm glad you got some rest."

"I was so tired. Thank you for letting me sleep."

His ears turn red. "Ready?"

I nod and touch the pepper spray in my purse, wondering, not for the first time, how my life has come to this. I curl my hand around the small canister, and we venture up the gravel driveway where a black Chevy Impala is parked. We continue to the dilapidated front of the house, crumbling with neglect. If something were to happen to me, would Ben fight for Quinn? I think he would.

"We'll just see if she's here and talk to her," he says.

I follow Ben up a small stone walkway leading to a porch, gray paint cracked and peeling. My ankle's still a bit sore, but I'm able to walk steadily. There are three orange rail planters, filled with pastel-colored flowers that brighten the otherwise sad little house. The sky is so blue and calm, the neighborhood so idyllic and peaceful; it's incongruous with the panicky rhythm of my heart.

Ben stops. "Should we knock?"

I take a deep breath and nod, even though I'm petrified. His knock sounds so loud on this quiet, serene street. Nothing happens. He knocks again, and a tinny voice calls out, "Coming!"

We wait for a full two minutes, both staring at each other, then the door opens. It's her, in the flesh: Donna. She's emaciated and pale. She doesn't look like a threat at all. But what stands out is her thick, wavy, blazing red hair. It's frizzy and unbrushed, an uncared-for mess. She could be the woman in the Prius. It's entirely possible. But I can't reconcile this frail woman with the stalker who has put us in danger.

Donna's hand trembles against the doorframe. She opens her mouth but utters not a word.

Ben stays perfectly still. I slowly step forward, so I don't spook her.

"Ms. Taylor, I'm Morgan Kincaid. And, of course, you remember Ben, though it's been a while." They look at each other.

"You're Nicole's brother. The one who came to get her after she . . . after Amanda died."

"Yes," he says, then looks down at his shoes.

"Ben and I wanted to ask you some questions, if you don't mind."

She quivers in front of me, as though I frighten her. "Why are you here?" she asks, her hand at her mottled throat. "Are you a reporter?" She puts shaky fingers to her lips and looks at Ben again. Tears fill her eyes.

Before I can say another word, she makes a move to close the door, and I put my foot in the jamb. I say, "Wait! Please! We just want to talk to you. There's a child at risk."

It works. I feel the pressure on the door relent. She opens it and stands before us, jittery and confused, but listening.

Then, she steps to the side and motions us in.

CHAPTER TWENTY-EIGHT

NICOLE

Before

It was 6:30 a.m. Nicole had been up all night, watching Quinn sleep. She couldn't sleep in her bedroom anymore. It reminded her of Greg, the husband she thought loved her, the man she thought would make a great father. How wrong she had been. These days, she slept on the couch, and Quinn was always only an arm's length away.

Tessa had stayed over the night before, in the guest room. She'd been thrilled when Nicole asked her to watch Quinn today so she could have a spa day. It was a necessary lie and a turning point, Nicole knew, that she had arranged to leave the house without her daughter. That she was being proactive and driving to Morgan Kincaid's apartment to talk to her, to make a real connection in person. She'd never received another message, but today she would find her and confess to her who she was. After all, Morgan had offered to help. And Nicole needed help so badly, but only from someone she could truly trust. Someone who truly understood her and the pain of her past.

Now that the time was here, though, she had misgivings. How could she walk out the door without her baby? What had she been thinking? What if Donna came while Nicole was gone? What if Quinn stopped breathing, or Tessa got distracted? She picked up her daughter and squeezed her so hard she cried out.

"Let me take her," Tessa suggested, coming into the living room, her heather Breathe romper splashed with water from the dishes she'd been washing.

It comforted Nicole to have Tessa there, but she felt awful about how many times Quinn had woken her up in the night. Tessa looked exhausted. Was she awake enough to watch over Quinn all day? Thankfully the awkwardness of their last visit had dissipated. Tessa didn't mention Breathe, and Nicole appreciated it. Yet she sensed a distance between them she'd never felt before. It was probably coming from her, though. Tessa was as calm and supportive as she'd always been.

"You don't need to clean up when I'm gone." Nicole clutched her baby, unable to let her go. "I'll run the dishwasher eventually. Just make sure Quinn is looked after."

"I don't mind. Now let me have her," Tessa insisted just as Quinn reached out and grabbed her braid. She laughed. "See? She likes me. She's trying to tell you it's okay to leave for a while."

Reluctantly, Nicole handed Quinn over, suppressing a warning to Tessa about holding her neck more firmly.

"It will be fine, Nicki. I just updated my CPR certificate. I know how to change a diaper. And you already made an appointment at the Peninsula. Their facials are incredible. You are going to take advantage and get more than a massage, right?"

Why was Tessa asking so many questions? Why was she pushing her to be away longer? Was she prying for info? But when she looked at her friend's face, it was peaceful. It was her guilt making her paranoid. Again.

Despite all the shades of purple she surrounded herself with, Nicole had never fully balanced her third-eye chakra, the center of her deepest awareness. But if she could just talk to Morgan, she knew she would finally see things the way they really were.

She looked at the clock. If she left now, she could catch Morgan at her apartment before she went to work. She would introduce herself; they would talk and share confidences. Nicole would know one way or another if this woman was truly the kind, loving, warm, nurturing person she seemed to be online.

Nicole stroked Quinn's velvety skin. "I don't know if I can leave her."

Tessa gave her a look she'd never seen from her best friend before. It was hard and unyielding. "You have to. If you don't, I will call your doctor."

Nicole opened her mouth to speak but thought better of it. Her friend loved her and only wanted the best for her, she reminded herself.

She waited for the usual weariness to set in, the debilitating fatigue she'd come to expect soon after she woke in the morning. Instead, she noticed that despite little sleep, she was awake and alert. She hadn't taken her Xanax yet this morning. Maybe she didn't need it anymore.

After a soft kiss to Quinn's cheek and another for Tessa, Nicole walked out her front door, alone for the first time since her daughter had been born.

Pausing on her front stoop, she looked left and right. No one was there.

Step by step, she kept going. Maybe, with Morgan's help, she could finally make things right and be the mother her daughter deserved.

CHAPTER TWENTY-NINE

MORGAN

Donna leads us into a living room where a chocolate suede sofa dominates the L-shaped space. There are no photos on the wall, no personal touches that make a house a home. I think to myself that Donna and Ben live in such empty, sterile spaces, making it hard to instantly gauge who they really are.

Ben and I both stand, my hand still on the pepper spray in my purse. No matter how fragile Donna seems, Nicole is dead, and we don't know what role she might have played in that.

"Did you do something to my sister?" Ben asks quietly.

Donna's eyes fill with tears, and she wrings her hands. "I never wanted Nicole to die."

I wait for Ben to continue. But he stays rooted near the wall across from the couch.

When he doesn't say anything, I do. "The police think someone was after her, and we have reason to believe that might be true. Did you stalk her? Have you been following us?"

Donna puts her face into her hands. Her shoulders vibrate, but no sound comes out. I stand back, helpless. I feel sick.

"Donna? What have you done?" Ben asks.

She brings her hands away from her face and looks at him. "A reporter called, then came to see me a couple of months ago. She said she knew things about Nicole's past, which is why she wanted to talk to me. She wanted to do an exposé on her and on Breathe. I'd already seen the article about her pregnancy in the *Tribune*, and I couldn't believe she was having a baby. I was furious. Why did she deserve a child when mine was taken away from me?" Tears roll down her face.

"No one ever wanted to listen to me talk about Amanda anymore. Not even Flynn, Amanda's father. 'It's all in the past. You have to let her rest,' he'd say. But how? How can a mother do that? I was so happy this reporter wanted to hear me that I told her everything about the day Amanda died. I told her I always suspected that Nicole was unhinged, that she killed my little girl." She blinks and the tears continue.

My mind is whirling. "Go on," I say.

"She listened carefully. It was clear she was on my side. For once, someone believed me. She left, but then she came once more. She was close to submitting the article, but she needed to make Amanda more real to readers. I showed her a few of Amanda's dresses that I'd hidden away. Not even my ex knew I had them. He threw everything else of hers out years before, against my will. I lent the reporter Amanda's baby blanket, the only one I kept, and the beautiful butterfly mobile Amanda loved so much so she could take pictures of them to include with her article. She mentioned she was very concerned about Nicole's daughter. Worried that Nicole wouldn't take care of her." Her voice breaks, and she uses the edge of the couch to stand.

Ben and I quickly exchange a look.

"Did you send my sister threatening letters, year after year?"

Her face goes tight and hard. "Yes," she says. "I was just trying to make her admit what she did. I wanted her to feel as anxious and distraught as I did when Amanda died. But I stopped those letters years ago." She grabs the neck of her loose white T-shirt, pulling it again and again. "I haven't sent a letter for five years."

I've worked with all types of people. I understand psychology. In front of me is a broken, delusional woman and we need to proceed with caution. But we also need answers. "Were you there on the platform the day Nicole died?" I ask, keeping my tone neutral.

"What? No," Donna says. "I admit I sent her letters years ago, but that's it. I'm happy she jumped. But I had nothing to do with it."

Ben takes a deep breath. It looks like she's telling the truth. She wasn't on that platform.

A thought is beginning to form in the back of my mind. "This reporter you mentioned. Do you have her name? Her phone number?"

"It's funny," Donna says. "She never left a number. She always called me; I never called her. And I never did see a single article or anything come out in the *Tribune* like she said it would."

Who is this reporter? Is she the one who followed me, who tried to kill us in front of Nicole's house? Was she after Nicole, too? Why would any journalist go this far for a story?

Ben looks at me, understanding dawning on him, too.

"Tell me," he asks. "What did the reporter look like?"

Donna looks from Ben to me, and back to Ben. "Young. And she had bright red hair, a lot like mine."

CHAPTER THIRTY

NICOLE

Before

Nicole opened the door to her wine-colored Lexus GS 350, her chest constricting with anxiety. She slid behind the wheel, the smooth leather seat almost consuming her. *I wish*, she thought, then stifled it. Today was the most alert she'd been in a long time, and she wouldn't let negative thoughts drain her.

She backed out of her driveway, and, on autopilot, turned onto North Lake Shore Drive. Her muscles remembered the dips in the road where potholes needed to be fixed, and the buses and trucks, taking their mundane routes, soothed her. She cast her eyes at the rearview mirror to check on Quinn, and when she couldn't see her, Nicole slammed on the brakes. A car behind her honked, and a man stuck his head out of the window. "Are you crazy, bitch?"

Yes, I am! Nicole thought about shouting back. He maneuvered around her and gave her the finger as he passed. She reminded herself Quinn was at home with Tessa, safe and sound. She just needed to get to North Sheridan Road in one piece and find Morgan.

She signaled to make a left onto West Foster Avenue, minutes from the apartment building. "I'm coming, Morgan," she said out loud as she checked her rearview mirror. Behind her, too close to her bumper, was a dark blue Prius. The woman driving had flaming red hair. Behind the woman, on the passenger side, she could see a car seat facing backward.

Oh my God, oh my God. Was that Quinn with Donna? She made the turn, pulled over, and used the Bluetooth to call Tessa. "Pick up, pick up, pick up!" Nicole screamed in the confines of her car as horns honked angrily behind her.

The Prius roared past her before she could get a second look.

"What's wrong?" Tessa asked when she heard Nicole's voice.

"Quinn. Is she there? Is she okay?"

"What? Of course. She's fine. She's sleeping in my arms. I sang her a lullaby," Tessa said.

Nicole rested her head on the wheel. "Thank God."

Nicole's shoulders relaxed.

Every day, her hallucinations got worse. Her fear was swallowing her whole. What kind of mother was she? She realized she was right outside Morgan's apartment building. What the hell was she doing? But it was too late to back out now.

"Are you at the Peninsula?" Tessa asked.

She had forgotten Tessa was still on the phone. "Yes, yes. Of course I am. I just pulled up." Despite the shabby building and cracked sidewalks, orange and yellow petunias exploded with color on a small patch of grass between the sidewalk and curb. Two women pushing strollers, dogs trotting beside them, chatted happily as they passed by her. Maybe the residents weren't wealthy, but did it even matter? It looked like a neighborhood filled with love and companionship, family barbecues and playdates. Nicole could barely take Quinn out of the house. What kind of childhood could she give her little girl? Her baby deserved a home filled only with goodness, security, and love.

"Enjoy every second. We're all good here. I'm proud of you for going out, Nicole. So is Quinn. Call me when you're on your way home, and I can order dinner for us."

Nicole hung up and parked on the street right outside the front door of Morgan's building. A few people were already heading out, but none of them were Morgan Kincaid.

What have you done?

Did Morgan hear that same question in her mind all the time? Nicole knew Morgan had been wrongfully accused. She was someone who was always looking out for others and who put herself last. Wasn't this the kind of person who'd help her keep Quinn safe? And she wanted a child of her own.

Alone for the first time in months, Nicole scanned every corner of the building. Her limbs loosened. The sun rose high in the blue sky, a brilliant yellow orb, the colors of the destiny chakra. This was where she was supposed to be.

A woman exited the building, her straight black hair, a shade similar to Nicole's, framing her narrow face. She was striking, though not conventionally beautiful. Her eyes were set too far apart, and even from here, Nicole could make out the fine web of crow's-feet at the corners.

Morgan Kincaid was a survivor.

Glued to her seat, she watched as Morgan turned down the street. She was getting farther away. Nicole had expected to talk to her before she left the building. She wasn't sure she had the strength to run after her. And she didn't want to scare her. Morgan might call the police when she took one look at how disheveled Nicole was.

She pushed open her car door and stepped onto the pavement. She followed a respectable distance behind, giving Morgan enough space not to feel someone behind her, watching and following. Morgan entered Bryn Mawr station on the Red Line. Was she going to work? Nicole followed her up to the tracks.

A train was about to pull into the station. Nicole made a quick decision. She'd follow her right on. They boarded. Morgan sat against the metal frame closest to the exit, head down, thick sheet of hair pulled over her shoulders. It was clear she wanted to hide her face. Nicole sat a safe distance away, her head low, too, keeping Morgan in her peripheral vision, so she wouldn't miss when she got off. How sad she looked. Morgan was still suffering, still paying for what her husband had done. Nicole understood. She paid, too, every single day she was alive.

A high-pitched cry from the front of the train made Nicole jump. It was a baby crying in its mother's arms. Morgan gazed at the child, smiling, then glanced away, as if she couldn't bear to look any longer.

The train pulled into Grand/State station. Morgan got up, and so did Nicole. She exited the train and followed Morgan down West Grand Avenue. Cars honked and braked, garage doors rolled up and down so loudly, her head pounded.

There were too many people. So much noise that she couldn't breathe. She wanted to be in her big house, with Quinn attached to her in the Moby wrap. Morgan turned left on North LaSalle Drive and dropped some money into a homeless person's cup. She chatted with him for a moment, and the bedraggled man smiled.

Nicole kept going. Morgan turned onto West Illinois Street, where there were fewer people. Nicole slowed, letting her get farther ahead. If Morgan turned around, she'd spot her. But she wasn't ready to approach her yet; now that she was finally so close, she didn't know what to say. She trailed behind as Morgan passed under a bridge and past a few shops. Then Morgan stopped at a small building set back from the road next to a church.

Nicole pressed herself against the side of the church as Morgan walked up a small gravel pathway. Was this the shelter? There was no sign, no one milling about. From her hiding place, she had a view of Morgan ringing a bell on the front door. Then Morgan whipped around. Did she sense someone staring at her?

Nicole was frozen. *Go to her now*, the voice inside her said. But she spotted cameras affixed to the building. Before she could do anything more, Morgan pulled a door open and disappeared inside.

Nicole rested her head against the rough brick wall and looked up at the cloudless blue sky. Quinn deserved so much better than Nicole. She deserved a fighter, and a mother who made the world a better place. A woman with a tragic past that was no fault of her own. A woman who deserved a second chance.

She knew then exactly what she had to do, how to stop Donna from coming after her and her daughter, how to make it all stop for good. It was probably best for Morgan not to know in advance. Safer for everyone.

Nicole had to disappear so Quinn could start a new life. With a new mother.

With Morgan.

CHAPTER THIRTY-ONE

MORGAN

We're in the car driving away from Donna's house, where we left her weeping on the couch. What she did to Nicole was bad—the letters every year, like clockwork, but she is not the one after Nicole. She is not the one after Quinn.

I turn to Ben in the car. We're both quiet, both obviously in shock, our minds racing. Who is the redheaded reporter? And why was she after Nicole? Why is she after us? I'm so out of my depth, and Ben looks ready to drop. He's got lines in his forehead I'm sure weren't there yesterday. "Should we call Martinez? Or Jessica? Tell them everything?"

He clears his throat and adjusts the sun visor. "Right now, I want to call Greg and make sure Quinn is okay." He scrubs his cheek with his hand. "I don't know what to do about Martinez. She thinks I'm an idiot for trusting you, or that I did something to Nicole. She said herself Greg has every right to Quinn. So, at this point, I feel like we're on our own. Let's get out of Wisconsin. I feel like shit. And I don't know what the hell is going on."

I nod. "Okay. Let's go."

We get on I-94 East toward Chicago. I'm lost in my thoughts. Ben fans his blue T-shirt, damp with sweat. He looks so frustrated. I am, too.

He nods at his phone on the dash. "Call Greg's number. But stay quiet and let me do the talking. If I ask outright about Melissa, or sound accusatory, I'll just piss him off. We have to be careful."

He's right. I find Greg's name and hit call then speaker. It rings three times before he picks up.

"What is it, Ben? I'm trying to get Quinn down for a nap."

"Just checking on Quinn. Seeing how her day's been."

"It's only been a few hours." He sighs. "She's good. I can't really talk now."

A female voice murmurs in the background.

I can't stop myself. "Greg, is that Melissa?"

"Ben, what the fuck? Why are you so involved with this woman? No, that's not Melissa. It's a friend of Nicole's, okay? There are people who loved her who are taking care of things. We don't need you, thank you very much."

Ben jumps in. "Which friend, Greg?"

He pauses then finally says, "Tessa."

"Tessa?" Ben asks.

"Yes, Nicole's best friend, her coworker. Tessa Ward. I've got to go."

"Wait! Is Tessa a redhead?" I ask.

"What? No. She's a blonde. Why are you even asking me this?" he splutters, and I hear Quinn cry.

The phone goes dead. If Nicole had a best friend, why would she file papers for me to be Quinn's guardian?

For the next few minutes the only sound is the tires rolling along the flat pavement. Without looking at me, Ben says, "I have something I haven't told you."

My heart does a frenetic dance.

"There's a reason Nicole hated me." He switches lanes. "When Breathe went public, Donna tried one more time to get back at Nicole. She filed a wrongful-death civil suit against her. Donna's attorney interviewed me, and I admitted to her that I thought Nicole was irresponsible when she was younger. She was. It doesn't mean I think she killed Amanda. The suit never went anywhere, because the statute of limitations was over. But the damage was done. Nicole found out what I said and never forgave me."

He looks at me for a moment with absolute sorrow, then turns his eyes back to the road.

"I told the truth, Morgan. It was a mistake."

His regret, and mine, weigh down the air in the car.

"I'm sorry," I say. "I'm sorry you and Nicole never had the chance to make amends. I'm sorry I didn't question my husband and that I never listened to my instincts. That I didn't dig into what was really going on with him. I'm sorry you had to hear from Martinez that Nicole wanted me to have custody of Quinn. You should have heard it from me. I've been so scared to trust you. To trust that our . . . friendship was real."

"Me too."

I look at him. "So, is that it? There's nothing else I don't know?"

He smiles, a genuine smile that makes everything okay, even for just this moment. "That's it."

"Then let's figure out what we know so far," I say. "Someone is following us. We don't know who. Greg said he's renting a place on North Astor Street, right? If Melissa's behind all this, if she's posing as a reporter, we need to confront her." Then I hit the heel of my hand onto my forehead. "I'm so stupid. I should have shown Melissa's company photo to Donna to see if she recognized her." I sigh. "And what about this Tessa? She's at Greg's now. Do you know her?"

He flicks the turn signal and moves into the right lane. "I met her once at Nicole's, years ago. But I don't know her."

Just as he's about to say more, my phone rings. It's Jessica.

I pick up and put it on speaker. I have nothing to hide anymore. The relief is immense. "Hi," I say.

"Where are you? I've been calling and there's no answer. I went to your apartment, but you're either not there or ignoring me."

"I'm with Ben. We went to Kenosha to talk to Donna."

"You what? Why?" Her voice is high and incredulous.

I fill her in on everything—Greg coming to take Quinn back, Melissa, the redheaded reporter, and Tessa Ward. I tell her about the letter slid under my door and the email with the horrible doll photo.

"Guerrilla Mail is an untraceable, disposable email address. It would be hard to prove *you* didn't send that photo to Ben."

There's something in her tone that I don't like. "You're not listening. We need to find this redheaded reporter," I say.

"We? Don't you think you should leave that to me?" She sighs, exasperated.

But I no longer care. I know I'm not guilty. I know I've done nothing wrong.

"How long will it take you to get back here, Morgan? Nicole's attorney filed her will into probate. It's now public. And Martinez got a search warrant for your computer and phone."

My stomach clenches. "A search warrant? What probable cause does she have?"

"Nicole's autopsy deemed her death undetermined, and not a single witness has come forward to say you didn't push her—at least not yet."

"I didn't do it," I say, my tone more forceful than I intend.

"It's just a theory. If there's no proof that you have any connection to Nicole prior to August seventh, she'll have to explore suicide and other persons of interest. But we have to give her your devices. The CSU did a search of Nicole's. The Post-its in the pantry with your name all over them aren't good. They also found a GPS tracker under the carriage of Nicole's Lexus, and a spy app on her phone and computer. They need to rule you out."

I can hear her suspicion. It's creeping into her voice. None of this is good news. Whoever's been after Nicole might know who I am.

"Track Melissa Jenkins," I tell her.

"I don't have enough information to go on. She was in New York with Greg when Nicole died, so she couldn't have been on the platform. The one strange thing, though, is that I got my hands on some footage from the blue Prius that hit you on the highway. And we already know Donna owns a Chevy. The license plate doesn't match the one you gave me for Melissa's car. But the Prius on the highway was rented in Nicole's name."

I shudder. Nicole's dead, and I'm still in danger. So is Quinn. "Did someone steal her identity to get the car? Does Martinez know?"

"I'm looking into it, and I'm not sure Martinez knows. I'll meet you at your apartment building. How long until you can get to your place?"

"About an hour."

"All right, see you in an hour."

I hang up and look at Ben. "Could you hear her?" I ask.

"Yes," he says. "Perfectly."

Flashes of my past flit through my mind in complete disarray. Ryan dropping to one knee and asking me to marry him. The middle of the night phone call telling me my father was gone. Nicole putting Quinn in my arms before jumping. Ben standing between me and Greg, defending me.

I think he's my ally.

"Thank you," I say to him.

"For what?" His eyes crinkle in the corners.

"Believing in me."

He smiles, and we spend the rest of the ride in companionable silence. Our separate lives have been entwined because of his sister and a baby we both care deeply about.

He pulls up to his house, where I left my car. We look at each other and laugh uncomfortably. This is all so insane.

"Now what?" he asks.

"I'll meet Martinez and Jessica at my place. You?"

"I guess I'll just wait."

"Of course," I say, though I'm disappointed. I've gotten used to him by my side. But we don't owe each other anything, and I can deal with this part on my own.

I put my hand on the door handle. "Okay, so, I'll let you know if anything happens."

He nods, both hands on the wheel. "Me too. I'll check in again with Quinn later and keep you posted."

I get out, and he does, too. Then, oddly bereft, I watch him enter his house and close the door.

When I drive up to my building and park, both Martinez's black sedan and Jessica's white Mercedes are waiting at the curb. The two women, one tall and lean, the other small and curvy, stand on the sidewalk. They stop talking when they see me approach.

Jessica smooths her dark hair. "I've informed Detective Martinez of all the evidence you've uncovered."

Martinez's face is stony. Does she believe any of it? Will she really follow the leads?

Without pleasantries, Martinez pulls a yellow form out of her pocket. She flashes it in front of my face.

I read the black print. "Search Warrant" is splashed across the top of the document.

I want to slap the warrant out of her hand. Again, I'm somebody's puppet.

Be strong, I tell myself. *Be brave.*

Martinez allows me to get my computer from my apartment and I hand it and my phone over to her. Wearing latex gloves, she puts them into bags, sealing them tightly.

"Please, Detective Martinez, I really think Quinn and I are in danger. Ben, too."

She pats the evidence bags. "Sociopaths are excellent liars. But they get caught because they think they're smarter than everyone else."

She stalks away, taking my only link to Ben with her.

Once she's gone, I rub my stomach, where a cramp has formed. Jessica stands there looking tense. "What if she finds something, Jessica?"

"If you haven't done anything, you don't have to worry, right?" She asks it as a question, which I don't like.

"This won't end for me until I find out how I'm connected to Nicole."

"That's actually not the most important thing right now. We need to clear you of any involvement in Nicole's death." She lays a hand on my arm. "Sometimes you don't get all the answers you want. You know that."

She gives my arm a squeeze, then gets in her Mercedes and drives away. I sit on the rough curb outside my apartment. There's only one person in all this who I would really like to meet. Nicole's "best friend." Tessa Ward.

If anyone knows something, it's her. Maybe she has all the answers I need to prove my innocence.

All I have to do is find her.

———

I walk over to the closest T-Mobile, buy a cheap burner phone, and beg the cashier to look up the address for Breathe headquarters. Then I send Jessica and Ben my new number. I've already memorized his. She texts back that she received my message. Ben doesn't text back at all.

It takes me twenty-five minutes to drive to West Armitage Avenue and North Halsted Street, where both the Breathe shop and main headquarters are located, and find a spot to park.

I'm terrified to face Nicole's friend. "You can do this for Quinn. And for yourself," I whisper.

My hands are clammy as I walk the quaint block toward West Armitage and push open the doors to Breathe. For all my courage, now that I'm inside the store that belonged to Nicole, that she created, I need to hold on to a clothing rack because my head spins. This is the closest I've felt to her, to Nicole.

The store, with its calming sea-foam walls and the light scent of essential oils infusing the air, is bustling with shoppers and salespeople. I don't see an entrance to the headquarters from in here. I go back outside and stride straight into the building next door, looking up to see four levels separated by glass railings, a skylight spilling sunshine onto the bamboo flooring below. There's a security guard manning the desk, and I'm sure there are cameras.

"I'm here to see Tessa Ward," I say as confidently as I can manage.

"And your name, ma'am?" he asks.

It's now or never. "Morgan Kincaid," I say.

He makes a call, then says curtly, "Come with me," and flashes a key card over the button for the fourth floor.

I'm in.

The elevator doors ping, and I step off into an elegant reception area. Pale blue walls hold framed photos of women and men posing in yoga wear under fiery orange sunsets and on golden-sand beaches. For a split second, I wish Ben were here beside me.

I'm very surprised when a minute later, a woman with white-blond hair and red-rimmed eyes steps in front of me. She's tiny, wearing a flowery sundress, definitely under five foot three. She barely reaches my shoulder.

She extends a slim hand for me to shake, and I do. Her skin is soft, her hand cool. "I'm Tessa Ward."

"Thank you for meeting with me. I'm . . . I didn't . . ." I stumble on my words, wrong-footed by her calm demeanor.

"Let's go to my office."

I follow her, curling my body to make myself smaller so I don't tower over her petite figure. She gestures toward two bright orange chairs in a room filled with hangers of athletic wear and shelves stacked with bottles of oils and tubes of cream.

I sit and watch her for signs of anger or hatred, but her face is composed, though her grief is evident in the black circles around her eyes.

I dig my nails into my neck. "I'm really sorry for barging in on you like this," I say. "I see you already know who I am."

"The woman on the platform," she says. "You called Greg earlier today."

I look down at my feet and wonder how much Greg has told her. "Yes. That's me. Look," I say. "I didn't know Nicole at all. And I feel weird coming here, but I really need some answers. Nicole was scared on that platform, before she jumped. She was very, very scared."

I look carefully at her turquoise eyes, hoping I can see the truth.

She doesn't respond to my ramblings. Instead she asks, "Can I get you some tea? We have a lovely herbal line I created when Nicole was sick. It's still under in-house development. We decided today that when it's ready for the market, we're going to call it 'Nicole.'"

This woman was her best friend, and I can see she's mourning a loss. I have a sudden urge to cry, but I fight it. "That's a really lovely gesture," I say. "I won't have any tea right now, but thanks for offering." I struggle to find the appropriate words. "I'm so sorry about Nicole." I wish that was the first thing I'd said to her.

"Thank you, Morgan. She was the closest thing to family I have, and I can't believe she's gone." She sweeps a hand along her glass-topped desk. "Tell me something: If you're a stranger, why would she want to give you Quinn?"

So she knows about the will. What she said is not spoken with malice, but it pinches. "I honestly have no idea."

She plays with the ends of her long braid. "I know who you are, like anyone who follows the news right now. But Nicole never mentioned you. She picked you over me, though. That's clear enough."

Why wouldn't Nicole have chosen this woman to take care of Quinn? Yes, she's young, likely not even thirty yet, but she's poised. I glance at the lime-colored clock with a lotus flower in the center on the wall behind her. The minutes are ticking by. Quinn is still with Greg and Melissa.

"Forgive me, but why do you think Nicole did that—named me as Quinn's guardian?"

She winces, and I feel ashamed for being so blunt.

"She knew I didn't want kids." She exhales a long stream of air.

A woman from the reception area brings in some files then leaves. Phones ring incessantly, and people walk back and forth outside her office, but Tessa's solely focused on me.

"Nicole slipped me a note with a name on it before she gave me Quinn. Before she died."

Tessa blinks. "What name?"

"Amanda."

Tessa nods. "Ah yes. The baby who died under her care. She told me once, then never wanted to talk about it again. But I should have made her. I should have realized more was going on than just postpartum depression." Her hands start to shake, and she folds them in her lap.

I have to press on. "I've learned some things about Greg's assistant, Melissa Jenkins. She drives a dark blue Prius. I thought she tried to run me down, but my attorney says it wasn't her car. Still, she might be involved in all of this. Do you know her?"

Tessa's eyes grow wide. "Nicole thought Greg was having an affair with her. But to be honest, I wasn't sure if that was real or in her head." Her brow knits together. "I live on North Vine, not far from headquarters, and I like to walk home from work, especially in the summer. Someone in a blue car, in large sunglasses, was following me the other day. Maybe it was Melissa. But why would she follow me?"

I lift my shoulders and let them drop. "I wish I knew. I didn't push

Nicole off that platform. And I think I'm being set up to take the fall for her death. Someone tried to kill me and Quinn."

I watch her already pale face leach of color. She seems genuinely stricken.

"And Ben, too," I say gently.

"Ben?" she says. The mood has become tense.

"Yes, Nicole's brother. Do you know him?"

Tessa's face is now harder, colder.

"Morgan, you know Nicole hated Ben, right? There was bad blood between them."

"Yes, Ben told me."

"Did he tell you he brought her prescription refills? Brought them right to her house?" Tessa holds my gaze. "Before she died, Nicole told me she kicked him out and never wanted to see him again. What if he had something to do with this? I hear his hospital is in deep trouble, that he needs money."

My hands start to shake. I feel the room get smaller. Everything I thought I knew could be so very wrong.

"That can't be right. He's been so devastated by Nicole's death. And so wonderful with Quinn. He was as scared as I was for her." Everything feels off. I feel off. I remember the article I read when I was looking for information about Nicole. It said Ben's hospital was slated to close. Could he have put the doll in the bassinet and sent himself that photo to throw me off track?

Tessa moves in front of me and rests against her desk. "Her will is now public. Nicole gave Ben the money he wanted, and it's a fortune. She gave it to the brother who wasn't even in her life."

Nausea churns in my stomach and my body goes cold. I told Ben the whole truth, but he didn't tell me anything about the money. I think of everything I've confessed to him about Ryan. My deepest worries. He's probably already filed for sole guardianship of Quinn and didn't tell me.

There are too many thoughts going through my mind at once, and I'm frozen in my chair. I feel sick and frightened. And so angry with myself. Have I been deceived by a man again?

"Ben and Melissa know each other," she says. "No matter what, he isn't the all-perfect doctor everyone thinks he is."

"What do you mean?" I say, my voice rising.

"Just . . ." She writes on an ivory piece of paper. "You can never really tell who a person is, you know?" She picks up the piece of paper and hands it to me. "This is my cell. You can always call me. Stay clear of Ben. If there's anything else I can think of to help you, I will."

"Thank you," I say. I take a scrap of paper from my purse, scribble my new number on it, and give it to her.

I say goodbye to Nicole's best friend and exit the lobby of Breathe headquarters. I'm a mess of tangled emotions. I have two choices: confront Ben or confront Melissa.

I make a quick call to Blythe & Brown, grateful my name isn't attached to this burner phone. A receptionist picks up. "Hi, I'm wondering if Greg and Melissa are in today," I say as casually as I can.

"I'm sorry, they're not. Can I take a message?"

"No, that's fine. I'll call back," I say, and hang up.

There's only one place to look for them. North Astor Street, where Greg told us he's staying. I want to see this woman's face again—the woman who might be working with Ben to destroy me.

I get back in my car, my heart pounding when I merge onto Lake Shore Drive, which is bumper to bumper. My mind keeps coming back to Ben. Would he really do this? Is it possible?

The traffic eases up, and I swing into the right lane to take the exit to IL-64/LaSalle Drive/North Avenue. The sky is overcast and dark, as though a storm is coming.

North Astor Street is just up the way, and it's not a long road. But the street only goes one direction, so I circle, driving up from the end of North Astor. I park and exit my car.

The neighborhood is eerily quiet; it must cater to professionals at work. Not a single person is out. As I get out of my car and walk down the street, I glance into the first-floor windows of every house. If someone sees me, I'm in deep trouble. But I'm in so much trouble already, I don't even care.

I spot a dark blue Prius up ahead. I squint. The license plate is different from the one I memorized outside the brokerage firm. I hear footsteps behind me. Something is pressed over my mouth, then I feel a hard slam into the back of my head.

I go down.

And everything turns black.

CHAPTER THIRTY-TWO

NICOLE

Before

The house was quiet as Nicole walked in. Her mind and body were quiet, too, for the first time in a long time. No scrambled thoughts; no fist of panic punching her in the chest. She had decided how to solve her problems. And she felt good about it.

"Nicki?" Tessa called. "We're in the living room."

She walked in to see Quinn lying peacefully in Tessa's arms. One day, when Tessa was a bit older and more settled, she would probably make a great mother. But it wasn't what she wanted, and Nicole had to respect that.

Nicole reached for Quinn, who opened her eyes and beamed at her mother. "Hi, my sweetheart," Nicole said. Her heart filled with the love only a mother can feel when she chooses her child's happiness over her own.

"How was the massage?" Tessa asked.

Nicole bounced Quinn gently. "Life-changing."

"I'm so glad," Tessa said. "You look . . . different. You look rested. Quinn was an angel." There was a book on the couch. It was *Goodnight Moon*. That was Nicole's favorite childhood book. Her father used to read it to her and together they would say good night to the moon and stars outside her bedroom window. Nicole choked on the memory.

"Come into the kitchen. I ordered dinner from a new vegetarian place Lucinda was raving about."

Nicole trailed Tessa into the kitchen and inhaled the lemony-fresh scent. It was as though all her senses were suddenly supercharged. Tessa had, of course, cleaned up. The dirty dishes were gone: only gleaming countertops remained. She'd spent so much time and money on redecorating and designing this house to suit her and Greg's lifestyle. What did it all mean now? Nothing, she realized. She didn't belong here anymore.

Nicole pulled Tessa into a tight hug, Quinn between them. When she pulled away, Tessa looked shocked. "What's that for?" she asked.

"You're an angel," Nicole said. "You've been such an amazing friend to me. I've never really thanked you. You helped me at work. You were my right hand. You even helped when I had panic attacks, and you kept your promise. You never told a soul." She broke off and swallowed hard. "You are my best friend, Tessa. Never forget that."

Tessa came closer and gently wiped a tear from Nicole's cheek. "Hey, you're my friend, too, Nicki. Jeez, you never get mushy. That massage must have been pretty incredible!" She laughed, and it lit up her beautiful face. "Besides, there's nothing I wouldn't do for someone I love."

———

Tessa left a while later, and Nicole closed the door behind her, knowing this would be the last time she saw her best friend. The scent of the sandalwood Tessa always wore lingered in the air. She armed the alarm, locked the dead bolt, and checked the door five times. She had to keep Donna—and her own fear—at bay for long enough to put her plan into motion. She held her daughter against her chest, willing all her love, hopes, and dreams into Quinn's tiny body.

But it wasn't time. Not yet. First, she had to make everything legal. On the couch, she waited until her attorney, Rick, sent a text saying he was outside her door. She'd told him the doorbell might wake Quinn if she was napping. *Never wake a sleeping baby,* she thought to herself, and the tears streamed down her face.

She wiped them away quickly and let Rick in.

He did a double take when he saw her. "You look exhausted," he said in his deep, rumbling voice. "I guess that's to be expected. My wife is still exhausted, and our boys are in college."

Nicole smiled, hoping he wouldn't notice how fake it was. As usual, though, Rick got right down to business. They sat at the dining room table, and he took the papers out of his sleek, brown leather briefcase.

"As I mentioned on the phone, now that I'm a mother, I figure I'd better get my affairs in order."

"Of course," he replied. "That's actually wise. A lot of people forget to do that when they have children, and it's important to make a plan for the worst-case scenario, all the while hoping that it'll never happen."

"Yes, exactly," she replied. "If I have everything in order, then I can rest knowing that whatever happens, Quinn will be safe."

"She's a very cute baby," Rick said, smiling at Quinn as she cooed in Nicole's arms. "You mentioned on the phone that you want a new guardian and executor of Quinn's trust? Are you sure Greg won't contest that? It's not like you're legally separated or divorced," he said.

She stroked her finger up and down Quinn's smooth neck. "He walked out because he didn't want this child. I'm fine with him seeing his daughter, but I don't want him being her guardian or the executor of her trust."

Rick arched his heavy brows. "Okay. And your good friend Morgan Kincaid is willing to take this duty on should the need arise?"

Nicole nodded.

Nicole asked Mary, her neighbor, to come over to witness her signing, and Rick agreed to be the second witness. It was over quickly, and Mary went back home. Nicole kept it together long enough for Rick to put the papers back in his briefcase and bid her goodbye.

It was done.

Her chest flared with hot poker jabs, so she downed two pills and had to drag herself to the computer. Her hands shook as she typed, hoping to express what she so desperately wanted Morgan to understand.

Lost and Confused: You deserve a child. You are good and kind. One day soon, you will be a wonderful mother. I know this with all my heart.

She stared at the computer, waiting for a message back. But an hour later, there was still no response. Quinn had fallen asleep, her head on her mother's shoulder. A soft sigh escaped her daughter's lips, her warm breath tickling Nicole's skin.

"I love you, Quinn. More than anything in the world. More than myself," she whispered. "I love you so much that I have to let you go."

CHAPTER THIRTY-THREE

MORGAN

I'm lying on my side, my face flattened against a hard floor. I move my head, and a sharp pain rips through my skull. I sit up, eyes blurry, and touch the back of my scalp where a bump the size of a walnut has formed. I look at my fingers. Blood.

My eyes adjust to the darkness. I'm inside a house, in a living room, judging by the couch against the far wall and the TV mounted on the opposite side of the room. I hear movement in another room, then a strange whooshing sound and the noise of running feet. I look up just in time to see a redhead fly out the back door of what looks like the kitchen and slam it shut behind her. There's a clock above the TV. It's 2:00 a.m.

Where the hell am I? And who just ran out that door?

I'm desperate to get up, but try as I might, my body won't

cooperate. It takes me a second to recognize the acrid smell making my eyes water. Smoke. It's coming from the kitchen the redhead just fled. And then, through the billowing haze, I see a body facedown on the ground at the bottom of the stairs, not moving. The smoke is getting thicker fast, and I crawl over, too unsteady to be on my feet. It's a man. I turn his head to see his face.

"Greg!" I say, coughing as the smoke fills my lungs. My eyes burn. He doesn't stir, and I feel for a pulse at his neck, feel it thud under my fingers. This is Greg's house. It's all coming back to me. But if he's unconscious on the floor, where's Quinn?

My own pulse races fast, and I try to pull Greg toward me, but he's too heavy to move. "Quinn! Where's Quinn?" I shriek, grabbing at my throat, which is closing from the thick smoke.

I hold a hand over my mouth and lower my belly to the floor, suddenly remembering the umpteen fire drills my parents used to run with me as a child. Go low; smoke rises. Flames burst out of the next room. Time is running out. On my stomach, I use my elbows to propel me toward the stairs, so I can get to the second floor. Quinn might be up there.

I hear the pop and crackle of the fire as it eats up everything in its path. The heat makes sweat drip into my eyes until I can barely see. I grab the stair railing and hoist myself to stand, taking the stairs as fast as possible, shouting, "Quinn! Quinn!" I can't see through the smoke.

"We have to get out!" someone yells. It's Ben's voice, calling out to me, but I can't see him.

"Where's Quinn?" I scream.

"I don't know! We have to get out of here!"

An explosion blasts from the kitchen and a beam from above lands right in front of where Greg is on the floor. Flames lick up the walls. I turn back and run down the stairs. With a strength I didn't know I possess, I pull Greg's leg hard. Then suddenly, he gets lighter, and I realize Ben has his arms. Together, we struggle through the smoke toward the front of the house. We find the door, open it, and drag Greg onto the grass.

Sirens blare in the distance.

Even outside, where there's less smoke, I can barely breathe. I look up at Ben, who is keeled over, struggling for air. I don't stop. I run right back into the house. The second I'm through the door, the flames come so close that I know they will kill me soon. But I can't leave without Quinn. I can't let her die. I drop low again and go forward.

An arm catches me out of nowhere and lifts me off my feet as though I weigh nothing. I'm being carried over someone's shoulder. Only once I'm outside, lying on the grass, do I realize it was Ben. He stands over me, calling out my name. Behind him, two firefighters storm forward, pulling hoses.

"Can you breathe?" he asks.

"I'm fine," I tell him, coughing and spluttering, trying to get my words out as an EMT appears and places an oxygen mask over my face. I push it away. "Where's Quinn?" I cry.

A window shatters from the second floor, flames roaring. More firefighters are running into the house. "There's a baby in that house!" I yell their way. "Please save her!"

"We know, ma'am. They're doing the best they can," the EMT says.

I lock eyes with Ben whose face is black with soot. My heart breaks into a million pieces.

The EMT helps me up and holds my purse out for me. "Is this yours? What's your name?"

"Morgan Kincaid."

Ben stands there as another EMT checks him out. Others are working on Greg nearby.

"Ma'am, we're transporting that man to the hospital. He has severe smoke inhalation and burns on his arms and legs. Do you know who he is?"

"His name is Greg Markham," I say. "Please, I have to talk to him."

I struggle past the EMT, who's calling out behind me.

"Ma'am! Please!"

I collapse on the ground by his side. "Where's Quinn?" I demand.

Greg's eyes are open. He knows exactly who I am. He groans and lifts his oxygen mask away from his mouth. In a guttural whisper, he says, "She took her."

"What?" I say, not understanding.

"She . . . did this. And she took Quinn."

Ben has stumbled over and is standing beside us. "Greg?" he asks. "Did Melissa take Quinn? Is that what you're saying?"

He can't breathe, can't speak. He puts the mask back on, shakes his head back and forth.

Ben puts an arm around me, and I sob, unable to do anything but watch as firefighters douse the flames until only thick black smoke rises to the sky. Two firefighters emerge from the front doors with a stretcher.

As the firefighters approach, I see they're carrying a woman with red hair, her face covered by an oxygen mask. Melissa.

I run over, Ben behind me. "Where's Quinn?" I say. "Is she inside?"

"No," she wheezes. "She's gone."

"What do you mean gone?" Terror runs through every part of me.

"Tessa," she says, gasping for breath. "She did this. And she took Quinn."

———

Quinn is missing, with Tessa, and Ben and I are stuck, lying side by side on stretchers in the overcrowded hallway of the ER at Northwestern Memorial Hospital. We've had blood taken and a pulse ox, as Ben calls it, and we're awaiting chest X-rays. My head throbs, my lungs burn, and my throat is raw from smoke inhalation and crying. But all I care about is finding Quinn.

I lift my oxygen mask. It hurts to talk, but I do it anyway. "Tell me the truth," I demand. "Did you drug Nicole? When you brought the prescription to her house? Do you want her money for your hospital? Did you set me up?"

Ben's mouth drops open. "Are you out of your mind?" He clutches his stomach, distressed.

"Why didn't you tell me Nicole left you money you needed for the hospital? When did you find out?"

"I never asked Nicole for money. Where did you get that idea? I work in one of the lowest-income areas in Chicago for a reason. Her attorney contacted me the morning after she died, and I felt sick about it. God, if she thought that's all I wanted from her . . . I just wanted to be in her life." He slumps defeatedly. "All I want is for Quinn to be okay. I've lost my sister. I can't take any more." Tears fall onto his oxygen mask.

My anger dissipates, and I reach out and touch his arm. "You saved my life," I say.

"You saved mine. And you ran into a burning house to find Quinn. You pushed us out of the way of a maniac driver. It's time we trusted each other, because we're all we've got right now."

Tears pour down my face, and my head pounds. His fingers find mine and squeeze. I squeeze back. So many lives have been destroyed. Tessa took Quinn. And we don't know where they are.

We both look up to see Jessica, her red-and-blue-striped dress a blur as she tears down the hallway. She comes to a halt, her phone in her hand, eyes scanning me from head to toe. "I left right after you called me, but the traffic was insane. Have you seen a doctor yet?" she asks.

I release Ben's hand and lift the oxygen mask. "Just tests. Does Martinez know? Have they found Quinn?"

"Martinez knows about the fire. She was there right after you were both taken away by ambulance. And she's tracking Tessa but hasn't found her. But you're no longer a person of interest, Morgan."

I don't dare believe this is true.

"And we now know how you're connected to Nicole. You posted on a website called Maybe Mommy about wanting to adopt a baby. Nicole responded in a private message to you, and you wrote her back. All those messages were found in your Maybe Mommy account on your phone's hard drive. The forensics team checked Nicole's computer, her hard drive, and linked the messages back to you. Her user name is Lost and Confused."

Oh my God. *Oh my God.* That site. I hold my hand to my chest and look at Ben, whose eyes are wide. And now it all falls into place. *Lost and Confused.*

"Yes, I remember now!" I tell Jessica. "We were total strangers, but we had a connection. Still, it wasn't enough for her to give me custody of Quinn. And it's supposed to be a forum for women who don't have children. I didn't even know she was in Chicago, never mind her name . . . She must have been so lonely." So was I. But I pushed her away.

"Well, that's the weird thing and the reason you're no longer a person of interest. There's a message between Nicole and someone who's supposedly you on August sixth. Nicole wrote that she wanted to give you her child, and M in Chicago agreed. This person said she'd take Quinn and that she'd meet her at Grand/State the next day. But your user name is 'Morose in Chicago.' The username on that account is 'M in Chicago.' Clever, but not clever enough."

Nicole wasn't a complete stranger to me. I'd felt something for her. And I'd failed her.

"Oh my God, she reached out to me. She wanted to know my name. And I got scared and backed off. Maybe if I'd answered her—"

I feel warm fingers on my cheek. "Morgan, stop. You didn't do anything wrong. Someone hacked Nicole's account."

Jessica's phone rings, and she answers. She listens for a minute, then holds the phone out to me. "Martinez wants to talk to you, Morgan."

"To me? Why?" I shake my head. "I don't want to talk to her. She always spins everything to be my fault. She probably still believes I'm involved."

"Please, Morgan. You want to take the call."

Ben shifts to the end of his stretcher and leans on his side. "Take the call. I'm right here with you, and I believe you."

I nod at Jessica, and she hands me the phone. I put it on speaker.

"Morgan, I'm very sorry this has all happened. Do you or Ben have any idea where Tessa might have gone?"

Her apology would be monumental were I not so frightened for Quinn. "I have no idea. All I know is that she's Nicole's best friend and works at Breathe. I don't know why she took Quinn. Please. You have to find them."

"Wait," Ben says, his voice scratchy. He motions for me to bring the phone closer to him. "Donna's the one who told us about the redheaded reporter. Maybe she's in on this, too. Tessa's got to be with Donna. They have Quinn."

"I saw a small redhead leave through the kitchen door at Greg's right before the fire got bad, and we know it wasn't Melissa. They could be at Donna's. In Kenosha," I say, already sitting up, ready to run.

We give Martinez the address. "Okay, I'm going to head there now. Just stay where you are," she says, and ends the call.

Jessica pockets her phone. "You two just wait for the doctor. It's all you can do right now. I'll keep you posted."

With a quick pat on my leg, she's gone.

Ben and I are alone, in a sea of sick and injured people. We're bruised and battered, but we're not broken. We'll only be broken if we can't find Quinn.

"We need to go, Ben."

He pulls his phone out of his pocket. "Okay, I'll get us out of here."

We are going to get that baby back if it's the last thing we do.

CHAPTER THIRTY-FOUR

NICOLE

Before

"'You are my sunshine, my only sunshine . . .'" Nicole held a sleeping Quinn in her arms on the couch. The Tiffany lamp on the side table cast a golden glow over her beautiful face. "I love you, my baby girl. So much. You're going to a safe place where nothing bad will happen to you."

Giving her baby away was the right thing to do. But it hurt so, so much.

The board had sent her a formal letter asking for her resignation as CEO, offering her a lump-sum payment to buy back her shares. She threw the letter in the trash. She could not and would not have anyone take Breathe from her daughter.

After today, everyone would know that Quinn was a part of Breathe forever. Nicole made sure of it. She looked at the message from Morgan on her phone. She had been overcome with happiness to receive it last night.

M in Chicago: I've wanted a child for so long, and I will accept your offer to take yours. Meet me on the northbound Grand/State platform on Monday, August 7 at 5:30 p.m.

In gratitude,
Morgan Kincaid

Nicole smiled to herself. Everything was in place.

She had accomplished something far more important than a clothing-and-wellness empire. She'd become a true mother to her child. It was the best thing she'd ever done in her life. She wasn't sure where she would go once Quinn was in Morgan's arms, but she would run. She would hide. She would disappear. That was all that mattered.

She waited, with Quinn laying against her breast, while her daughter peacefully slept. Once Quinn awoke, she bathed her in the small baby tub, careful to wash her neck and little fingers and toes, softly massaging shampoo into the black tufts of hair that always stood up. Her baby slapped gleefully at the water, oblivious to what was about to happen. Her daughter would never remember this, but still, she poured all her love into the tiny person who meant everything to her.

Unlike all the other days at home with Quinn, this one passed so quickly, and suddenly it was time to leave. With Quinn nestled against her, she went to the kitchen to prepare her baby's bottle. She passed the silver toaster and looked at her image, so distorted, yet true to how she felt. It occurred to her that someone at Grand/State might recognize her as the CEO of Breathe. She couldn't risk anyone stopping her. She gently placed her daughter in the vibrating seat and pulled the scissors from the wooden block of knives. Then she began to cut the beautiful hair she'd had her whole life. She snipped and snipped, until the blades of the scissors scraped her scalp.

Now she looked nothing like Nicole Markham. Or Nicole Layton.

She went into the pantry and looked at the Post-its covering one entire wall. A sea of purple that had never brought her any clarity at all.

Name card. Redhead. Missing pills. Letter. Mobile. Door. Shattered chandelier. Photo. Box. Text. Exhaustion. Help me. Shelter. Widow. Morgan Kincaid.

She added one more note.

Mother.

It was the anniversary of Amanda's death, the last day Nicole would ever see her daughter.

She was ready to say goodbye.

CHAPTER THIRTY-FIVE

MORGAN

After being discharged for minor smoke inhalation, Ben and I exit the hospital into the bright sunshine. We are wrecks. We've been told to rest, but we're desperate to find Quinn. We don't know what to do, or where to go. We hail a cab and ride silently back to our cars on North Astor Street, where Greg's house is a charred ruin.

"What now?" I ask, wanting to do something, anything, to find Quinn.

Ben shrugs. "We wait, I guess, for Martinez and Jessica to call."

His phone rings, and we both jump. He rushes to yank it from his pocket. "It's Martinez," he says.

My heart slams against my rib cage.

"Detective, I have you on speaker," Ben tells her, and his eyes lock onto mine.

"I went to Donna's. She wasn't there. But there was a weird shrine to Nicole and Amanda. There was a baby dress laid out on the kitchen table with old newspaper clippings from the case of Amanda's death. The front door was wide open, and Donna's Chevy was in the driveway."

Then she pauses.

"I don't know how to tell you this, but there was blood in the entryway, as though there was some kind of struggle," Martinez says. "Please, if you have any idea where Donna might go . . . We need to act fast."

"No, no, no!" I cry, then immediately wipe my tears. There's no time for self-pity or fear. I grab Ben's arm. "If Donna's taken Tessa and Quinn, where could she go to hide?" Before he opens his mouth, it hits me. "Nicole's! If Donna's the one who put the spy apps on Nicole's phone and computer, she must have access, or Tessa gave her access! It would also be the best place to go because no one's living there."

"All right, I'm on my way, but it will take some time to get back from Kenosha. Hang tight. And stay right where you are." Martinez ends the call.

I tap my foot frantically on the pavement. "We're a five-minute drive from Nicole's. We can get there first."

Ben hesitates.

"For Quinn."

We jump into his Altima and fly down West North, barreling from street to street until we screech right onto North State, the squealing tires shockingly loud in this restrained, upscale neighborhood.

My leg jitters as he turns left onto East Bellevue Place.

My seat belt is off, and I grab my pepper spray. We get out of the car and run toward Nicole's house. On her driveway, Ben yanks me back before I make it to the door.

"Wait. We have to do this carefully. If Donna's in there with Quinn and Tessa, we don't want to scare her."

I pull out of his grip. If Donna's hurt Quinn in any way, I will wrap my hands around her neck and squeeze as hard as I can. But he's right. "Let's go around the back and look through the windows."

We tiptoe around the side of the house, crouching down under the railing of the deck just off a sliding glass door. On the second floor, there's a small terrace off a room. The doors are wide open. A baby's cry echoes from above.

I look up. A redheaded woman holds Quinn, her back to us. She steps onto the terrace, Quinn so close to the railing, and a twenty-foot drop, that I instinctively reach out my arms to catch her should she fall.

The woman turns around.

It's not Donna.

It's Tessa.

In a red wig.

Ben and I bolt around the front of the house, but the door is locked. In a frenzy I search for another way in. Tripping on bushes and slipping on the stones, I race to the side of the house and spot a double-hung window. I slam the heavy glass with my elbow, but it doesn't even crack.

Ben rushes past me. Without anything to cover his fist, he smashes the glass again and again until pointed shards rain down. He hoists me through the broken window and pulls himself up.

We're in a powder room.

"Let's go," I mouth to Ben.

He nods, blood dripping from his hand, and goes ahead of me. With my pulse pounding in my neck, we head to the second floor, to a bedroom.

Then I stand stock-still. Huddled against the wall, next to the terrace, sits Donna, knees pulled to her chest, tears streaming down her face. It's then that I notice her hands are zip-tied, and a bloody gash runs the length of her cheek. There's a red wig on the floor, next to an open bottle of pills.

"It's not me!" Donna says, no louder than a whisper.

"Don't move!" I hear from behind me. Ben and I turn. Tessa stands, her blond hair tangled and disheveled. Quinn is in her arms, held too tightly. "Get your backs against the wall, next to Donna." She swings her body around so hard that Quinn's head thuds against her arms.

Slowly, Ben and I walk over to Donna, who's trembling on the ground by our feet. She looks up with those watery blue eyes so full of pain, and so much regret.

We stand against the wall as Tessa instructed. I can feel Ben vibrating beside me. I focus on Quinn, whose beautiful eyes are filled with fear.

Ben leans forward. "Tessa, what do you want with Quinn?"

Tessa edges closer to the open doors of the terrace. She smiles beatifically. "I'm saving her. I'll tell the police Donna was stalking Nicole. Because she knows Nicole killed Amanda. I found Donna here, but it was too late. Overdose. Quinn was alone and screaming," Tessa says. Her face is composed, but her eyes are wild. "Then her auntie Tessa will get custody of her."

Donna is curled on her side. She whimpers, "This is all my fault. I'm sorry. She's the reporter."

I look at the floor and the orange bottle of pills. Nicole's name is on them. I tap Ben's hand once and slide my eyes to the pills. His eyes follow.

"What kind of pills are in that bottle, Tessa?" he asks gently, carefully.

She kicks the bottle with her foot, so a few pills spill out. "You should know, Ben. You brought them to Nicole."

Ben peers at the round, white tablets and breathes in so sharply I hear it. "Those pills aren't the Xanax she asked me to bring. Those are zolpidem. Generic Ambien. Nicole should *never* have been taking Ambien."

"As far as anyone knows, she texted you and *you* brought her Ambien instead of Xanax. The generic brands all look so similar, but you'd think a doctor would be able to tell the difference. Unless he wanted his own sister to become paranoid."

"And suicidal," Ben says. I hear him struggle to control the fury in his voice.

"Shame she already had a panic disorder. Those pills really tipped her over the edge. Literally." She carelessly dangles Quinn over her arm so her neck flops back.

"You sent me that text from Nicole's phone, didn't you? Asking me to pick up her prescription."

I dig my nails into my palm until I draw blood. If I could just take Quinn from Tessa.

Ben lets out a soft stutter of pain. "You switched my sister's pills."

She slams Quinn against her chest, making the baby howl. "What the fuck did you ever do for Nicole, Ben? Nothing! Was I worth nothing to her? What do you think?"

He doesn't answer. I look at the red wig on the floor and recall the terror in Nicole's eyes on the platform, looking everywhere for someone who might hurt her and Quinn.

"You stalked Nicole and us, pretending to be Donna or Melissa," I say quietly, scared to set her off even more.

"You don't get to ask questions anymore," Tessa hisses. "You weren't a part of Nicole's life. *I* should have been acting CEO. Nicole never even asked or gave me voting power. *I* should have gotten Quinn! And those shares of Breathe? They should be mine." Tessa advances on me quickly. The baby wails, and the sound pierces my soul. "What kind of fucking mother trusts her child to a total stranger?"

One who didn't trust anyone she loved. One who was on drugs that cause paranoia and depression.

In a shaky voice, I venture, "You made Nicole believe Greg was sleeping with Melissa, didn't you?" I go one step further. "Were you sleeping with him?"

"Nicole should have paid more attention to her husband. I stepped in to help." She presses Quinn too hard to her chest. The poor child won't stop screaming.

So Greg and Tessa were having an affair. Was he involved in

Nicole's death, too? I don't ask because Donna moans and tries to stand, but Tessa kicks her legs out from under her. I stifle my scream, horror nailing me to the wall. I feel Ben touch my hand, and I grab his in return. I'm desperate to reach for the pepper spray in my purse, but she'll see me and kick me before I can get to it.

I'm afraid to push her any further, but I have no choice. "We know you're M in Chicago, Tessa."

She whips her head to glare at me with eyes devoid of humanity. "It's always the husband, isn't it? Greg's the one with access to Nicole's phone and computer. And he's dead."

"No, he's not," Ben says.

Tessa jerks her head back in shock. "Greg told us everything, Tessa," I lie. "Us and the cops. They'll be here any minute."

Quinn screams and screams, and Tessa shakes her. "Shut up!"

"It's over, Tessa. There's nowhere to run. No one left to blame." Ben steps an inch forward.

She moves closer to us. Then she transfers Quinn into one arm and reaches into her back pocket. She takes out a small-silver-and-black gun.

My vision gets fuzzy, and I will myself to focus. All I can see is Ryan lying in a pool of blood on the floor. My insides turn to liquid. Ben is completely frozen beside me.

Tessa is pointing the pistol at us both.

I think I hear the sound of sirens in the distance.

Tessa's eyes glaze over, and she waves the gun violently. It hits Quinn's temple.

Adrenaline surges through me, unlike anything I have ever felt before.

"No!" I yell, and I fly at Tessa and grab the baby as the deafening crack of a gunshot rings out in the room.

Donna screams, and Ben slams Tessa to the ground. The gun lands beside her. She reaches for it, but Ben kicks it out of the way.

The carpet swims up to meet me, but I don't go down. Not with Quinn.

"I've got you, baby. You're safe." I wrap my arms around her, feel her face against my palpitating heart.

Ben holds Tessa down as footsteps bang up the stairs. I swivel my head to the door and see Martinez charge into the room with a team of cops. I look to Donna, who's crumpled on the floor, blood spilling onto the cream carpet. There's a bullet hole in her leg.

"Everyone down! Now!" Martinez yells.

I sink to the floor with Quinn underneath me, screaming but safe. Ben hits the floor, and Tessa scrambles to get up, but Martinez puts a knee into her back. "Don't move an inch." She gestures to officers at the door, who cuff Tessa's hands behind her back.

"It's Tessa, Tessa alone!" Ben says. "She shot Donna. She needs an ambulance."

"Okay," Martinez barks. She relays the message into the radio attached to her shoulder. Police or emergency response people—it's hard to tell—rush into the room and head right to Donna's side.

Martinez looks from Ben to me. She steps forward and helps me gather Quinn in my arms and stand. I feel her hand on my wrist.

"It's okay, Morgan. We know everything. I'm sorry."

I try to speak, but I can't. All I can do is rock Quinn and soothe her.

"Greg gave up Tessa to cut a deal for himself," Martinez says. "He confessed to having an affair with her. They planned to destroy Nicole, and they wanted to take control of Breathe."

I can't believe this. How could a father do this? And how could a best friend? They conspired together to bring down the woman they both claimed to have loved. I feel sick and horrified and so sad for Nicole, this struggling mother who became my friend online. She was right all along. The people closest to her weren't to be trusted.

Tessa's face is red with rage as the officers lead her out and down the stairs.

I'm so weak that my arms feel like leaded weights. Quinn's cries are easing off. I'm clammy and shaky and can't stop my body from trembling. I'm so cold.

As we all exit the house, Ben stops and looks at a rack of keys on the wall. "My keys aren't here." He points to the empty peg. "Nicole had a copy of my house keys. Tessa must have taken them and put that doll in the bassinet."

"She must have found a way into my apartment, too," I say through chattering teeth.

Martinez turns. "We think she jimmied the lock to your fire exit. You really need better security in that building."

Once we're all outside, two paramedics rush toward Donna with a stretcher, lifting her onto it. Ben pulls me into him. We stand as a unit, protective around Quinn.

Tessa is escorted into the back of a police car, and as Donna is whisked away in the ambulance, another pulls up to the curb. Ben and I climb in and we sit together on a stretcher while the paramedic checks on Quinn, who seems afraid but otherwise unharmed. "Here you go," he says, handing me Quinn while he disinfects and bandages Ben's hand. Martinez crouches across from me.

"Did Greg tell you if Tessa was on that platform the day Nicole died?" I ask her. I want to know the truth.

"I didn't get to ask," Martinez says. "Greg confessed to me that he and Tessa had a plan to be together. But he didn't know how far Tessa would go. He was worried for Quinn. I was about to ask him if she was on the platform on Nicole's last day alive, but I didn't get a chance. After confessing to me, Greg died of acute respiratory distress."

I taste salt as tears leak out of my eyes and into my mouth. So much senseless loss. Ben envelops me into a hug that doesn't need words. But Quinn is safe with us, where she belongs.

Martinez observes me. "You interfered with an investigation. You put yourself in danger."

My anger and resentment rise to the surface. "I—"

"But you saved Quinn, Ben, and yourself. I'm not saying what you did was smart, but it was brave." A small smile appears on her face. "Someday, you're going to be a really good mother."

A hard lump forms in my throat, and I nod. "Yes, someday I will."

CHAPTER THIRTY-SIX

NICOLE

Before

Nicole dressed Quinn in a clean onesie and wrapped her in a plush, yellow blanket her own mother had made for Nicole when she was a baby. She used to sleep with it after her parents died. She wanted to make sure her baby girl would have something special made by her grandmother's hands. Quinn's feet stuck out at the end. As Nicole slid little white socks over her daughter's tiny toes, she swallowed back tears.

Goodbyes were never easy.

Morgan would know never to put a blanket in her baby's crib. She would never harm Quinn the way Nicole harmed Amanda. Donna kept the AC so jacked up because she'd read somewhere that babies should sleep in cool environments, but it had been so chilly in Amanda's nursery that day.

Nicole had draped the blanket over Amanda as she slept peacefully, careful not to tuck it near the baby girl's mouth and nose. Then Nicole went to the living room and fell asleep on the sofa. When she awoke and went to check on Amanda, the blanket was covering her face. Nicole tore it off, and picked the baby up to make sure she was okay. Amanda wasn't okay. She was dead. And it was all Nicole's fault.

Before she called 911 and before Donna came, Nicole stuffed the white blanket in a drawer then waited for the fate she deserved. But when the autopsy report came, SIDS was the only cause of death.

Nicole had never told a soul about the blanket. But she always believed Donna knew. Even without absolute proof, a mother always knew.

The weight of that blanket had suffocated Nicole for almost twenty years. She would never know for sure if Amanda had died of sudden infant death syndrome or accidental suffocation.

Nicole closed her eyes and saw the violet light of her third-eye chakra. And she surrendered to the unknown.

But no matter how careful Nicole was with Quinn, she would never stop being afraid for her daughter's life.

She stuffed formula and bottles into her designer diaper bag and slung it over her shoulder. Then she unlocked the deadbolt. The alarm was already disarmed. Whether she'd done it or not didn't matter anymore.

They arrived at Grand/State. Her heart began to race now that it was really happening. Quinn nestled against her. "You're the best thing that ever happened to me."

She rooted in the diaper bag for her phone to check the time. 5:15 p.m. She saw the Post-it notes and took one off the top.

Morgan would never see the notes on her pantry wall. She might never be aware of the lurking danger. If Donna was really out for revenge, Nicole had to warn her, just in case Donna didn't stop. It was almost 5:20. She had time for only one word, and so for the first time in almost twenty years, Nicole wrote Amanda's name.

She paid for her fare and stood at the top of the escalators lead-ing to the platform. There was no working elevator today. Her eyes blurred when she looked down, so scared her baby would fall from her arms and crash to the bottom before she could ensure that Morgan would be Quinn's mother.

Quinn started snuffling. Dread flared, quick and sudden, in Ni-cole's chest. *Please don't cry. Please don't call attention to us.*

A woman leaned over and cooed, "Oh, what a gorgeous baby. Look at that hair! How old is she?"

"Seven weeks."

"Well, she's just precious. Enjoy her. It all goes so fast." The woman disappeared down the escalator.

When she was gone, Nicole took a deep breath and rode down to the platform. Her eyes darted left and right until finally, Morgan walked by. Nicole bit her lip so hard she tasted blood. Morgan's glossy black hair hung in a thick sheet down her back, and her white eyelet dress was simple but pretty. She kept her head down, avoiding the crowd of commuters. Any second now, Morgan would see her.

Nicole would pass Quinn to her.

Quinn would be safe.

Morgan would have everything she ever wanted.

And so would Nicole.

All it took was a few more steps.

A tiny figure in black, like a shadow, peeked out from the column behind them. She wore tight black yoga pants and a hoodie, pulled over her head so her face wasn't visible. Was it Donna? Had she fol-lowed her here?

It was time.

"I know what you want. Don't let anyone hurt her. Love her for me, Morgan."

She thrust Quinn into Morgan's arms, and Morgan caught the baby. Nicole retreated a few inches, so she was too far away to take her daughter back.

Nicole thought she smelled sandalwood. She looked over at the column again.

The person in the hoodie lifted her face.

Nicole gasped. No, it couldn't be. Had she had it wrong all this time?

The train came closer.

It must have seemed fast to everyone watching, but for Nicole, time slowed to a crawl. She watched as Morgan cradled her daughter so close to her chest. She knew that Morgan would keep her safe and love her.

Nicole had one last thought before she hit the tracks:

Goodnight moon. Goodnight my child.

CHAPTER THIRTY-SEVEN

MORGAN

Seven Months Later

"Ben, can you grab me the polka-dot leggings from the dryer?" I call out as I'm changing Quinn's diaper in her nursery on the pretty, white table Ben and I bought right after I moved in with him. I tape the diaper shut, kiss her forehead, and smile when I'm rewarded with a drooly grin. Quinn's two front bottom teeth have come in.

Her room is sunshine yellow. On the wall next to her crib are purple flowers, and the billowy curtains over the window are covered in little moons. Above her bookshelf is a framed photo of Ben and Nicole on Halloween, a brother taking care of his little sister. Now he takes care of his niece, and I'm with him every step of the way.

With Greg gone, Ben and I were able to file together for nonparental guardianship of Quinn, agreeing to share the same residence to give Quinn as stable and safe a home as we can. In four more months, if we don't screw it up, we will be granted full custody and we can officially adopt her. Quinn's birth father never wanted her, but by giving evidence against Tessa, he made it possible for us to love her.

And more has come to the surface about him. Martinez dug into his financial records. He'd been a client of Ryan's. Like so many other people my husband destroyed, Greg had invested and lost his entire savings in the scam. Greg went along with Tessa's plan to get Quinn's shares of Breathe because he was in such deep financial trouble. Nicole never knew. But Tessa did.

Poor Melissa was simply a victim. She'd only worked for Greg a few months when Tessa realized she was the perfect redheaded decoy. New and inexperienced, she just wanted to impress her boss, and agreed to take care of Quinn the day Tessa set fire to Greg's house. That's why she was in the passenger seat that day. She's fully physically recovered since that horrible tragedy, but if there's anything I know for sure it's that the scars of trauma run deep.

Tessa was hoping, it seems, to kill all of us in that fire. Destroy as many witnesses to her treachery as she could.

It's still hard for me to wrap my head around what Greg and Tessa did, how far they would go for love and money—if you can call what they had love. I guess you really can't. It's more like obsession, and madness.

For her part in this, Donna was full of regret and guilt. She never meant to contribute to Nicole's downfall, and she knows what she did in the past was wrong. Nicole never killed Amanda, and accepting that has meant Donna has started to heal. We keep in touch with her to this day. She has a soft spot for Quinn and lights up whenever our baby girl giggles.

As for me, Martinez issued a formal statement clearing me of any connection to Nicole's death. My skin no longer rises with welts. I've become a case study at the University of Chicago Law School about how an innocent bystander can become the wrongly accused. Blogs and podcasts have followed. How quickly the tides turn on social media.

My mother called from Miami after my name was clear. We've spoken a few times. I'm not ready to fully forgive her for believing the worst of me, but family is family. It's time for all of us to move forward.

"Ben! The leggings, please!" I roll my eyes, assuming his head is stuck in a medical text, like it usually is when he doesn't answer me right away. I grab the gray leggings with the tulle skirt Quinn was wearing before. She looks so cute. I pick her up and nestle her, amazed as always that I now have a child, that I'm a mother and that loving her is my right and privilege.

Don't let anyone hurt her. Love her for me, Morgan.

When I take her downstairs, Martinez is there, standing next to Ben. My instant reaction is to bristle, but she smiles, actually smiles so her dimple shows.

"What's going on? Was Tessa released?" I tighten my arm around Quinn.

I can't imagine that's possible, but I still have trouble trusting the system meant to protect the innocent.

Tessa was arraigned and pled guilty to first-degree murder charges and arson for Greg. She's also facing kidnapping and unlawful restraint charges, and attempted murder of Donna, Ben, and me. She pled not guilty to all charges related to Nicole's harassment. She's being held without bail, with more charges likely to come after discovery is complete.

"A trial date is finally set for June. I thought I'd be the first to tell you," Martinez says.

I exhale a long breath of relief. Ben's face reddens and his hands curl into fists. "Tessa killed my sister. She should go down for first-degree murder and a whole lot more."

Martinez pulls her ponytail tighter. "That's the other reason I'm here. Can we sit for a minute?"

We all go into the living room. I place Quinn in the safari-themed exersaucer she loves so much, and she immediately jumps up and down with glee. I sit on the couch, and Ben sits next to me then reaches for my hand.

Martinez speaks. "The coroner finally closed Nicole's case as a suicide. There's no evidence on the CCTV that Tessa was ever on that platform." She looks at Ben. "We believe Nicole took her own life. I'm so sorry."

I've watched the video countless times to try to spot Tessa in every shadow and blur. But all I see with certainty is Nicole's heel dangling off the edge of the platform and the fear in her eyes before gazing at me and Quinn. Then she's gone.

I gently touch Ben's arm. "I'm so sorry."

I promise myself to be there for Ben the way no one was there for me. Nicole's death isn't his fault. Ryan's wasn't mine. I believe that now.

Martinez crosses her legs. "It's clear Tessa and Greg caused your sister to fall apart. They are responsible for that, and Tessa will pay for that. The State's Attorney is adding a charge of involuntary manslaughter. It's the most we can hope for. Everything will come out at Tessa's trial, but I felt you deserved a preview." She coughs and smooths her ubiquitous black dress pants.

"Would you like a glass of water?" I ask, then almost laugh out loud. If someone had told me two years ago that I'd invite Martinez into my home and offer her a beverage, I would have fallen over in shock.

"No, thank you. I don't want to keep you too long." She fiddles with the collar of her white blouse. "As you know, the GPS tracker placed on Nicole's car was identical to the one we found on yours. We finally located Tessa's laptop, too, which she'd hidden in a storage room at Breathe. We found a copy of the letter we discovered in Nicole's bedside table. Donna never sent it; she really did stop all that nonsense years ago. And we found emails on her hard drive using different Guerrilla Mail addresses. And of course all the Maybe Mommy messages between you and Nicole, and Tessa as 'M in Chicago.' Basically, it's a gold mine of evidence." She smiles sadly.

I shudder to think of how close we all came to dying.

Quinn babbles at the small mirror in front of her. As always, I'm overcome with love for her. Ben and I look at each other, no words necessary. We're the lucky ones.

Quinn raises her arms for me to pick her up. I hold her so she's facing Martinez.

The detective beams. "She's beautiful."

"She looks exactly like my sister," Ben says. "My sister was a good person."

"A good person who trusted the wrong people. It can happen to anyone." Martinez locks eyes with me, her expression kind and gentle.

I have a recurring dream in which Nicole and I are on the platform. I grab her arm and pull her toward me, away from the tracks. I hold her close to me and whisper, "I'll help you." And she doesn't die. Instead, she cradles Quinn and points forward, to someone on the platform. But I can't see who it is.

Martinez takes her leave. Ben and I stand at the door, watching her drive away. Quinn is in my arms. The air is unseasonably warm for March. The sun-dappled elm creates a canopy over the lawn. A haven for us all.

Ben takes my hand. "Are you happy?"

All I feel is affection, warmth, and gratitude for this man. "I'm happy, yes," I say. "But you should put the toilet seat down once in a while."

He laughs, and so does Quinn. I'm so lucky to have them. I'm lucky to be alive, and free. And to finally know the truth. I no longer blame myself for Ryan's immorality, his greed and lies. I've learned that good people don't always recognize evil, because we don't understand it.

I won't go back to social work ever again. But not because I don't like it. I've decided to do a master's degree in counseling psychology online. This way I can get my degree and spend as much time as possible with Quinn.

Ben is back at Mount Zion, at the newly minted Nicole Markham

Emergency Department, and now that he's settled—now that *we're* settled—he's devoting time to fixing a lot of the hospital's problems. The profit margin this year should finally be above the bottom 25 percent of safety-net hospitals, which will ultimately enable Ben to hire three more ER doctors and two triage nurses, and add a rapid medical exam area to decrease wait times and increase patient flow.

Breathe took a severe hit on the stock market, but Lucinda Nestles, executive chairperson of the board, was appointed the new CEO. She admitted that Tessa had fed her information about Nicole's instability. She felt awful for perhaps exacerbating Nicole's panic by sending a letter asking for her resignation. Just another unwitting player in Tessa's game. She's managed to sell more shares to new investors, and though the turnaround is slow, Breathe will recover. Quinn's shares are held in trust by us. Though neither Ben nor I are financial experts, we are learning, because we're both wary of putting our faith in a broker.

Quinn squirms, the way she does when she wants to feel her feet on the ground. She's now using all the furniture to pull herself up to stand. Before we know it, she'll be walking. We head down the steps onto the wet grass and I hold our independent, strong-willed girl upright. Then I turn to Ben. And I kiss him.

He cups my face in his hands and kisses me back. Quinn pulls her hand out of my mine, and I open my eyes. Ben and I turn our attention to our daughter. She reaches for something flying in front of her.

It's a butterfly with purple details on its wings. It comes so close to Quinn's cheek that it might have even touched her.

Then the butterfly soars above all of us, up and away.

ACKNOWLEDGMENTS

Woman on the Edge took over six years to write, revise, and publish, with an incredible team of people. I could never have seen my dreams realized without them, so please bear with me because I have so many to thank and finally have the chance. If I've missed anyone, please forgive me. I promise to catch you in the next book.

My fierce, tireless super-agent, Jenny Bent, plucked this book from the slush pile and saw into my soul what I wanted it to be. Then, draft after draft after draft, she taught me how to turn my idea into my debut thriller. Because of Jenny, my wildest wish came true when she sold the book to Nita Pronovost at Simon & Schuster Canada, whose brilliant editing transformed my manuscript into a novel I never knew it could be. Nita and editor Sarah St. Pierre gently guided me, word by word, enhancing my voice and story in ways I didn't know were possible. I am so grateful and so lucky to work with all of them. I actually want Nita and Sarah to now follow me wherever I go, editing my every sentence, because what they can do with my words is magic.

Simon & Schuster Canada is based in my city of Toronto, and the offices have become my home. The entire editorial, marketing, publicity, and sales teams are incredibly hardworking and dedicated, and I'm indebted to president and publisher, Kevin Hanson; assistant to Kevin and Nita, Sophia Muthuraj; VP of marketing and publicity, Felicia

Quon; senior publicist, Jillian Levick; marketing associate, Alexandra Boelsterli; associate director of publicity, Rita Silva; director of sales, Shara Alexa; assistant editor, Siobhan Doody; marketing manager, Jessica Scott; and director of sales, Mike Turnbull, for everything they do to make sure as many readers as possible know about my book, while keeping me laughing all the time. Thank you to copy editor Erica Ferguson.

Huge thanks to Sarah Hornsley at The Bent Agency, who was also instrumental in shaping the book and finding it a home in the UK with the loveliest, most supportive editor, Sherise Hobbs at Headline. I'm honored to be with Headline, which publishes so many of my writing idols. The minute I saw the cover for *Woman on the Edge,* my jaw dropped, because I could never have envisioned something so spectacular. Huge thanks to uber-talented cover designer Caroline Young. And so many thanks also to assistant Faith Stoddard; my eagle-eyed, genius UK copy editor, Penelope Price; Jo Liddiard in marketing; Rosie Margesson in publicity; Frances Doyle in sales; and Rebecca Bader, sales director. And to Rhea Kurien, who I only had the privilege of working with for a short time, though it was wonderful.

Everyone at The Bent Agency who collaborated with me, from edits to submission to foreign rights, I owe you a lifetime of gratitude: all the interns, and especially author Kevin van Whye and agents Molly Ker Hawn, Amelia Hodgson, Victoria Cappello, and Claire Draper. A huge thank you also to Sam Brody and Eliza Kirby for their hard work on my behalf.

To the publishers who will translate *Woman on the Edge* into so many different languages, I thank you for bringing my book to readers all over the world.

I needed the expertise of many professionals, and I'm so thankful to the following people for their time and generosity: criminal defense attorney Donald J. Ramsell, attorney and private investigator Tracy M. Rizzo, Detective Constable Minh Tran, psychotherapist Mitch Smolkin, Dr. S. Bazios, Dr. Elana Lavine, and the Circuit Court of

Cook County Guardianship Assistance Desk for Minors. Any errors are my own.

To Lauren Erickson, massage therapist extraordinaire, who suggested Morgan's name and also untangles the pretzel I twist into when writing.

To all the women who so openly shared their experiences with postpartum depression, anxiety, and mental health struggles, I thank you so very much.

I am so blessed to have the best, most honest beta readers and critique partners, who gave me invaluable feedback from the very first draft to the last: Lisa Brisebois; Jackie Bouchard; especially Francine LaSala and Meredith Schorr, who must have read a hundred drafts; Eileen Goudge; and Lydia Laceby, my best author friend in Toronto, whose talent amazes me.

Francine, Meredith, and Eileen are also part of my beloved writing tribe, the Beach Babes, along with Jen Tucker, Julie Valerie, and Josie Brown. We convene every year for a week in Santa Cruz, and I love and appreciate their phenomenal ability and wicked senses of humor. They are my family, and their friendship sustains me.

To the friends who have encouraged me for so many years: Miko, Michael, Nicole, James, Jenny Z., Catherine, Lesley, Helen, Val, Karen, Christine, Caroline, Jessica, Beth, Maggie, Cheryl, Erin, Lise, Leslie, Laura C., Siobán, Kailey, Rachel, Patty, Simone, Jenny R., Kathy, Matt, Jen S., Deb, Lisa G., Melanie, Sylwia, Jon, and Amanda.

I am a voracious reader and my persistence through years of revising was fueled by the many authors whose words inspire me and whose support is invaluable to me. It would take an entire book to thank them all, but I would like to give special thanks to Jennifer Weiner, Caroline Kepnes, Brenda Janowitz, Lori Nelson Spielman, Lisa Steinke, Liz Fenton, Kristin Harmel, Roselle Lim, Rachael Romero, Maggie Morris, Janis Thomas, Jean Pendziwol, Meredith Jaeger, Mark Leslie Lefebvre, Whitney Rakich, Jill Hannah Anderson, Wendy Janes, Amy Heydenrych, Marissa Stapley, Hannah Mary McKinnon, Karma

Brown, Jennifer Hillier, Laura Russell-Evans, Anita Kushwaha, Amy Stuart, Rebecca Eckler, Mary Kubica, Roz Nay, Robyn Harding, Catherine McKenzie, Gilly Macmillan, Kimberly Belle, Samantha Downing, Daniela Petrova, Christina McDonald, Emily Carpenter, Andrea Bartz, Kaira Rouda, Heather Gudenkauf, Laura Sims, Paula Treick DeBoard, Kate Moretti, Sonja Yoerg, Natalie Jenner, Halley Sutton, Lisa Barr, Jen Griswell, Jess Skoog, Julie Lawson Timmer, and Danielle Younge-Ullman.

I am so grateful to the bloggers, bookstagrammers, and readers who give so much of their time to support authors and keep me stocked in book recommendations: Elizabeth Gunderson; Melissa Amster of *Chick Lit Central*; Marlene Roberts Engel; Suzanne Fine; Kaley Stewart of *Books Etc.*; Dany Drexler; Andrea Peskind Katz of Great Thoughts' Great Readers; Athena Kaye; Jamie Rosenblit of Beauty and the Book; Kristy Barrett and Tonni Callan of A Novel Bee; Kate Rock of *KateRock LitChick*; Sonica Soares of *The Reading Beauty*; Barbara Bos of *Women Writers, Women's Books*; Tamara Welch of *Traveling with T*; Judith D. Collins; *Books and Chinooks*; Nic Farrell of *Flirty and Dirty Book Blog*; Shell of *The Big Fat Bookworm*; *LindyLouMac's Book Reviews*; Suzanne Leopold of *Suzy Approved Book Reviews*; Cindy Roesel; and all the others who are the reason readers know about our books.

And thank you to the booksellers and librarians everywhere who will stock *Woman on the Edge*, recommend it, and help me find the books I want and need to read. They are the unsung heroes.

I will always be grateful to my eighth-grade teacher, Malcolm Crawford, who gave an insecure little girl the English award at graduation and told her she had talent.

My family has never stopped believing in me: Jonah, Perlita, Hannah, Mikey, Eileen, Ron, Lindsay, Scott, Felix, Bassie, Todd, Lori, Brynna, and Owen. I love you all so much. How lucky I am.

I dedicated this novel to my parents, Michael and Celia, because I grew up reading. I read while eating and walking, and often banged into poles because my head was in a book. In stories, I found myself.

ACKNOWLEDGMENTS

My parents never stopped me from reading any book I wanted (the ones they knew about), and they instilled in me the confidence never to give up on my dream. I can only hope I do the same for my children.

Finally, and most important, I could never write without the support, love, and excited encouragement of my husband and children. They give me the space to write, the inspiration to create, and the love and laughter that is my world. Brent, Spencer, and Chloe, you all fearlessly follow your own dreams and passions, and I am so proud of all of you. You are my sun, moon, and stars.

And to you, my readers, who wanted to read *Woman on the Edge*. I only get to live my dream because of you, and I thank you with my whole heart.

ABOUT THE AUTHOR

Dahlia Katz

SAMANTHA M. BAILEY is a Toronto-based novelist, journalist, and freelance editor. Her work has appeared in *NOW Magazine*, the *Village Post*, and with Oxford University Press. She was a writer-in-residence for Kobo Writing Life at Book Expo America 2013. She is the cofounder of BookBuzz, a promotional and interactive author-reader event held in New York City and Toronto. *Woman on the Edge* is her debut novel. Connect with her on Twitter **@sbaileybooks** and on her website at **samanthambailey.com**.